6/14 ✓

T

VATICAN WALTZ

Center Point
Large Print

**This Large Print Book carries the
Seal of Approval of N.A.V.H.**

VATICAN WALTZ

ROLAND MERULLO

CENTER POINT LARGE PRINT
THORNDIKE, MAINE

This Center Point Large Print edition is published in
the year 2014 by arrangement with Crown Publishers,
an imprint of the Crown Publishing Group,
a division of Random House LLC,
a Penguin Random House Company.

The text of this Large Print edition is unabridged.
In other aspects, this book may vary
from the original edition.
Printed in the United States of America
on permanent paper.
Set in 16-point Times New Roman type.

ISBN: 978-1-62899-116-1

Library of Congress Cataloging-in-Publication Data

Merullo, Roland.
Vatican waltz / Roland Merullo. — Center Point Large Print edition.
pages ; cm
ISBN 978-1-62899-116-1 (library binding : alk. paper)
1. Women—Religious life—Fiction. 2. Vatican City—Fiction.
3. Boston (Mass.)—Fiction. 4. Large type books. I. Title.
PS3563.E748V38 2014
813′.54—dc23
2014007842

For my mother,
Eileen Merullo

And for my mother-in-law,
Judy Stearns

All shall be well, and all shall be well, and
all manner of thing shall be well.

—JULIAN OF NORWICH

An important fruit of contemplative prayer is
to be purified of our childish ideas about
God. As our idea of God expands, there is no
word, no way, no gesture, that can articulate
it anymore. Hence we fall into silence, the
place we should have been in the first place.

—REV. THOMAS KEATING,
Intimacy with God

Some who have been called to grace may
wrestle for years with their fearfulness before
they are able to transcend it so as to accept
their own godliness.

—M. SCOTT PECK, *The Road Less Traveled*

BOOK ONE

CHAPTER ONE

My name is Cynthia Clare Piantedosi—a big mouthful of a name, I know—and the story I have to tell is a story about God and faith and prayer.

I grew up in an unsophisticated way, in a place half insulated from modern America by a blanket of Old World traditions and beliefs, but I'm not naive. I know very well that many people are put off by the words "God," "faith," and "prayer." Who can blame them? For untold generations those words have been used like clubs; people have been beaten over the head with them, sometimes tortured or killed because of them, or left unharmed but made to feel they were nothing more than sinners. They were labeled, locked up in titles—atheist, agnostic, Christian, Jew, Moslem, Hindu, Buddhist—while their full, wonderful, quirky humanity was taken away from them like a prisoner's street clothes and never given back. My question is this: If there is some kind of Divine Spirit organizing this impossibly complicated universe, does that spirit really worry about what we call ourselves?

The God I imagine and worship, the Being I give thanks to for every breath and pulse, doesn't care as much about labels as about love; and my style of prayer isn't so much about asking for things (though I sometimes ask) as it is about searching, in an interior silence, for my truest self, my reason for being here, in this place, in this body, at this particular point in the endless sweep of time. I was born and raised in the Roman Catholic tradition, and to this day I hold a good deal of reverence for those rituals and beliefs, but my story is really about what happened as that label fell away, as I found the courage to un-name God, as I came, so slowly, to understand who I really am.

IF I'M GOING TO TELL this story right, I should begin with the great sadness in my life: I have no memory of my mother. She died when I was an infant—"heart trouble," relatives said, but for years no one offered anything more specific than that. I was raised by my father, an older man, gruff but not unkind, and my mother's mother, who moved in with us after her daughter's death. My father, mother, and grandmother grew up in Italy, not far from one another, in fact, and they left that country soon after the end of the Second World War. My parents were married in America, far apart in age but linked by heritage and language and the strong twine of fate.

I should say, too, here at the start, that I have always been a strange soul. I am mellow and quieter now, more sure of my destiny and purpose, but as a child I was feisty and sometimes troublesome, the kind of girl who fought with boys and argued with teachers. I had a few close friends, but also a natural inclination toward solitude—not exactly an Italian American tradition. We're a gregarious people, fond of social clubs and the hairdresser, card games, big families, meals with cousins and aunts. Not me. In high school and college I never even had a boyfriend, not a real boyfriend, in any case. Part of that was because of an intense shyness about romantic relationships that for many years fit over my head and shoulders, tight as upholstery. And part of it was simply the fact that I considered myself unattractive. Though I hoped one day to have a husband, and though I always wanted very badly to bear and raise a child, I was sure, for a long time, that those things would never happen.

I grew up on Tapley Avenue in the small city of Revere, Massachusetts, which sits along the shore at the northern end of the subway line from Boston. Revere has a nice beach—fine gray sand and smooth stones—but the rest of the city is a modest territory of close-set houses and crowded streets. It has always been a place that welcomed new Americans, and when my parents first settled in Revere as newlyweds there were a lot of Italian, Irish, and Jewish families there. Later, those families were replaced by waves of newer immigrants, people from Cambodia and Somalia, Guatemala, Ethiopia, Brazil. But we stayed on, my father and grandmother and I. Our new neighbors watched the soccer channel in Portuguese or wired money to Mogadishu. There were halal stores on the corner where once you could buy mortadella and real Genoa salami. Friends' families fled to the suburbs. We stayed on.

From the time I was a little girl, living a ten-minute walk from St. Anthony's Church, I started to have what I thought of, at first, as "spells." *Visions* would be another word for them, though that sounds pretentious, and to me, those experiences were as familiar and ordinary as the peeling paint on the house across the street. Whenever those spells or visions came over me, I'd feel like I was being carried away on an internal wind, a kite lifting up, rocking and tilting and sailing happily there out of reach of the everyday world. It was like traveling, inside my mind, to another planet. Maybe that's why I was so content for so long with my plain exterior life, with our simple routine—no trips, no adventure, no romance.

We had a small backyard—a swing set there when I was very young and then, later, an oval swimming pool, above ground. My father—fifty-three years and one month old on the day I was born—worked as a mechanic in the garage where the MBTA buses were repaired, and my grandmother worked at home, cooking and cleaning, gardening and praying. She was—or seemed to be—an unspectacular soul: not particularly beautiful, not rich or famous, not well educated, no one who would stand out in a crowd. But I always felt that she and I were linked at the heart, that God had spun us out of the same dust and blood and set us down together for some good purpose.

Nana, I used to call her (though the Italian word for "grandmother" is actually *nonna*), and as a young girl I spent hours and hours with her, conversing in two languages at the kitchen table, watching her prepare meals; eventually, like all Old World girls, learning to sew, clean, and cook. She was short and round, with a bun of gray hair and beautiful green eyes, an unselfish woman who denied herself many pleasures. But she loved coffee, and when I was only six and seven she'd serve me cups of it with a lot of milk and sugar and we'd sit at that table with its plastic tablecloth and bowl of plastic fruit in the center and we'd drink and eat and talk. She was the first person I told about the spells—the only person for a long time—and when I described them to her she said, "*Cinzia, ho visto queste cose dalla tua giovanezza.* Cynthia, I've seen those things since you were very young. They are God's gift to you. I know what they mean."

"What, Nana? Tell me."

"Someday I'll tell you. Later. Not now."

Naturally, after a nonexplanation like that, I

would assault her with a hundred questions. But she would close up, a pot with a tight lid, and, though in later years she made a few comments about the spells, the promised explanation never materialized.

When she died, the saddest day of my life, I was nine and a half years old. I remember it was an unusually hot July night, with boys setting off firecrackers in the street and a radio tuned to a Red Sox game in the house next door. Nana had been ill for several weeks, at home, and every day I took her soup or water, or tore out the soft insides of loaves of Italian bread and fed them to her. I sat with her for long stretches or knelt next to the sofa bed she lay on in the small TV room and recited the rosary while she moved her lips to the Hail Marys. When the prayers and the food were finished, we would sometimes talk for a few minutes, but by the end, she didn't have much energy for conversation. After a couple of sentences she'd clasp my wrist in her right hand and just hold on to me, not in a fearful way—there was no panic in her and no complaint—just as an expression of her love, a way of reassuring me, maybe, that death wasn't some terrifying monster. The last time I spoke to her she could barely open her eyes, but when she heard my voice she tried to smile and she said, so quietly I could barely hear the words, "You'll have a child . . . to make up . . . remember."

"Remember what, Nana? Make up for what?" I wanted to ask, but my throat was closed up with a choking, full-body sadness and all I could do was put my other hand over hers and beg God to let her live a little longer. An hour or so after those last words she fell into a deep, quiet stillness, and a little while later she died.

For months and months after her death I wandered the hot streets of the neighborhood like a lost child. It felt as though God had ripped all the love out of the air, transformed the bones of my face into lead weights, turned down the light of the sun. Make up for what? I asked again and again. Make up for what? The fact that she was leaving this world? Could a child ever take her place? Remember what? The time we'd spent together? Her love? Her strength and warmth and her unshakable faith that all things both good and bad had a purpose? I'd sit in the shade on the back steps and stare at the ceramic statue of the Virgin Mother, not praying, not asking for anything in particular, just sinking down into a sad trance. Sorrow, yes, a deep, piercing sorrow that nothing and no one could soften, but the main emotion I felt then was confusion. Once or twice, before I realized it was hopeless, I turned that confusion on my father in a fusillade of impossible questions. "Why do people die, Papa? Where do they go when they die? Why can't we see them and talk to them? Why does God make this happen?"

The answers he gave were the predictable ones I imagine a local priest had given him after my mother died: that God was mysterious; that we couldn't ever know why He did what He did; that we had to accept what He wanted for us and not complain too much. That Mama and Nana were in Heaven, we'd see them there after we died.

Explanations like that didn't work very well for me. I spent hours on my knees in St. Anthony's, praying for my grandmother's soul, asking her to visit me, hoping I'd dream of her in my hot bedroom on the second floor of the house on Tapley Avenue, hoping I'd at last be given some explanation for the mysteries that seemed to wrap themselves around me like vines around a thin young tree. But there were no visits, no messages or answers, nothing more than the fleeting sense of her in a few brief dreams, and a thousand scraps of memory.

As time went on, the wound of her absence grew slightly less painful, but it never stopped aching. My devotion to the Church and to prayer survived and grew stronger, sometimes even to the point where it tried my father's patience. He was a good Catholic, but for him, as for so many of the other Catholics we knew, Mass on Sunday and holy days, the occasional confession—that was enough. And for me, as had been the case with my grandmother, God asked something more of people, a consistent devotion that bled into the daily run of minutes like colors in a plain white wash. God was there for us in every breath, not encased within the walls and rules of the Church but right there, in the kitchen, at the beach, as I pulled the quilt up over my shoulders on a cold winter night.

After my grandmother died and before I was old enough to cook well, my father, a capable cook himself, prepared our meals. Many times, dozens of times, having lost myself in prayer in the half dark of St. Anthony's nave, I'd come home late for supper. He wouldn't be angry, exactly, but he'd question me in a way that made me feel abnormal. Why couldn't I be out playing with friends? At the beach with my cousins? Why was I spending so much time in the church? What was I really doing there?

"Praying, Papa," I always said, but that didn't change his mood. He grumbled, shook his head, grabbed my plate from the table, and, instead of just heating it up as most people would have done, made a fresh portion. That was perfectly typical of him: he believed the human world should run like a bus or train engine, according to fixed rules. You did not reheat pasta. You did not miss Mass. The father was the undisputed head of the family, and it was his job to earn the money and make all the important decisions.

Beneath all that was a tender side, though, and after he'd taken the time to make me a hot meal, and after we'd endured a little stretch of uncomfortable silence, he'd always say something to break the bad air. "The gravy she came out good today." Or "You should bring over your friend, Lisa, for the pool." Or "Tomorrow she's gonna snow, the TV says." I could see the shyness in him then, the urge toward love and warmth, and the confusion about how to show or ask for it.

THAT FALL A NEW PRIEST was assigned to St. Anthony's. His name was Father Alberto Ghirardelli (like the chocolates, he used to say), and he was the only priest I'd ever met who made jokes. Sometimes even during Mass he'd joke. If an altar boy accidentally rang the bell a few seconds before the host was elevated, he'd glance over at him and in a hoarse whisper say, "Mikey, can't you wait?" Once he tripped on the altar step, and my friends and I thought we heard him let out an exasperated "Oh, shit!"

He spent much of his time visiting the sick, going to wakes, playing cards at the nursing home with men who were too old to drive or walk to Mass. Father Alberto, as everyone called him, had a tremendous sweet tooth and loved to eat, and he said—even sometimes hinting from the pulpit—that the best part of being a priest was the invitations to local homes for dinner. Whenever my father invited him—for squid stuffed with ricotta, for peas and pasta, for wine and fried peppers and *pizza dolce*—he'd eat with great gusto and compliment him a thousand times, and when he said hello and good-bye, he'd always hug me the way an uncle would, a strong, real hug, nothing timid or wrong in it.

I began to go to Father Alberto for Saturday-afternoon confession. Even there his gentle humor surfaced and sparked. "What big sins do we have this week, Cynthia?" he'd ask. "What heavy sack of guilt are we carrying around the city on our back?" Or "What did your father make for supper last night, anything good?"

After a while I came to enjoy those brief exchanges so much that I'd always try to be the last one in line in the pew so I could spend a bit of extra time with him. As the weeks went by, I began to have the feeling that Father Alberto enjoyed the conversations as much as I did. Eventually I told him about the spells, and he asked me in detail about what I saw and what I felt and went to great lengths to assure me that there was nothing wrong or sinful about the experiences. I wasn't crazy, I wasn't weird. "Well, maybe a little weird, Cynthia, but that's okay. I'm weird, too. We can start a club. No normal people allowed. . . . For your penance, bring me a slice of *pizza dolce* next time. Wrap it up nice, okay?"

When I mentioned that Nana had told me the spells were gifts from God, Father Ghirardelli agreed, "Yes, yes," he said so enthusiastically that a bit of saliva flew onto the confessional screen between us. He laughed and wiped it off with the sleeve of his shirt. "That's just what they are. Gifts. Exactly right. Look at the mess I'm making."

"But what do I do with them?"

"For now just accept them, the way you accept a birthday present. Just say, 'Okay, God, thank you.' That's all. Don't ask too many questions of Him. Don't be a pest, a little *skutchamenza*. And don't worry about what they mean. Later on He'll help you figure it out."

It was comforting to hear that, but at the same time, as I grew into my teenage years, all of it—the spells, the absence of my mother and grandmother, the deaths of uncles and aunts, the conversations with Father Alberto, the distance I was starting to feel between my friends' lives and my own (Lisa said she went to bed thinking about Joey Alimonte's eyes; I went to bed wondering what St. Lucy had actually looked like. But I couldn't say that, of course; I couldn't let myself say it.) was like an accumulation of puzzlement for me, a great pile of question marks overflowing my closet and drawers. Lisa and my other friends were becoming interested in boys; they'd sneak cigarettes and swear as if it were a badge of adulthood; they liked to go to the beach and sit on the hurricane wall, flirting, talking about makeup and dates and each other. I did some of those things, too. I was, as one of my friends put it, "seminormal," but at the same time I kept feeling a magnetic draw to the church. Part of it was simply the beauty of that building in comparison to what surrounded us. Revere was not a rich community. In our part of the city the houses weren't fancy, and though they and the yards were mostly well kept, there were stingy landlords who wouldn't fix loose siding on a duplex and homeowners who didn't have the money for a paint job or a new front door; people drove old, dented cars or had a television antenna hanging from their roof like a sign that they were out of date, too poor for a satellite dish or cable, too tired to go up there and do the repair. They worked in the factories in Lynn or as plumbers or painters or clerks. They had a place to live and food to eat and small flecks of enjoyment here and there—the dog track, the movies, clothes shopping, the beach—but their lives were denim and gray wool, not satin and silk.

St. Anthony's Church, in comparison, was a work of art, a temple to the hope of something better, a spectacularly large building made of light brown irregular stones with a red tile roof and a seventy-foot bell tower and heavy front doors. When you stepped inside, what you saw was perfectly orderly and neat, the red carpet running up the center aisle like a ribbon of welcome, the pale wood pews to either side, elaborate stained-glass windows, square columns faced with marble, a white marble altar rail, and above it a complicated mural of Jesus floating with Mary and his apostles. There were four confessionals, two on either side; they had red velour drapes, and an octagonal light went on above them to show if one side or both was occupied.

I loved that building, every part of it, inside and out, and even though it wasn't open during the week, I made friends with Matilda the caretaker—red hair, three hundred pounds, a smile that sparkled with one gold tooth—and if I knocked on the side door of the rectory where the priests lived and ate their meals, she'd let me in and lead me through the baptistery into the dark, cool nave and leave me alone there for as long as I wanted.

Some days I wouldn't kneel or pray; I'd just sit and look at the altar flowers or the shiny tangerine-colored marble blocks on the walls to either side of the altar, etched with the names of people who'd given money, eighty years earlier, so the church could be built. My own grandparents' names were cut into one of those rectangular stones, and sometimes I'd look at them and think of my grandmother and try as hard as I could to feel her presence. And sometimes I did feel it, so much so that the skin on the backs of my shoulders would prickle and jump and I'd turn around to check the empty pews. I'd be almost certain I heard her voice again—a whispered "remember," a forceful assurance that I'd been given a great gift and that with it would someday come a great responsibility. Those hours in church were a peculiar mix of pleasure, excitement, and fear: I sometimes believed I could reach across a thin membrane and touch the world of the dead.

But I almost never had a spell in church, and that was another pebble in the huge pile of puzzlement that filled the rooms of my mind. Those spells would come to me in home room and the cafeteria, in my bed, or as I was walking on the frozen beach in wintertime, alone, my collar turned up against the wind, a wool hat pulled down over my eyebrows, the cold salt air biting the skin of my cheeks and lips. Sometimes the feeling would be so intense I'd have to stop walking and sit on the hurricane wall. I'd perch there in the cold wind and soar into another part of my mind, a place that was very still and clear and warm and untroubled. There were no thoughts. There wasn't much in the way of images, but there was a calm, sweet, silent joy, a sense of welcome. It was as if, like a beloved pet, that quiet space had been waiting all day for me to come home.

On Saturdays I'd go see Father Alberto and we'd talk about what had happened during those moments, and I'd ask him for the fifth, tenth, or fiftieth time what he thought they meant, and he'd say, "God knows, Cynthia," and lend me another book. He was a brilliant man, well read, open-minded, mostly self-educated, and he infected me with his love of learning, lending me books on history and philosophy, the writings of Teresa of Ávila, biographies of the saints, the history of the popes. I read them, of course, but at that age I appreciated them in the most superficial way, like a person who overhears a conversation in a foreign language she barely understands and catches only a few familiar words. Once, near Christmas, on a visit to our house, he gave me a coffee-table book of pictures of Italy and told me he was sure I'd get there one day—he'd had a vision of his own, he said—and I paged through it every night for months, studying the buildings and people, imagining myself in the squares and churches, wondering what it had been like for my grandmother when she was a girl in those places and why, exactly, she and my father and mother had decided to leave. "Mussolini," my father said when I asked. "The *fascisti*. The war. Everybody, he was hungry alla time. Everything, she was on fire. The kids crying, the dogs and chickens runnin' around, smoke in the air, big piles of stones in the street. What? You wanted to stay in a place like that?"

"Did you know Nana and Mama then?"

"What, know? I was twelve, thirteen. You *nonna*, she was twenty, twenty-five, from another village, how was I gonna know her? You mama was born over there, I was already here. Nineteen years was always the difference."

"How did you meet her, then?"

Another shrug. "She knew my cousin over there. My family."

"Any more details than that, Pa?"

"What, details? You meet, that's all. God makes you meet."

"Who's this cousin?"

"Franco, his name is."

"You never mention him. Don't you like him?"

"What, like? He's a cousin. Rich. I didn't see him two times in a year when we were little."

It seemed, with my father, that anytime the conversation turned toward the past it pierced a bubble of bad feeling. A sour tone came leaking out over the tops of his words and I wondered if his early years had been only misery—Mussolini, the war, having to leave his homeland, then losing his young wife—or if there was some secret pain or regret there, and the sourness was his way of steering the conversation back to better times.

OUR PATTERN OF LIFE—harmony without much warmth, connection without much talk, good meals, the routine of weekly Mass, his work, my spells—went on unchanged well into my teenage years, and then, one night, a new thread was sewn through the middle of it. As I often did when I had a little time and a certain kind of urge—for wildness, for escape, for the feeling of being in nature—I decided to walk to the beach, only a mile or so from our home. The sun had just gone down. The air was cool. I sat on the waist-high wall and looked out across the bay, past the islands of Boston Harbor, still visible. The last light leaking out of the world gave everything an air of mystery, and for a little while it seemed that I could sense the whole sphere of the earth, all of us living out our small dramas on that stone ball, whirling around in the middle of empty space, everything—oxygen, water, sunlight, temperature—set up perfectly for our survival. I moved my eyes to the water, the tide slowly receding, the wet, slick, gray sand at its edge, the seagulls coasting, the shells and stones along the shore, one or two shadowy shapes walking there, and I could suddenly feel every atom, all of it thrumming with life. That life energy was clearly connected to the places I went in my spells. Looking at the scene in front of me, I felt I was touching something familiar, setting my finger on the pulse of a person I knew and sensing the life there, the mystery of the taken-for-granted working of the heart. It was a kind of language without sound, a communication with something unknown and unnamed. A rumbling, sparking mystery. And for the first time in my life that mystery took over the place, in my mind, where the man-shaped God had always stood. *God*—that word—could hold the shape of a person, but it could not possibly hold the vast, seething, spinning dimension of the world I was touching then. For the first time, no word stood between me and that mystery, no word, concept, or image.

As I was walking home that night, three boys came by in a car and rode along next to me, very slowly, saying things, threatening, mocking. I don't remember exactly what they said, but I remember that I was completely unafraid. After a minute or so I just stopped, turned to face them, and looked at them calmly as they glided along in the darkness, heads and arms out the windows, taunting, threatening. The car stopped. I thought they'd get out. But then my lack of fear seemed to pass across the air between us, a signal, a soundless voice. I remember the small splash of shame on the face of the boy in the back seat. He said something to the others; they sped away. After they were gone I felt surrounded by a cloud of calm strength, and for some reason I began to count my steps. And I think what happened was that the counting and the sense of fearlessness I felt served to focus my mind in an unusual way, and when I was several blocks from the house it seemed to me that the cocoon of my ordinary thoughts and hopes burst open. The wonderful place I was used to going in my spells gave way into another larger, brighter place that was so magnificent I had to stop walking and stand still on the sidewalk again and simply bathe in that light.

Gradually the new feeling dissolved, leaving only a sweet memory, but I felt I'd opened a door into another room in the enormous castle or mansion I was being given glimpses into now and again. I felt that I had traveled to a part of the stratosphere where fear couldn't breathe. It's really impossible for me to put this accurately into words, but the impression of that evening stayed with me, a kind of interior fireworks, beautiful, startling, unforgettable. It was as if, behind the old God of my imagination, this enormous, new, unnamable spirit was sliding across ancient grazing fields into a twilit landscape, and I was being asked to follow. The memory is like a chip in the kind of stone that has colorful crystals beneath a gray surface. It sparkles there, deep, deep inside me, even now, beyond every worry and hope.

CHAPTER **TWO**

I always did well academically—thanks, in part, to Father Alberto's unofficial tutoring—and when I finished high school I was admitted to Boston University Nursing School, something that made my father proud. If I wasn't going to have boyfriends and travel the familiar path toward marriage and family, at least I'd have a secure job to go to every week. If I wasn't going to act like a normal girl, at least he could tell his friends, "My daughter, she's the nurse," and that would serve as a decent enough explanation for my strangeness.

I did have a few dates in those years. For whatever reason, though, the boys who asked me out to dinner or a movie (or once to play pool) seemed only half interested, as if they were going through the motions, trying to prove something to themselves: that they could go out on a date with a girl, that someone would say yes if they asked. They ventured a kiss, not much more. It was completely unintentional, but something about me seemed to set up a barricade of cool refusal around my innermost self, and though I was curious and felt the usual desire, it seemed that the world of intimacy was walled off to me, a country that would never issue me a visa. Before those dates I always looked at myself in the mirror. I'd been told—by relatives mostly—that I was pretty, but what matters is what you believe about yourself, not what others tell you, and I saw nothing particularly beautiful in that mirror—thick black hair with a few rogue curls in it, dark eyebrows, the long nose and large lips—nothing that matched the faces of the beautiful women I saw on TV or in magazines. Maybe the way I felt about my looks somehow magically infected the boys I was with: their kisses were almost apologies, as if they didn't want to insult me by shaking hands.

But for some reason, I really didn't know why, the absence of a serious love in my life was not a devastatingly sad thing for me at that point. There were times, especially alone in my room at night, when I'd ridden the subway home to Revere after my nursing classes, when I'd made a meal for my father and cleaned up afterward, when I'd finished my homework, climbed the stairs to my room, and was lying there looking at the ceiling, there were times when I felt a species of deep loneliness, a want of another person to confide in, to do things with, a body to hold my body against. Really, though, the pain was not as intense as it seemed to be for friends who talked to me about their own loneliness, their boyfriends and breakups and sexual fun, their waiting for the phone to ring or a text tone to sound, their anxiety —one way or the other—about pregnancy tests.

My closest friend, Lisa Dixon, had an on-again, off-again relationship with a boy we'd both known in high school, and there was so much drama and pain in it that it seemed to me more like torture than intimacy.

"Are you gay?" she asked me once when we were out for pizza and I told her, for the seventieth time, that there was no special man in my life.

"No."

"Just not interested?"

"I'm interested. It just never works out for me."

"You don't like sex?"

"I've never had sex."

"You're joking, right?"

I shook my head.

"Well, we'll have to fix that," she said, as if she had a particular man in mind for me, and detailed plans about what this man and I would do.

AS I GREW OLDER THE conversations I had with Father Alberto—so different from the ones I had with Lisa—evolved to fit my new understanding of things, my new stage of life. I'm sure he did that on purpose, guiding me like any good soccer coach or violin teacher, gently expanding my horizons with more complicated reading material—Julian of Norwich, St. Augustine, Dostoevsky—ramping up the conversations so that we were wrestling with the idea of free will, imagining what must have happened at the Last Supper, pondering Jesus' final lament on the cross, his unforgettable "My Lord, my Lord, why have you forsaken me?"

Father Alberto was a quiet, unassuming man with short salt-and-pepper hair and a belly that pushed out in front of him like the middle of a wine barrel. If he wasn't visiting the sick or having dinner with parishioners, you'd often find him on the grounds of St. Anthony's, shoveling snow or pulling weeds in the parking lot or on the big stone patio—something, of course, that wasn't part of his job description. If you went up to him when he was working there, he'd always stop, stand up, slap the snow from his gloves or the dirt from his hands, give you a big smile and a hug, and invite you into the rectory to have coffee and cheesecake with him and Matilda in the kitchen. He was, at those times, as soft and gentle as the sash on a dress. But especially in later years, when he put on his vestments and stood at the altar, he changed into a different man. He seemed to grow taller and more broad-shouldered. He walked with more confidence, his head tilted slightly back. He lost some of his kindliness and said things that made older couples in the pews squirm and look at each other.

Sometimes when he gave those sermons—again, this happened more in his later years; I was well into college by then—he'd actually leave the altar and walk back and forth in front of the communion rail, occasionally even venturing half-way down the center aisle. No other priests did that, none that I'd seen or heard about anyway, certainly none of the priests in Revere, and soon he developed a reputation for being eccentric, weird, as he himself put it, a radical priest in a place where radicals of any kind were as rare as palm trees in Canada. If, on a given Sunday, he became particularly excited, he'd wave his arms and raise his voice and talk passionately about the

Church ("the capital C Church" he always called it in those sermons), his love for the Church, how wonderful it was that it had existed for thousands of years and that the rite of the Mass had remained almost unchanged over all that time, how much money Catholic charities had given to help the poor all over the world, the good that was done in Catholic hospitals and Catholic colleges and schools, how much comfort the faith brought to people when they were sick and dying, when they lost someone in their family, when they were suffering through an emotional or psychological crisis.

At the same time, he said, the Church had many flaws, and, if we were to be fully rounded, honest-living Catholics, it was important for us to acknowledge them, too.

He was one of the few priests I knew who spoke openly about the sex scandals of that time period. "Lives have been ruined," he would say, waving his arms and speaking so loudly that his voice echoed high up into the corners above the choir loft. "Lives have been ruined by some members of this Church, an organization that's supposed to stand for love and kindness and godliness. Let us look at the way we've hidden those grievous failings all these years. Let us admit our own culpability. And let us acknowledge the fact that we still exclude certain people. We exclude those who've been divorced, for one good example. We exclude those whose sexuality is different from that of the majority. Yes, that's what I'm talking about. If it gets me in trouble, I don't care anymore. If I upset you, let me ask you to consider something: Is exclusivity something Jesus would have condoned?" At a point like that in a particularly forceful sermon, Father Alberto would turn his back on the congregation, walk all the way up and stand behind the altar rail, as if it might offer him some protection. "Jesus," he'd repeat, nodding his head respectfully, as we were all taught to do when saying God's name. "If you read the Bible, our Jesus stands for forgiveness, for inclusiveness, for wrapping his loving arms around the most marginalized in society, the poor, the sinners, the outcast. That's the Jesus we worship, isn't it? So tell me, what are we doing in the modern era? Inventing a new Jesus? A stricter, more hateful, more exclusive Jesus, somebody who likes the in-crowd, the safe majority, the ones who stayed married but not the ones who didn't? The ones who love a certain way? Who live a certain way? Let us think about that, can we? I'm going back now and I'm going to sit in my chair and not say a word to you for five full minutes, and I want everyone in this church to sit quietly, too. Kids, listen, you sit as quiet as you can and let your mother and father think for five minutes, and when you get home they'll give you a treat. Chocolate or something. Ice cream. Understand?

I want us all to ponder the way we've been trying to remake Jesus, the way we cast certain members of the human family outside the embrace of his loving arms. Why are we doing that? What's in it for us? What do you think He would say if He were here?"

Then he'd go back and sit silently for five minutes at the side of the altar.

It drove some parishioners crazy. You'd hear men and women muttering, coughing, moving restlessly in the pews, little kids crying and asking their parents what was going on, people kicking the kneelers and knocking their missals onto the floor, and even a few of the angriest ones walking out, and not trying to be very quiet about it either, as they opened and closed the heavy front doors.

Gradually, as our relationship deepened, the tone of our conversations in the confessional, and even at the table in the rectory over cups of coffee, began to change. As I grew older, Father Alberto began to speak about those things more and more openly with me. "Cynthia," he'd say, "I value your opinion, so tell me, what do you think about the stuff I got into at Mass on Sunday?" Usually I'd begin by saying "I thought it was wonderful, Father. I thought it was exactly what we needed to hear."

But he could tell I was being saccharine and polite. "Come on, now," he'd say, "be real. Speak the truth. What do you think?" And we'd go from there into a conversation that sometimes lasted twenty or thirty minutes. My knees would hurt because I'd be kneeling in the confessional for so long, and once Father realized that, I started to say my confession face-to-face with him in one of the small conference rooms of the rectory, and then our talks sometimes lasted as long as an hour or an hour and a half. We'd argue, debate, discuss Church history, the lives of the saints. He'd talk about a certain cardinal's behavior and how much it bothered him that some of his fellow priests, abusive, hurtful, deeply troubled men, had been protected in order to protect the reputation of the Church. We'd talk about the lawsuits and the court cases and friends of my father who were divorced, and we'd talk a bit about sex, too, although he was always careful to let me have my privacy in that regard. Not that there was much to protect. Lisa's promise to invigorate my sex life had never amounted to anything. I'd kissed three boys in my brief adulthood. That was as far as it had gone and for years as far as it would go. When I went out, it was almost always in small groups of men and women, nursing school friends, a fun environment without much risk or thrill in it.

Then, as I moved into my third year of college, the tone of those conversations changed yet again. I'd stopped mentioning the spells, but Father Alberto started asking about them in a new way, and when I told him how the experiences were changing, he said he'd been meditating on them all that time and he'd come to the conclusion that I had a calling, that there was something special I was going to do on this earth. "Becoming a nurse is fine," he said. "It's valuable work, godly work. But I feel sure now that there's something else for you." He didn't know what it was, he said, but he had a sense of it. "Intimations" was the word he used.

Then, a bit later, when he thought I was ready to hear it, he said his intimations told him my true calling would bring me great difficulty.

That part upset me, naturally. I didn't want any great difficulties in my life. But, if I'm going to be perfectly honest, I have to admit that a small, hidden part of me didn't really believe what Father Alberto was saying anyway. I knew by then that our friendship was as important to him as it was to me, and I wondered sometimes if, as he'd grown older without a wife and children, a nagging loneliness had taken hold of him and that loneliness was unconsciously leading him to make me out to be something I was not. I sometimes even wondered—I'm not proud of this—if our friendship might be a substitute for not having lovers in our life. I didn't feel any particular physical attraction to him, and I doubt he felt any for me. I don't mean it that way. I mean only that I worried about the temptations of the solitary life, the places it might lead us in our thoughts.

• • •

AT SOME POINT AFTER I finished my next-to-last year of college and was thinking about where I'd end up working, Father Alberto started to tell me he was getting into more and more "hot water" for his sermons, that the pastor of St. Anthony's, Monsignor Zanelli, who'd always been a friend and supporter, was about to retire and finding it harder to protect him. He said he was receiving phone calls calling him "the Satan Priest," and worse. "It won't keep me from speaking the truth, Cynthia," he'd say. "It won't stop me. I have my own understanding of God, and the older I get, the surer I am of it. I'm a priest. It's my job, precisely my job, to pass on that understanding. I'm not going to keep quiet about it."

Calls came to his room in the rectory late at night, and when he answered he knew someone was on the other end of the line, taunting him with silence. He started to talk openly with me about an organization called Lamb of God, which was gaining popularity in the parishes around Boston in those difficult years. The Lamb of God people covered a spectrum from ordinary good Catholics with conservative social opinions to absolute fanatics who would violently disrupt school board meetings when the issue of birth control and sex education was being discussed, and they'd sometimes be seen on the television news making hateful comments about "the deterioration of the American moral fiber," spoiled children, lazy workers, lenient priests. More and more often in those years the radical factions were speaking for all of Lamb of God, and I worried, even then, where it would lead. Obviously, the kinds of things Father Alberto said in his sermons were not pleasing to those people. "I'm on their radar now," he told me, and he suspected that some of the more irrational members of the movement were the ones who were calling him up and sending him the hateful letters.

I've never been a very political person. My father, a fairly typical parishioner at St. Anthony's, wasn't political either, certainly not about matters of the Church. When Father Alberto asked him to sit silently for five minutes and contemplate this or that question, he tried to do that. When a priest said the Church was being unfair to society's outcasts, my father probably agreed in theory, but he had no comment and made no move to do anything about it. Issues like that were simply not a matter for discussion in our home. He went to Mass, did what he was told, and didn't seem to think about it much, and so in that way—and in others—we had very little in common with Lamb of God Catholics. There was a kind of cushion between us and them. Father Alberto was the antithesis of their mentality, a man of love, not rules, a man who tried to unify, not divide, to sow understanding and compassion, not hatred and harsh judgment.

But like a lot of men and women of love—Jesus and Mary come to mind; Gandhi, Martin Luther King, Abraham Lincoln—that desire to unify, not divide, was exactly the trait that would eventually bring him trouble.

CHAPTER THREE

Near the beginning of my last year of college—it was September 24, about eight p.m.—Matilda called from the church, hysterical with grief, and said that Father Alberto had been in a terrible accident. He'd gone to someone's house for dinner, she said, probably had a few glasses of wine, and crossing in front of St. Anthony's—a place where Revere Street makes a ninety-degree curve—he'd been struck by a car. The driver didn't stop; the police were looking for him. Father was in the intensive care ward of a hospital in Boston (the same hospital where I'd done my clinical practice and was hoping to work one day); could I give her a ride?

That news, sent through the phone line in Matilda's frantic voice, hit me like a beam falling from the roof. I grabbed the keys to my father's car and picked her up, and we drove into Boston, too fast, and parked in a no-parking zone in front of the hospital (the car was towed) and hurried inside.

Father Alberto wasn't conscious, the nurse told us, and wasn't expected to regain consciousness. No visitors were allowed, but she'd seen me on the wards and she remembered me and I talked to her for a while, told her that Matilda and I were as close as he had to family, and, as nurses will occasionally do in those situations, she bent the rules. Matilda was weeping so hard that she took two steps into the room, made the sign of the cross, and went out again, but I sat by Father Alberto's bed, watching his chest move up and down in too-small bumps, praying under my breath, glancing up at the heart monitor as if that one pulse were the ticking clock of God's kingdom on Earth. I put my right hand on Father's wrist and squeezed, and, as if that touch had all the force of my love in it, his eyes fluttered and opened and I could see him slowly becoming aware of his surroundings. His irises wavered for a moment, as if he were having trouble controlling them, but I squeezed his hand again and he began to focus.

After a minute or more of just staring at me, he said the strangest thing: "I see who you are."

I nodded. "Cynthia."

He shook his head, said, "No," faintly, and let his eyelids drop closed. I couldn't tell if the shake of his head meant he was trying to tell me there was no hope for him or if his brain wasn't working right and he was saying "no" to the Cynthia part, mistaking me for someone else. When people are close to death, they sometimes believe they see their mother or father or husband or wife at the bedside, even though that person has been dead for years. Doctors consider it an hallucination, nothing more than a change in brain chemistry brought on by the stress of dying or a combination of medicines. I wasn't so sure. I loved science, but what I didn't like was the certainty of some scientific minds, as if the known laws of chemistry, biology, and physics explained absolutely everything. What if those people *were* seeing the spirits of their loved ones? Why, given all the other miracles that surround us—sunrise, for instance, or childbirth—was that so impossible? I squeezed Father's hand a second time. His eyes opened again, but just for a moment, as if raising the lids required the same amount of will and strength as lifting a heavy weight above his head.

"Father," I said. He didn't respond. I squeezed his hand gently a third time, I waited. Before my throat closed up completely, I said what I hadn't been able to say to my grandmother: "Thank you."

There was a twitch of what might have been a smile at the corners of his lips. The nurse came in, checked his IV line, the heart monitor, then hurried out to fetch a doctor. In the course of my training I'd seen a number of people die. Some struggled. Some, like my grandmother, drifted off into what looked like a peaceful sleep, the burdens of life left behind them like too-heavy luggage on the start of a long trip. Some tried to get out of bed or yelled or screamed, their faces twisted up in terror. I watched Father Alberto for any of those signs, I glanced up at the monitor, and when I looked back at him I saw that his eyes were open again, just barely, a quarter of an inch between the lids. His lips moved. "Can't give up," I thought he might have whispered. Or maybe "Don't give up." I leaned down and kissed his lips, and then the nurse and a doctor came hurrying into the room and Father Alberto's eyes closed and the lines on the machines wavered a last time and went flat. I stepped away to let them work on him—it's such a violent exercise, trying to keep someone in this world. Instead of leaving the room as they told me to, I stood in the doorway and watched. I could clearly see Father Alberto's spirit gathering itself, almost the way a person brings his arms in close to his body and bends his knees before making a big jump. But this spirit didn't have any shape that resembled a human body; it was something else, not ghostlike exactly but outlined in light, supple, electrical. Somehow—I could never say how—it contained, not his looks and personality, but Alberto Ghirardelli's *essence*. There was a signature stamped on it. I watched that essence preparing itself, gathering itself up through his chest and throat and in the features of his face—just the smallest flexing of the smallest muscles there. And then it flickered a last time, like a candle flame going out, and made its leap into the next world.

The doctors and nurses worked and worked—they're required to by law—but I could have told them it was no use. I said one Hail Mary, helping him on his way, and then, carrying a familiar sad weight, feeling an all-too-familiar hole opening in my world, I went out into the hall to find Matilda.

ON THE DAY AFTER FATHER Alberto's death, Monsignor Ferraponte—who had taken over a group of local churches after the retirement of Monsignor Zanelli—put out a brief statement saying, basically, "We are all saddened by this loss." To my ear at least, the tone of it was half sincere. There wasn't a single good word about Father Alberto, no praise, nothing about how beloved he'd been, and it struck me as doubly strange that the monsignor didn't preside over the funeral Mass and wasn't anywhere to be seen among the thousand or so people who crowded the church.

In the days and weeks following Father Alberto's death I felt as though I inhabited a great cold emptiness. It was all I could do to make myself go into Boston for school, to come home and finish the chores I was supposed to do around the house. My father seemed frightened by the depth of my grief. At the funeral he watched me as if I might melt. And later, at home, he was like a knight clanking through the kitchen and living room in a heavy armor of self-consciousness. Father Alberto's sudden death had taken hold of his world with two big hands and shaken it so hard that the things he'd always done easily—snapping green beans off a vine, gluing and clamping a loose leg on an old kitchen chair—seemed suddenly beyond him, as alien to his hands as the French language to his tongue.

"What's wrong, Pa?" I said at last.

"Nothin'."

"You're not yourself."

A grunt. A silence. Then: "You best friend you lost now."

I looked at him through a quick lens of tears, but even in that sad blur I could see the fear on his face, a cold-weather tan. I *was* sad, of course, wrapped up in sadness from eyes to knees, but I wasn't afraid. "I'll see him again," I said, because that was—and is—a certainty in my world. I know it like I know red from blue: God doesn't bring souls together for a few years in the ocean of eternity and then separate them forever. What sense would that make in a world that, even judging by the known laws of biology, chemistry, and physics, is otherwise so meticulously ordered?

"Nobody knows it for sure," my father said,

then he made a quick retreat to the consolation of television, that leaping, seductive, electronic world, a deathless universe.

Though the state and local police conducted an investigation—Matilda told me they knocked on every door in the neighborhood, hoping to find someone who'd seen or heard something on the night Father Alberto was killed—and though there were articles in the paper and notices on the TV news asking for help, the hit-and-run driver, drunk, careless, or an assassin, was never found. I went to the police station and told the officer on duty about the phone calls and veiled threats. I asked him to look at the Lamb of God movement for possible suspects, but even I knew how useless that would be. They'd have to trace the calls, somehow connect them to the hit-and-run driver; it would be the next thing to impossible.

I kept going to St. Anthony's, of course. I'd sit in the cavernous darkness and pray for Father Alberto and try to make contact with his spirit, just as I'd done with my grandmother after she died and with my mother for so many years. Even though he'd shaken his head when I said my name, I tried to make myself believe he'd known it was me there beside him in the hospital room and that what he'd said was "Don't give up." In the echoing emptiness I ran our conversations through my mind over and over again, searching them for something I'd missed, some nugget of wisdom, some finger pointing me in a certain direction. What I remembered most, to my frustration, was his insistence, in our last few visits, that there was nothing more he could do for me.

"Can't we keep talking, Father?"

"Of course, yes, we'll always keep talking. We'll be gabbing and snacking forever in the kitchens of eternity. But there's nothing more I can tell you, Cynthia. You're so far beyond any point I'll ever reach. You need to find somebody higher up, somebody wiser about this kind of prayer. You need, most of all, not to be so damn modest! If you can't come out and admit God is touching you in a special way, that's a kind of sin, too, don't you see?"

I laughed at that, changed the subject, but I filed it away where I filed everything else he'd ever said to me.

"Somebody higher up" meant, to my simple way of looking at things, the new monsignor, Father Alberto's immediate superior. Sitting there in the church, I decided that he'd been advising me to go and tell Monsignor Ferraponte about my spells. Explain the messages I thought I was getting from God. Ask his advice.

"What good will it do, to talk to somebody else, Father?" I'd argued. "What can somebody else tell me that you can't?"

"It's not a question of good, Cynthia. It's a

question of your calling. How many times do I have to tell you this? You are being asked by God to do something. You have been given these special gifts. Believe me, I've heard the confessions of thousands of people in my life. No one I've ever met has had this kind of communication with God. It's not something to fool around with. God doesn't do things without a purpose. He's pointing you toward something, and I'm not a good enough man to know what that something is."

I stalled and procrastinated. I kept telling him I had too much schoolwork, that I was too busy at home, but he knew the real reason as well as I did: more and more as the years passed, I hated making any kind of fuss about myself. The spells and visions were something I'd been living with for so long that they felt as much a part of me as my hair and hands, and it simply wasn't in my nature to lift my head above the tide of everydayness. I was very much like my father in that way: he did his work and came home. He didn't make any trouble, as if he believed that there were always snipers in the neighborhood and to lift your face above the wall everyone else crouched behind was to invite a bullet. But it was more than that. Most of my young feistiness—most, not all—had, over the years of visions and prayer, been rubbed smooth like a stone's sharp edges in surf. I was borne along in a near-constant peacefulness. I watched chips of Lamb of God protests on the nightly news, wondering if any of the angry faces I saw belonged to the person who had killed my friend. I read about the movement in the paper, but anger like that—anger that wanted some sinful Other to rail against—felt as alien to me as loud music in a library. I didn't want to add anything to the trouble on this earth. The last thing I wanted was fuss or confrontation.

Still, in spite of my natural reticence and solitariness, after Father Alberto died I started to let myself think about the possibility of finding someone else to talk with about the experiences I was having in prayer. If I did make an appointment with the new monsignor, I thought, what was the worst that could happen? He'd yell at me, chase me out of his office, call me a lunatic, a mad egotist, a foolish girl. So what? Maybe Father Alberto had been wrong, and that kind of rejection was exactly what I needed. Maybe my "calling" in life was simply to be a good nurse and daughter. Wasn't that enough?

The spells went on and on, like someone who calls your house and calls and calls and won't give up until you answer the phone. One night I was so buried in prayer that I stayed on the subway car after my stop—which was the end of the line—and the conductor had to come and shake me and tell me to get off before they made the loop and headed back to Boston. Week by week the spells seemed to take me further from ordinary life, to go on longer, to leave me with the stronger and more lasting certainty that I was touching another universe, a place where very different laws applied.

At about that same time, one after another, Catholic churches in Revere were closing. When I was a young girl, there had been seven of them in our city. By the time I started my last semester of college, there were three. As the doors closed and the parishioners were sent elsewhere, as real estate signs went up in front of the stone-and-wooden three-doored buildings, the assignments of the priests were changed, too. St. Anthony's was one of the three churches that stayed open; the empty spot created by Father Alberto's death was filled by a Father Gerencia, who was from Chile. As I've said, after Monsignor Zanelli resigned, Monsignor Ferraponte, who'd been the pastor at St. Ann's in Beachmont, had been made the monsignor and pastor of all three churches in Revere.

Near Christmas of that year the visions changed. They intensified and became even more frequent, and with the new intensity, the message God was sending me began to take a clearer shape. That shape—so surprising, so strange—broke my neat bowl of contentment into three dozen ceramic shards. I tried to pretend to myself I was "hearing" it wrong, that my inner world had grown cluttered and noisy and God's words had become garbled.

Finally, when spring arrived, I couldn't bear this new stage of things any longer and I called and made an appointment to see Monsignor Ferraponte. I was haunted by a new kind of impatience and irritation. I think part of the change and part of what prompted me to finally do something was connected to my feelings about Father Gerencia, our new priest. He was so small, spiritually, in comparison to what Father Alberto had been, his sermons so empty of anything provocative, original, or interesting to me. His whole demeanor on the altar and his tone in the confessional—cool and detached, a sacrament machine—was something that, to my own shock, I found difficult to respect. I still went to Mass two or three times a week—avoiding Father Gerencia when my schedule allowed it—and nothing could have kept me from the quiet hours of solitary prayer I spent there. But in the past, whereas I would leave a Mass said by Father Alberto exhilarated and deeply satisfied, I now left Father Gerencia's masses feeling as though I'd showered with a sour-smelling body wash. He seemed to me to be going through the motions, like a mechanic changing a set of spark plugs, and I treasured the rite of the Mass so much that it felt almost sinfully wrong to me not to perform it with enthusiasm. Here you were, creating God's body anew, reciting prayers that had been spoken for thousands of years by worshippers all over the world. It wasn't something to be done in a luke-warm way. I don't really blame Father Gerencia; that was just the person he was. He was . . . neutral, unimaginative, a kind enough, good enough man, but—and may God forgive me—it seemed to me that his understanding of the spiritual life was kept in a thin drawer in his head. There was no whole-body richness to it as there had been with Father Alberto, no risk, no real pleasure, no sense of awe.

I was starting to feel my love of the Church unraveling like a blouse with a pulled thread. I still had my prayer life—more intense than ever—but the Mass, the most sacred rite of my faith, had started to lose its beauty and power, and that terrified and upset me. In a very real way, the act of attending Mass stood at the center of my life. It meant more to me than schoolwork or career. It was like anything else people look forward to for comfort and meaning—seeing their children, making love with their spouse, a favorite meal, a visit with friends, a run on the beach—not so much an addiction as one of the main pillars of my happiness. Father Alberto's death had been like an earthquake; the pillar had cracked and become unstable. Every time I sat in the pew and listened to Father Gerencia's flat voice pronouncing stale platitudes like "God is love, and because God is love, we must love one another as God loves us,"

I could feel the pillar tilting and shifting, the life above it sliding down and to the side, more and more of my prayer time being occupied with a stony, dusty bitterness.

So finally I made myself take out my phone and call St. Ann's and ask for an appointment to see Monsignor Ferraponte. The woman I spoke with there told me that the nearest available appointment was three weeks away, a Wednesday afternoon, three o'clock. After that, it would be another month. Should she write my name in?

Wednesday afternoons we had our regular tour of the wards at Mass General, not the best part of the school week to skip. But I knew that if I procrastinated any longer, I'd never do it, so I said yes, fine, and on the appointed day, just before three o'clock, I got off the train two stops early, walked down to St. Ann's, and climbed the creaking wooden steps of the rectory.

The woman who made the appointments at St. Ann's was very much the opposite of my friend Matilda at St. Anthony's (I think sometimes that people and places have a magnetic charge and that charge attracts certain kinds of people and repels others). I don't remember her name; I just remember how cold she was and how protective she seemed of the monsignor. I walked up to her little window, the kind of glassless window where you pay parking tickets at the police station, and I said, "Hi, I'm Cynthia Piantedosi. I have an appointment at three o'clock with Monsignor Ferraponte."

She looked at me as if I were a terrorist bringing a bomb into the building. She checked her book, saw my name, and told me in a wary voice to go and sit in one of the chairs and wait, the monsignor would be with me as soon as he was free. I stood there for a few seconds, until she looked up from her appointment book and made eye contact; then I felt my commitment to peacefulness breaking open and I said, "How about being a little more polite?"

A shiver of nastiness went across her face. She pinched her eyes at me the way kids used to do in high school and said, "Yes, your highness," and built a smile out of two parts meanness and one part private, closed-off world.

I went and sat in one of the hard-backed chairs, sneaking glances at the receptionist. I've always been blessed with the ability not to care much what other people think of me. It's a great gift, really, something that's allowed me, over the years, to grow and change and not feel locked into the person I'm supposed to be in others' eyes. It gave me courage, even in the rough waters of my teenage years, to listen to something inside myself, a small voice telling me who I was, what I should and shouldn't care about, and it helped me ignore, to some extent at least, the rip currents of peer pressure and local opinion.

But sitting there—I waited nearly twenty minutes, nervous and upset—I couldn't help wondering if the woman was that cold to everyone who came through the door or if the fact that I'd been close with Father Alberto was known to her and had branded me, in that parish at least, as some kind of troublemaker. It was odd to think of myself that way. Until then, outside of the rectory at St. Anthony's, I'd felt almost invisible, a shadow that slipped around the city unnoticed, a plain-faced Revere girl who rode the subway five days a week, blending into the plastic chairs and scratched-up windows, who could make sense of an anatomy textbook and start an IV and go out for a drink with friends and cook for her father and not cause so much as a ripple of upset on the pond of Greater Boston life.

The squeak of rubber-soled shoes on linoleum—a hospital sound—knocked me out of my troublesome little daydream. Around the corner came a tall, trim, good-postured man in black pants and a black, long-sleeved shirt. We had never spoken before, but I recognized him from the times he'd come to St. Anthony's for a holiday Mass. I stood and introduced myself. Monsignor Ferraponte shook my hand with his arm held out straight. I walked half a step behind him down the gleaming hallway, and then we turned into an office—plain as a boardinghouse room—and I sat in the chair he indicated.

Monsignor Ferraponte closed the door with a soft click, then walked over to a chair opposite me, hitched up his pant legs by taking hold of the cloth between thumb and second finger just above the knee, and sat. From things I'd heard around St. Anthony's over the years, I knew a bit about the new monsignor's story—he'd been born in Cuba, he and his father and his sister had escaped on a homemade raft, venturing out in darkness toward the hope of freedom, drifting across ninety miles of shark-filled water. His mother had stayed behind, and his sister had died of thirst on the crossing. Despite those awful things, people said, he'd never lost his devotion to God, and, though he wasn't allowed back into Cuba, he went to the Dominican Republic every winter and spent a month with poor children there, not just administering the sacraments but working alongside their families, building houses, running sewer lines, and so on. There were less flattering stories, too—mostly having to do with his less-than-kind treatment of altar boys and his affection for a group of politically powerful Lamb of God friends—but Father Alberto had told me not to pay attention to them, it was just rumor, gossip. "If he could ever get the stick out of his ass," Father Alberto said once, in an unguarded moment, "Ferraponte would be a great priest."

Looking across the table at him, I tried not to dwell on that remark or on my theory of magnetism. It wasn't easy. The monsignor had the posture of an offended state trooper. His eyes were blue blue, the top of his head bald, the hair to either side as black as his shirt and pants and cropped short. My father had a favorite expression for certain people, "If he smiled, his face-a she break," and I was trying not to think of that either, as I looked at the monsignor.

"How can I be of service, Miss Piantedosi?" he asked.

What was the point of speaking to him if I couldn't be fully honest? "I'm sure you know, Monsignor," I began, "that Father Alberto and I were very close."

He pressed his lips together and nodded. "We were sorry to lose him."

"Yes, very sorry in my case. He was almost like a father to me."

"I understand he was your spiritual adviser."

"I never thought of him that way," I said. "He was a friend. I went to him for confession, for years, since I was a young girl. We used to like to sit in the rectory and eat and talk."

The monsignor seemed not to be listening. "I'd be happy to take over that role if you'd like," he said, "if that's why you've come. I've heard a great deal about you and your prayer life."

"You have? How?"

"Don't be falsely modest, Miss Piantedosi, that's not an attractive trait. You're quite well known in these parts for your devotion to the faith. I understand you spend many hours a day in prayer."

I knew he was lying about the well-known part, perhaps trying to flatter me in the only way he knew, but I hid that thought and said, "I've had an urge toward prayer since I was a young girl. I can't really help it."

"Nor should you. . . . Are you married?" he asked abruptly.

"Not yet. I'm only twenty."

"Boyfriend?"

"No, Monsignor," I said.

"Lesbian?" he asked, the word bursting out of his mouth in a strange, snapping way, almost as if he were spitting or as if the gate that protected his thoughts from running out into the air had been blown open in a gust of wind and the word had leapt out before he'd had a chance to catch it.

I was so surprised I couldn't say anything for a few seconds. "No, no. I'm just a, I'm a shy person. I live with my father. I'm going to nursing school."

"All very good," he said, "and forgive me for asking. We've been besieged lately with what I suppose you could call 'protests' from various women's groups. Boston. Cambridge. They're feminists. I can't imagine what they want with us, really."

"I don't think of myself like that. I mean, I'm not part of any group, not even—"

"How can I help you, then?"

I began to tell him in detail about my experiences in prayer, how I'd been having the spells since I was a little girl, how close I felt to God, and how I was trying to understand what direction He wanted me to go in. When I'd said almost the same things to Father Alberto, it had been a simple recitation of the truth; there, in that office, I felt as though I should mount a defense of every sentence.

"Did Father Ghirardelli give you advice in this matter?"

"I wouldn't call it advice. We used to talk about it, he gave me some books—"

"Which, may I ask? What kinds of books?"

"St. Teresa of Ávila was the one I liked most. *Interior Castle.* I try to reread a bit of it every night. Even though I'm not really sure it's so, Father Alberto said he thought I had a gift, a calling. He kept saying I should speak with somebody."

"Well, that's fine, we can have regular meetings."

He started to say more, but I interrupted him. "Monsignor, I've been getting a particular message lately, in prayer. If I don't tell you about it, I'd feel like I was being deceitful."

"Speak freely."

"It's something strange . . . I feel," I paused at that point, watching him. I'd realized, shortly after the "lesbian" question, that it had been a mistake,

61

that I should never have come to speak with him, but I was there; it made no sense to pretend I'd come for some other reason, or to get up and walk out. "I feel," I said, "that God is calling me to be a priest."

The monsignor hesitated a second, then laughed. It was a high, sweet sound, tinkling glass. I watched him, and when he stopped laughing he said, "Would this be some kind of prank? A joke?"

I shook my head.

"But you're a born Catholic. Surely you don't need me to tell you that isn't possible."

"I know that, Monsignor, yes, of course. And, believe me, it's the last thing I want. I'm not a very outgoing person. I could never imagine myself doing what I saw Father Alberto do, what you do. But I've been having these very clear messages from God for months now, and though I keep trying to pretend they aren't what they are, I've come to realize I can't do that."

"You're serious."

"Very serious. Nervous. Worried you're going to throw me out. But serious as I can be."

He shook his head, a shiver of disbelief. "The parish is in an uproar, don't you realize that?"

"About Father Alberto?"

"Nothing to do with Ghirardelli. It's the false allegations, the court cases. One or two bad actors, yes, we had them, but now you have hundreds of people making up stories of abuse, years after they supposedly occurred. This is really not what we need now, another troublemaker in the parish."

"I'm not a troublemaker. You have to believe me. I would never even be here unless I felt I was being given messages from God. I feel very close to Him."

"I'm sure you do, but that's not the issue."

"Shouldn't it be?"

"Perhaps it should. But let's examine the facts. You are, like me, a Roman Catholic. That means we live according to the rules of our faith. You know the position of the Church, don't you? You understand it?"

"I do, and I love the Church. I just feel so strongly that God is asking me to change that position. I think it might be part of the troubles the Church has been experiencing lately. I came to ask for your help."

"Then you came to the wrong place."

A silence fell over us, bitter as moldy bread. Behind or beneath it I felt that I could hear our thoughts doing battle with each other. I felt a surge of anger against him and I tried to let it dissolve before I said anything else. He looked at his watch.

"I'm sorry to disturb you, Monsignor, but I—"

"You're not disturbing me, you're disturbed. You need to see a lay counselor. You need to pray to our Lord for help. You need to understand,

Miss Piantedosi, the way Satan works his evil magic in this world, the tricks he plays. If he had been a true spiritual adviser, Father Ghirardelli would have warned you about this years ago."

"We talked about it, Monsignor. We—"

"The Church is the bride of Christ, his earthly spouse, do you understand? The ordained priest is the representative of Christ on earth. As such, he and the Church form a union of masculine and feminine, as it were, in a symbolic sense. Were females to be allowed to be priests, that relation-ship would become a homosexual one. Unnatural. The Vatican has been very clear and consistent on this doctrine."

"Homosexual?"

"Yes, exactly. Outside the laws of God and nature."

"So you don't think the rule has any chance of being changed? Not now, maybe, but—"

"I don't think it can be, nor do I think it should be."

"Should priests be allowed to marry?"

"That is not for me to say. I took a vow of celibacy and obedience, as did Father Ghirardelli, I might add, as does every priest."

"But, Monsignor, forgive me. I'll only take another minute of your time. Just in this city, just in the last two years, four churches have closed. When I was a little girl, there were five Masses on a Sunday morning at St. Anthony's and the parking lot was full for all but the earliest one. People are leaving. Millions of people are leaving the Church."

"In many parts of the world she is gaining members and influence, thriving in fact. There is, in Africa and Latin America, an abundance of new vocations."

"But not here, Monsignor."

"No, not in North America, not in most populations, at any rate. But remember this: the Church has a track record of two thousand years and of not abandoning her principles in difficult times."

"But we've seen changes. Saturday-night Masses. Meat on Fridays. My father says they used to have to wait three hours after eating before taking Holy Communion. Those things have changed."

"I'm aware of those things," the monsignor said coolly.

"And from the books I've read, the rules weren't always what they are now. For a thousand years or so after Christ's death priests were allowed to marry. Some popes were even married. Many of them had children of their own, and some of those children later became popes. And women were being ordained as late as the fourteenth century."

"I'm not here to argue a legal case, Miss Piantedosi. I'm not a scholar of the Church, and neither, I'm afraid, are you. These stories you cite are not facts but Satanic bits of revisionist history. I have a schedule so full now—we have a new priest arriving next week—I'm afraid I can't—"

"I'd ask you for just another minute, Monsignor," I said. "I've been in this parish my whole life."

He pressed his lips together, and I watched him breathe through his nose. "This is an exceedingly difficult time."

"I know it is, and I am sorry, but I believe with all my heart and soul and with complete respect for the traditions of the Church that God is speaking to me and instructing me to serve Him as a parish priest. I've had visions of myself at the altar. I—"

I stopped there because a change had come over the monsignor's face. His eyes had shifted to the side and down. The muscles along his jawline flexed. "Nothing in the world is as clever as Satan," he said. "Nothing."

"This isn't from Satan," I almost shouted, and something changed in me, too. I felt a strength rising up from behind my veil of shyness, something absolutely new. I wanted to be polite and respectful as I'd always been, but underneath that the water was boiling, the steam swirling into a new shape.

The monsignor seemed to see it. His face softened. He said, "How does one know?"

"How does one know anything, Monsignor? At

some point you have to believe in the way you feel, don't you? How do we know there's a God?"

"From the sacred scriptures."

"But how do we know we can trust the scriptures?"

"You are stepping very very close to the edge of blasphemy."

"I don't think so," I said forcefully. "I'm a good woman. I do no harm in the world. I go to Mass three times a week. I spend at least two hours a day in prayer. Father Alberto and I had dozens of conversations about the possibility of being deceived—"

The monsignor raised a hand to me, palm forward. "Stop," he said. "Stop there, please. I don't think it wise to rely on the spiritual guidance of a man like Father Ghirardelli, may God rest his soul. Some of the things he said from the pulpit I would never have allowed had I been his superior. We have priests who succumb to the temptation of lust. We have priests who succumb to laziness. And we have priests who succumb to the temptations of power and ego, who enjoy the attention one garners by being different, radical, extreme. The same can be said for people who have so-called 'visions.' What I'm telling you is that you should be careful that these visions you say you are having are, in fact, not coming from someplace other than God."

"I feel like I can tell the difference."

He let out a breath. "If this visit was to ask me to help you become a priest, then the answer is no. Categorically. Absolutely. The rest of this is, given the circumstances, I'm sorry to say, a poor use of the hour."

"All right," I said. "Is there anyone I can appeal to?"

"Any and every appeal would be useless."

"Then I won't take any more of your time."

He stood quickly, before I had a chance to change my mind. "I appreciate that." His tone was more conciliatory then, his posture less stiff. At the door he shook my hand and said, "I'll make the offer again. If you'd like me to be your confessor, I'd be willing to do that."

I don't know what came over me then. From the moment I'd stepped into St. Ann's I had felt annoyed and off balance. The place seemed to me to echo with hymns being played in the wrong key. I said, "Two things, Monsignor. First, may God bless you, may He give you every blessing, a deep and abiding peace."

"Thank you."

"And second—I have to ask you this before I go: Do you think there's any chance that somebody associated with Lamb of God killed Father Alberto?"

I admit, though I'm not proud of it, that I thought the question might upset Monsignor Ferraponte. As I asked it I watched his face very closely, but nothing remotely like surprise showed there. He pushed up the middle of his lips the way some people do when they're considering an interesting question, and then he said, "Ah, I see what this is about now."

"He was receiving threatening phone calls before the accident," I said, but the monsignor's face had hardened.

Instead of answering my question he half closed the door and said, "Good-bye, Miss Piantedosi . . . and be careful."

BOOK TWO

CHAPTER **FOUR**

I felt as though I'd gone in to see Monsignor Ferraponte carrying some delicate hope, a fine sculpture made of thin sticks and rare paper. I'd lifted it out of its protective box and handed it carefully across the table to him, and he'd taken it into his hand and squeezed hard, once, crushed it to pieces, and handed it back to me, ugly and broken.

But after I'd walked a few blocks from St. Ann's, replaying the conversation in my mind, I felt a new personality growing inside me, pushing out hard against an old skin. It was almost as if, with the breakage of my delicate sculpture, a shell had broken open, too, and a stronger, more forceful, more assertive Cynthia Piantedosi had been brought to life. It began to seem to me that the monsignor, with his ramrod-straight posture, his fear of the Devil, his need to put people into boxes, might have done me a peculiar favor, punctured the shy and polite surfaces I'd been living beneath for the past few years, and allowed this new woman to breathe.

"God works in mysterious ways," Father Alberto had been fond of saying. A cliché, sure, but on his lips the truth of it pushed up through the surface and sprouted fine, white blossoms of understanding. "You think something bad has happened," he liked to say, "the last thing you want, and then a little time goes by and you see it differently. The pain is like fertilizer on a fruit tree. It stings, it smells, it hurts your eyes, but then by and by you have this beautiful sweet peach."

I believed that, in theory at least. Walking away from St. Ann's, I thought it might be possible that something good would come from the meeting, a change in me, if not in my Church.

STILL, DESPITE THIS HOPEFUL NOTION, the overall effect of the conversation was that, for a time, I completely gave up any ideas I might have been holding on to about changing the Catholic Church. It began to seem not that the Devil was the source of my visions but that my ego might have gotten involved. I was a simple person, really, not stupid but provincial, a nurse in training who lived with her father and had seen almost nothing of the world. And here I was, going to the offices of important men and trying to convince them to do things that were unprecedented and obviously impossible.

So for a month or more after that meeting with Monsignor Ferraponte I kept to my quiet routine and bothered no one. As I feared it would, the investigation into Father Alberto's death yielded nothing beyond a few dead-end leads and two suspects with alibis. It eventually shriveled into a dusty file in the police station. Father Gerencia was a persistent disappointment to me, but I went to Mass as I'd always done, spent many hours alone in the church, cooked for my father, and, with each course and examination, each hour of clinical training in a different hospital ward, moved a step closer to becoming a nurse.

As that was happening, as I was living out my days in what people said was supposed to be the prime of my life, I felt as though the new creature inside me was being wrapped up and strangled like an insect in a spider's web. For a few days after the meeting at St. Ann's I'd felt her stretching her strong arms and legs, lifting her head high, pushing away the old walls of bashfulness. But then steadily, day by day, my usual routine and habits wound her up again in sticky gray filaments.

What risks had I ever taken? I started asking myself. I'd lived my whole life in the same small city, in an upstairs room in my father's house. I had a few friends and a lot of loving relatives, but other than going to college in Boston, only a subway ride from home, I'd never ventured out of my safe little circle. As the weeks passed—winter to spring—a virus of impatience infected me. It was as if, half wrapped up and frustrated to the marrow of her bones, this new me was being held hostage in a room with a loudly ticking clock. The sound had burrowed inside her brain and would not be scalpeled out. Looking back on that time now, I think it was almost as if Father Alberto— the memory of him or his actual spirit—was urging me out of that safe enclosure, cajoling me, pushing me. Some days I woke up and I was sure I'd heard his voice in a dream.

MY FATHER HAD SAID MANY TIMES, in both the languages he used with me as well as with bits of Neapolitan dialect, that I shouldn't feel I had to come home every night and cook him supper. "I can make the pasta, you know. I can fry up-a the saw-seege." The truth was, though, that I enjoyed cooking for him. From the days when I'd watched my grandmother at the counter and cutting board, I'd always loved the sensual aspect of preparing a meal, the textures and colors, the sound of uncooked pasta being poured into a pot, the fragrance of simmering garlic. I liked being able to perform a simple service for him. More than that, I enjoyed having a dependable routine. Probably I would have been happy as a cloistered nun, all decision and uncertainty removed from my life, a time set for waking up, for prayer, for work, for meals, for sleep. Probably, if there had been a convent still active in Revere, I would have been tempted in that direction.

Instead I made a semimonastic routine for myself: I woke up early and prayed, ate an egg or a bowl of oatmeal, some fruit and coffee, took the bus to the subway station, the subway to the hospital or to school. Afterward, I'd retrace that route and stop in at St. Anthony's for an hour before going home. I'd make dinner, ask my father how his day had been, take a walk or a short run, read a bit, go to bed. On days off I'd occasionally accept an invitation for lunch with a friend or a cousin or, in summer, spend a few hours swimming and sunbathing at the beach or working in the garden. For whatever reason, I wasn't a person who liked surprises or change.

So it was unusual for me that, one April afternoon, instead of getting right onto the subway and heading back to Revere, I left the hospital and went for a stroll around downtown Boston. Without any particular destination in mind, I meandered up the back of Beacon Hill, through its narrow old streets and past the brick town houses and flower boxes, the small-paned windows and wrought-iron railings; then I cut behind the State House and found myself at the north edge of Boston Common. There was some kind of music festival going on there, and I didn't feel like being part of a crowd—just the opposite—so I turned left and followed the edge of the Common toward Tremont Street, headed for a different station on the same subway line.

Before I reached the T station, though, I passed a small Catholic church I'd never noticed before. It was set there, improbably, squeezed tight between brick office buildings. Three red doors right on the sidewalk, a crucifix, a schedule of Masses in a glass box out front. I tried one of the doors and was surprised to find it open. The nave was more modern than St. Anthony's, the pews set at an angle facing a stylized altar festooned with colorful banners. Not exactly my kind of religious motif, but I knelt and prayed for a while, then sat back in the pew, closed my eyes, and let my mind be still and quiet. "Contemplative prayer," St. Teresa called it, as opposed to "vocal" prayer. Wordless, imageless, just a stillness, an interior silence. That kind of prayer had been my hobby, my passion, my addiction since I'd been old enough to speak. I found it a strange and wonderful fact that saying and doing nothing had so much joy in it. We're a society of doers, people who believe contemplation is suspect, the province of the lazy and foolish, but that stillness always lit a fire of pleasure inside me, and it does so even now.

After a time I heard footsteps, and after another few minutes I opened my eyes. A small man in jeans and a T-shirt, with crew-cut gray hair, was walking across the altar with a polished candelabra in one hand, and I knew, somehow, that he was a priest. There was something refreshing in the way he was dressed—like an electrician or a taxi driver—and in the way he crossed the altar without the slightest self-consciousness or fuss, as if it were a place exactly as sacred as every other place on Earth. I felt an immediate kinship with him, one invisible person to another, and decided, right then, that I would try going to Mass at his church.

The Paulist Center, it was called, and I knew from the first Sunday that I'd made the right decision. The small priest's name was Father Welch, and his sermon might have been taken from Father Alberto's notebook. Inclusiveness. Kindness. Charity. Openness. "These qualities," he said, "are precisely what the term 'imitation of Christ' actually means."

I loved it when priests took a biblical phrase I'd been hearing my whole life and turned it in a slightly different way, allowing a new light to shine on it. I remembered Father Alberto doing that with "in the fullness of time." "Think about that," he'd said, so happily. *"In the fullness of time!* There's two parts to it. First, if we're really living, if we are hearing with our ears and seeing with our eyes, as Christ told us to, then the day has a richness and fullness to it that gets diluted if we spend the hours worrying, doing five things at once, or desperately hoping for something that might or might not happen. If you spend all day thinking about being rich, for example, then time isn't full at all. It's just a rickety bridge to some imagined future. You don't care about *now,* all you care about is some imaginary *then* when you'll be rich. It's like a child wishing away his youth so he can be grown up enough to drive or go to work every morning!

"And second, by *the fullness of time* the biblical writer could have meant eternity. God's eternity! Think about it! Year after year, century after century, filled with all kinds of different opportunities to move closer to Him. There's your free will. That's what it means, if you ask me. Absolute freedom in how we use the time that's been given to us. Now, you might say, Father, I don't have no freedom of time. I gotta be at work at nine a.m., Monday to Friday, fifty weeks a year. Sure, okay. But when you're at work, when you're cutting that two-by-four for a new house or filling a tooth or answering the phone or selling a chocolate-glazed donut, where are you, really? What are you doing? Are you *there?* Or are you picturing the beer you're gonna have in front of the TV that night or the new dress or car or swimming pool you're gonna buy after you hit the lottery? You see my point here? You can do those things creatively, see? In a way that brings you more in touch with God's world."

It was almost as if I could hear Father Alberto's voice there in the modern surroundings of the Paulist Center, almost as if his spirit, or a kindred spirit, had taken possession of Father Welch and was speaking to me in a kind of liturgical poetry, the new meanings opening up like a cracked walnut, the sweet rich flesh there nourishing me again after all those hungry months with Father Gerencia.

I liked the Paulist Center, too, because it kept its doors open during the week. Father Welch didn't quite have Father Alberto's passion and sense of humor. He didn't have anything close to his abilities as a speaker. He didn't walk down the aisle waving his arms and getting his parishioners excited or angry. And he didn't force anyone to sit quietly for five minutes at a time contemplating the nature of the modern Jesus. But he was my kind of priest.

So I began going regularly to his Masses, and to confession there, too. Little by little, in the confessional, I found myself speaking about my moments of silent prayer. "It's more than a conversation with God," I heard myself say, the sticky filaments snapping one after the next as the new woman inside me awoke, stretched, and stood up. "Not that I feel I *am* God—I'm not crazy, Father, and I don't think I'm conceited—but that God really is alive in me. The only thing is, that word—*God*—it doesn't fit anymore and hasn't for a long time. I grew up thinking of God as a big man in the sky or Jesus on the cross, but this God is more a kind of loving energy, and I feel it not just in myself but in everything and everyone. Does that sound ridiculous?"

At first Father Welch didn't offer any opinion. He didn't ask many questions about my prayer life, the way Father Alberto had, and didn't seem particularly curious or helpful. After two or three conversations in the confessional, though, he invited me to meet with him in his office. We sat there in the small, cluttered upstairs room, and he asked what my upbringing had been like, which people I'd been close to, exactly what happened to me in prayer, how that had changed over the years, what I thought was the origin of those moments and visions. He asked if I'd ever been in therapy, and I said that I had not. He asked if there was any mental illness in my family, and I said that other than my father's love of gambling at the dog track and my grandmother's somewhat compulsive cleanliness, I didn't think so. He laughed at that, and from then on the conversations were easier for both of us.

Every Thursday afternoon I met with him in his office and we talked about the same things I'd discussed with Father Alberto—though in a slightly more intellectual way. The lives of various saints, their experiences and challenges, the ways one's own ego, mental difficulties, or stress could cause one to have the kinds of experiences I was having. We talked about temptations to be wary of—feeling special, superior, judging others, even wanting the experiences to go on and on instead of accepting them as precious gifts, given according to God's timing and purpose.

"In your case," he said, "it's highly unlikely that

these moments are caused by stress, unless you were particularly stressed out as a four-year-old. The issue about becoming a priest, though, is a little bit different. I've had a few people in my counseling sessions who've spoken about a prayer life that was somewhat similar to yours, but no one had the experiences with as much intensity, and no one had them over such a long time, and none of the women felt they were being called to the priesthood. I don't sense any kind of ulterior motive here. You certainly don't seem like the kind of person who wants attention. You don't seem particularly angry at the Church or anything or anyone else—with the possible exception of your monsignor. The only question, as far as I can see, is how to act on this. How long to wait for God to give you that answer."

I sat there listening. I had come to trust him, and although I didn't feel as close to him as I'd once felt to Father Alberto—he was more formal, better educated, less warm—I took his advice seriously. "Tell me," I said, when he'd finished, "how do I pursue it? Where do I go? I feel like if I don't do something, I'll really lose my mind, or my faith, or both."

He sat there and looked at his hands for a few seconds. I can see now that it would have been very easy for him to have left it at "Well, let's just go along as we've been going and wait to see where God leads you." That would have gotten him off the hook with me and kept him out of trouble with his superiors. But Father Welch was braver than that. After a moment he said, "I was in seminary with our present archbishop, did I tell you? Seve Menendez. I think the next logical place to go would be to him. He's the supreme liturgical authority in these parts, and I can't think of anyone who'd be a better person to speak with at this point. You realize, I'm sure, that the chances of anything very satisfying coming out of it are practically zero."

"By now, I've figured that out, Father, yes."

"The Church, when it changes, changes at a glacial pace. Maybe in a hundred years, or three hundred years, we'll see married priests or female Roman Catholic priests. Maybe. There is a group of women who've been ordained or who consider themselves ordained. I respect them, but they haven't been acknowledged by the Vatican, of course, and it seems to me that what you're after isn't so much personal satisfaction as a change in the Church at large. Before we go any farther, I have to caution you that this could end up in a way you neither expect nor want."

I told him what I'd told Monsignor Ferraponte: that I really had no desire to stand up in front of a congregation, to visit the sick and have dinner at people's homes. "I'm more private than that," I said. "But over these past few months I've come to understand that if I just hear these messages and do nothing, I'll get so twisted up inside that I'll end up being a person I don't want to be. At this point, I'll try anything you recommend."

"I think I can arrange a meeting with Menendez," he said. "I won't tell him in much detail what it's about. He's a very . . . I don't want to say *cagey* man, but he keeps his cards close to his vest, as the saying goes. It may be that Monsignor Ferraponte has alerted him to your situation and the two of them see it the same way and he won't let you make an appointment, or he'll use the meeting as an opportunity to give you a lecture of some sort. But let's try it anyway. Let me contact his office. I'd offer to go with you, but that would make it seem like I'm sponsoring you or leading you, and I'm not. I'm happy to have you use my name, but I think the actual meeting with him, face-to-face, is something you should do on your own."

I thanked him, and as he was seeing me to the door he said, "You know where this could lead, don't you?"

"Probably to my getting in trouble."

"I mean geographically. Unless Menendez completely shoots down the idea, I think the next place you'll be going is Rome."

I stood there and stared at him. We were almost exactly the same height, our eyes probably three feet apart.

"You look shocked," he said, smiling one of his rare smiles.

"Father, I've never been to Canada. I've been to New York City once in my life, to Maine once. Going to Rome, for me, would be like going into space. How would I get there? What would I do there?"

"I don't know, frankly," he said. "But my guess would be, if the archbishop senses, as I do, that there's a legitimacy to your prayer life, and if he is, as I suspect him to be, the kind of man who doesn't like to make difficult decisions, then I would think he'll try to pass you up the ladder, to a cardinal in Rome, perhaps, or a cardinal's assistant. He could just as easily tell you to go home and mind your own business. I mention the Rome option only so you'll be ready."

ON THE SUBWAY RIDE BACK to Revere that day I tried and failed miserably to picture myself anywhere near Vatican City, in any cardinal's assistant's office, for any reason. Even the idea of going to see the archbishop had made me start to fret from the minute I'd heard his name spoken. I wondered if this would end up being a kind of ongoing torment, a penance for the sin of my presumptuousness, my spiritual egotism: I'd be sent from one office to the next for a series of humiliations.

It was late by then, but instead of going directly back to Tapley Avenue, I went by St. Anthony's, still the home of my heart. Matilda let me in, and I sat in a pew about halfway up on the left side, where I usually sat, and I looked up at the mural of Jesus floating there among the people who loved him, and I thought that the quality I'd neglected to attribute to him was courage. Kindness, compassion, assertiveness, wisdom, godliness, yes, always, but, on the human level, the pure bravery of doing what he did was something I hadn't really given enough thought to before. It seemed to me that the most important quality we could have on Earth besides kindness to others was courage. The tremendous courage required of someone like Mary, pregnant, unmarried, too young, who said, when she discovered she would bear a holy child, "Let it be done to me according to Thy will."

I vowed then that I would make Mary my patron, my supporter. I would let her move me where I needed to be moved. If that meant meeting the archbishop and having him mock me, I ought to be able to have the courage to deal with that. I would pray to her in particular from that moment on. I would ask her to give me the strength to face my humiliations and failures. And I would let God take me where He decided I should go.

CHAPTER **FIVE**

In the last year of nursing school the ratio of classroom to hands-on work flips fairly drastically and we spend most of our time in "clinicals," making the transition from theory to practice. It's one thing to know that the liver cleans toxins from the blood and then passes it on to the kidneys for further cleansing; it's something else entirely to care for a patient who's dying of kidney failure. It's interesting to read about the role of the placenta in a pregnancy, but that's like a small, hummed tune next to the painful, messy, glorious symphony of an actual birth.

My classmates and I were rotated through various parts of the hospital—Med-Surg, Ob-Gyn, Pediatrics, Psych, and so on, partly to give us a broad base of experience, and partly so we could make an educated decision about where we eventually wanted to specialize.

It was during those last months of training that I discovered I could affect people's health by touching them. Not every patient, not every time, but it began to happen fairly often, and I began to be able to tell when it was happening. Sometimes it wasn't a matter of actually healing or curing them as much as lessening their discomfort, and it's possible some of that came from the simple power of one human body touching another.

But in moments of complete honesty I knew it was more than that. I also knew it had been going on long before nursing school. When I'd touched my grandmother in her last weeks, when I'd put my hand on Father Alberto after his accident, there had been the feeling of something passing from me to them, a spark, a line of love with a silent force to it. This was difficult for me. On the one hand, I knew it was common for people, when they're very ill, to respond to the voice or touch or presence of a person they love. Any nurse has stories of patients awakening from a coma long enough to say good-bye to a spouse or child. On the other hand, especially as I spent more and more time in the hospital, I saw— beyond any denying—that I could often change a patient's condition just by laying a hand on him or her.

I tried to hide it, naturally. It's a precarious time, the last half of the last year of nursing school. You're trying to soak up and hold as much information as you can, you're under constant scrutiny, already thinking about taking the Boards and applying to the hospital of your choice. The competition is stiff (though there is a particularly strong sense of camaraderie among nursing students). So the very last thing you need is to give any sign that you're flaky, unstable, even overly emotional. The people who will decide your fate—mostly senior nurses, but certain physicians and professors as well—are watching you for any signs that you won't be able to handle the real trials of the profession: the long hours, the life-or-death decisions, the blood and guts and smells and complaints, the everyday, unspectacular, quietly efficient care that can make the difference between a patient walking out of the hospital unassisted and sinking deeper into his or her troubles. Does Piantedosi regularly check the charts? Does she wash her hands enough, even when she's under pressure to get to the next patient? Can she insert a catheter into a man who's afraid and upset? Can she keep her focus through a four-hour intestinal operation?

Those are the kinds of things that decide your fate, not, Can she cut someone's pain in half by placing a hand on his shoulder?

So I never mentioned it to anyone—friend, superior, or coworker. I tried to deny it at first, even to myself. But then I understood how selfish that was, and I kept hearing Father Alberto chastising me about false modesty, and I started to let the healing energy move through me without so much resistance. One of my patients was an older man suffering from late-stage emphysema. He had an almost unbearable amount of trouble breathing, probably a week to live. Patients always have quirks, and his quirk was that he liked to lie there with one leg outside the sheet. I'd go in, and if there was no one else in the room, I'd put my hand on his right leg and I'd notice immediately that his vital signs would change. His breathing was still labored, but less so; his heartbeat dropped from the high 100s to something closer to normal.

It wasn't as though I could stand there beside his bed for a whole shift, touching him, and it wasn't as though I could go around from room to room, fondling patients who were in pain. Sometimes I wanted to. It's one of the hardest aspects of a nurse's life—being around so much suffering and not always being able to completely take it away. There were days when I had an urge to grab a nurse-supervisor by the arm, drag her into a room where someone was suffering, and say, "Watch this." But I suspected that the response would be something like "No, *you* watch *this*" as I was banned from the hospital and thrown out of school. I suspected, too, that if there was even the smallest element of egotism involved, the tiniest bit of showing off, then whatever healing magic God was sending through me would immediately be extinguished.

So I did what I could, surreptitiously putting my hands on the patients who seemed to need it most, never when there was anyone else nearby. Some patients noticed. One woman—she'd been in a car accident and had a broken collarbone and a broken pelvis—said, "Whenever you touch me my pain is less." I smiled, made a neutral remark, and was especially glad when she improved enough to go to a rehab unit.

It was in that time that my last surviving aunt, my father's sister, Chiara, fell ill. She'd suffered from kidney disease for many years, but at that point in her life she had to be hospitalized. It would turn out that she would die during the six months of my clinicals, and I would be able to see her in Mass General while I was working there and help her a bit. When she started to suffer, like most patients with kidney disease, she had horrible shooting pains in her legs, so every night before I went home I'd spend half an hour in her room, massaging her calves and feet, making sure she had anything she wanted in the way of food and drink and blankets and medication. My father had always been very close to her, and he took to spending hours in the room with her, too, sometimes talking but more often just sitting there with his hands folded in his lap, watching her, watching me whenever I came in. There was something almost boyish about him in those last weeks of her life, as if he were remembering the days when the two of them had been very young, marching through the town square in uniform, starting the school day with a pledge to Mussolini that my father still partly remembered: "Nice, Corsica, Malta, all these belong to the great Italia. . . ." My father was, as the saying goes, not good with death, and I could feel the fear coming off him in waves; he'd seen his wife and mother-in-law die; he didn't want to be left alone again. Sometimes, if the timing was right, we'd leave the hospital together and ride back to Revere in his car, and if he said anything on those rides, it would never be about his sister's illness. "Do we have the milk?" he'd ask. "Do you want me to start the tomatoes now, inside, or wait?"

Two or three times Aunt Chiara said something like "Cynthia, you've almost taken the pain completely away." But if my father noticed, he never mentioned it to me. He thought, I'm sure, that his sister was just trying to make me feel useful and appreciated. She'd been raised as an Old World Italian girl, unfailingly pleasant, polite, kind, thoughtful, considerate, always putting others' needs ahead of her own. We'd had a good relationship, but I'd always felt I couldn't get as close to her as I wanted to, that she was surrounded by a soft cushion of *niceness* and it kept her from being completely real with me.

In my aunt's last days I massaged her legs as often as I could, and it seemed to bring her real comfort. I wasn't there at the moment of her death, and I regret that. It seems to happen that way so often. I was with her and with her and with her, my father was with her, and then he was exhausted and left to go home and I stayed. It was midnight; I knew she was failing. I took a short nap. It was two a.m. Finally I stepped out and walked down to the cafeteria to get myself a cup of coffee, and when I came back to the room she had died.

My father's reaction surprised me. He was a different kind of Old World soul than his sister. He was on the gruff side, as I've said, often distant and aloof, a man's man. He'd always worked with men, he gambled with men, he bowled with men, he was good to me but not particularly affectionate, and really, after I turned eight or nine we never had much in the way of a substantive conversation. Certainly, despite the Italian American stereotype, he was never a man who showed a great deal of emotion, but after Aunt Chiara died, he had periods of being almost inconsolable. He spent those days watching television or pacing the back yard, buried in grief. I'd come home from work and find him with tears on his face, standing at the stove. He wasn't cooking anything, he wasn't even making tea, just standing there, crying.

One night that spring, tired from the long day and the loud subway ride, I spent half an hour in St. Anthony's and then went home, intending to make my father supper, and found him sitting in the living room. That wasn't so unusual. But the TV was turned off and it was getting dark and he was sitting there with his hands on the arms of the chair, staring out the window. When I stepped through the door, he looked at me, and it was as if he were seeing me for the first time. Familiarity breeds contempt, people say, but I think it's truer that familiarity breeds taking for granted. When you live with people day in and day out for years, you become so accustomed to them that you can stop seeing them. You half look at them, you stop listening. And I think what had happened with my father was that his sister's passing had made him understand that he'd been doing that with me for probably my whole adult life.

That night when I came into the living room and said hello, he looked at me, and there was something so new and different in the features of his face that I was about to ask him what was wrong.

"Cinzia," he said, and even the fact that he'd chosen the Italian pronunciation of my name was different. I thought for a second that there was more bad news, that he'd been diagnosed with something horrible or that someone else we knew had just died and he'd been sitting there in shock, preparing himself to break the news.

"Let me take you out for supper," he said in Italian. "Your aunt left you two thousand dollars. She left me some money, too."

I thought I might fall over backward. Not because of the small inheritance but because my father was willing to spend some of it. He'd grown up poor in an Italy ravaged by political turmoil and war. During his working life, he'd made just enough money to pay the mortgage on our small house and put food on the table and gasoline in his five-year-old Pontiac (financial aid, loans, and summer jobs had gotten me through nursing school). During my childhood it was an exceedingly rare event for us to go out to eat, in part because my grandmother was such a good cook, in part because my father, after a day of work, didn't particularly want to come home, shower, get dressed up, and step back out into society. But mostly it was because he was so careful with money, as if he expected another dictator to appear any day, another war to start, another long stretch of hunger and deprivation like the one he'd been forced to live through in the last years of Mussolini's Italy.

So when he said, "Cinzia, let me to take you out for supper," it was as unexpected as if he'd said, "Cinzia, we're moving to Norway. Pack your things."

"You sure, Pa?"

"Winthrop," he said, switching back to English as he often did. "Rossetti's."

Rossetti's was a place I'd been to exactly twice, once for a family reunion and once on a date. It was a wonderfully authentic Italian restaurant just across the road from Winthrop Beach. Probably a twelve-minute drive from our house.

"Are you sure, Pa?"

"*Sì, sì*," he said, as if convincing himself. "*Andiamoci.*"

I went upstairs and showered and changed my clothes. He dressed up and put on a pair of shoes—which was unusual because he almost always walked around in work boots—nice pants, a long-sleeved white shirt, and a sweater, and we climbed into the front seat of the Pontiac and set out as if for a drive across North America. It took a long time to find a parking space on Winthrop's narrow streets. And we ended up having to wait about fifteen minutes on the sidewalk outside Rossetti's. But when we were seated and had opened the menus there was another surprise.

"I think you should have the lobster ravioli," my father said.

I'd already noticed them by then—I had a soft spot for ravioli—but I'd also noticed that they were one of the more expensive items on the menu, and, in deference to him, I'd shifted my eyes to the simpler pasta dishes.

"And wine," he said. "*Una bottiglia.* We gonna drink it together."

I was able, after a few seconds of internal struggle, to relax and let him be generous. The lobster ravioli were fancier versions of the crimped, ricotta-filled squares my grandmother had fashioned on a dish towel on the kitchen table; it seemed decadent to see such things—a peasant dish, really—filled with lobster meat. I had a salad beforehand, one and a half glasses of wine. My father had a small steak—which he cut, piece by piece, with a mechanic's precision—and pasta on the side. The food was delicious, perfect, the service tinged with a particular kind of local friendliness I'd always loved. A light mood encircled us, as though the owner had hung silvery curtains by our table and arranged for the Neapolitan sun to shine through them. A mood like that was so unusual where my father and I were concerned that I found myself wondering if he might be undergoing some late-in-life personality change brought on by a tumor or a new medication.

We decided to share a dessert of *pizza dolce*, a ricotta cheesecake that must have five thousand calories per slice. We sat for a while over coffee, too, and then he asked for the bill and paid in cash, keeping his scarred, rough hands under the table so I couldn't see how much our great indulgence had set him back. When we were finished, he suggested we go to Revere Beach and take a walk. Another surprise. Another first. "We live near there all this time, you and me," he said, "and when do we go? *Mai.* Never."

It was a clear night, cool near the water, the waves taller and more exuberant than anything I'd seen there in months. At age seventy-five, my father was in excellent condition, and we went along on the firmer sand at a good pace. Something hovered in the air between us, a moth of discomfort on that pretty landscape. After a few minutes he said, switching into Italian and staying with that language, "I understand now, why you go to church so much. All these years I saw you praying and praying, going to Mass even during the week, being quiet in the backyard or in your room, reading religious books. I never really understood. *Adesso capisco.* Now I do."

I kept silent, chewing on my surprise like the last bits of the meal, worried I'd break the spell he was under and he'd stop talking and close the door again on the neat, masculine room where he guarded his feelings.

"Because you know what I don't know," he said. "You knew it all along. What I knew in my mind, like a thought, you knew in your heart—that this life goes by."

I hooked my arm inside his.

"It goes by, Cinzia. And then what? Heaven? What's Heaven? How old are we in Heaven? All the people who died, where do they go in Heaven? How do they know each other? Are they married again? Are they still brother and sister or friends? How can that be, something like that?"

Still holding his arm, I turned him so we were looking out to sea and I said, "*Guardare, Babbo. Guardare il mare.* Look, Pa. Look at the ocean. I like to come here and think of everything that's in it, the way it comes in and goes out every day, like our breath, and we barely notice. Something much bigger than us has to have made that, don't you think so?"

He studied the bay for a few seconds, then turned and looked at me again with that same puzzled expression on his face, as if I were a new creature in his life. "See," he said, "you can say things like that. You can talk that way. See what you are?"

"You're the same as me, Papa," I said. "We're made of the same stuff."

"Sure," he said, in English now, as if, standing near the noisy surf on the empty beach, he no longer had to worry about being overheard and mocked for his accent. "The trucks I fix at the garage, they made of the same stuff like a Cadillac, too."

"I'm the same as I always was," I said. "A little bit fatter after that *pizza dolce*."

My attempt at humor passed him by completely. "Sure, just the same," he said. "Why would you be different? But when I go, you pray for me, okay? With you praying for me, I'll have a chance."

I held on to his arm and tried to move my mind nowhere into the future or the past. I wanted that moment in its fullness.

When we were walking back south along the beach, the wind at our backs, I said, "There's a chance, a small chance, that when I finish the clinicals in a month or so I'll have to go to Rome."

"For work?"

"No, not exactly."

"A boyfriend?" he said hopefully.

"I don't have a boyfriend."

"You should have one," he said, "a beautiful girl like you."

"I'm special, I'm beautiful. I think you had something to drink before I got home."

He didn't laugh.

"It has something to do with the Church. I'm not sure, but I think I may have to go and meet with somebody in Rome about Church business, about my prayers."

"To become a nun?"

"No," I said, and for a moment I thought I might explain the whole situation to him, but I said only "A priest I know in Boston wants me to go."

"I have my cousin there, still, all these years. Franco. I told you about him. You can look him up. Right near Rome he lives. Rich now . . . the lawyer."

"Want to come with me, Pa?"

"No no no no," he said, forcefully, and the lightness was suddenly falling away from him like dry leaves from the bed of a speeding, overloaded pickup truck. I almost looked behind us to see the trail. "What I left, I'm-a never goin' back to."

"It's different now, Pa."

"No no no no," he said again. "The memories

ain't different. They half sleepin', the memories. Who wants to wake 'em up?"

After we'd walked another little ways he said, "You gonna stay over there?"

"No. A week, maybe two weeks, that's all. I was thinking I could use the money Aunt Chiara left. For the plane tickets and everything."

"You can stay if you have to."

"I'm fine, Papa. I'm happy here."

"How?" he asked. "You work, you come home and clean the house. Where's the happy part? Tell me?"

"Praying makes me happy."

He looked out at the water. The waves were slapping the shore in a slow, hard rhythm, streaks of brown seaweed showing in each small curl. "Show me about it," he said. "When we get home. Show me what you do to be happy like that when you say a prayer."

CHAPTER SIX

Father Alberto had told me many times that he was sure God had a sense of humor. "He's a big trickster, Cynthia," he liked to say, putting one hand flat on his large belly as if preparing to laugh but not actually laughing. "He takes the things we want—to be rich, beautiful, healthy, to live forever—and He turns them this way and that like a magician and plays His tricks on us with those things. Sometimes He gives us what we want for a little while, or partly, and then He takes it away and watches to see how we react. It's like He's saying 'Is this what you think you're here for? Do you think I made you so you can have a nice face and have it forever, and everybody will give you compliments on it, and every time you look in the mirror you'll have a little puff of pride?' You think that's what the whole machine is for? The lungs and heart and skull and blood? I went to all that trouble so you could look in the mirror?"

On the day I was scheduled to meet with the archbishop I had reason to remember my late friend's God-as-trickster theory. It would be a long ride, I knew, and I'd wondered about, then decided against, asking to borrow my father's car. For one thing, going through the heart of Boston from north to south like that is suicide by traffic, and for another I hoped that the time on public transportation would allow me to prepare what I was going to say, to wrap up my nervousness in a kerchief and stuff it down into a corner of my purse. First, I had to take the bus down Revere Street to the subway station, then the blue line into downtown Boston, then switch to another line there, ride that line all the way to the end, and then take another short bus ride or, depending on how much time I had, make a long walk to the offices of the archdiocese. I knew it would take an hour and a quarter at least, so at the first subway station, to pass the time, I bought a newspaper I wasn't fond of, a tabloid known for gossip and big headlines. I don't know what made me do that—there was a photo of a pregnant actress on the front page, I had the smallest twinge of envy—but when the train came and I took my seat and opened the paper, I felt a shock that was like the pain of a broken bone.

On the second page my eye was caught by a story with this headline: HOW ARE YOU MAKING OUT, FATHER? There on my lap—one of God's painful jokes—was a photo of Father Welch kissing a woman. In Franklin Park, the caption said. Some enterprising photographer had either followed him there, based on a tip, or by the purest accident recognized him on a bench in Boston's huge, inner-city park. There was my confessor and adviser, clearly kissing a woman in a way that was more than friendly. The woman was black, Father Welch was white, which, of course, made the story that much more titillating. I stared at the picture for a long time and read the caption and the short article twice. At the end it said that the matter had been referred to the archbishop's office and would possibly result in Father Welch's being forced to leave the priesthood.

I set the paper down and looked out the opposite window. A flash of blue bay. Airport runways there. The timing of it was simply awful. There was no way on earth a person like me would have been granted an audience with the archbishop of Boston if it hadn't been for the intercession of Father Welch. A twenty-two-year-old nurse-in-training? A Revere girl, plain as a tree trunk in all respects, meeting with a man who rubbed shoulders with governors, senators, and popes?

I had a moment of wondering, as I folded the paper and set it on the seat beside me, if the news about Father Welch meant that the archbishop would refuse to see me. I was aligned with another radical priest, one who obviously wished there wasn't a vow of celibacy involved in his chosen profession. Though I knew beyond a doubt that it wasn't so, it would look like Father Welch had sent me to the archbishop for selfish purposes, to help his own cause.

Where would he go now? I wondered. What became of priests after they were fired?

The event and the tawdry press coverage raised a breaking wave of sadness in me. The subway train plunged into the tunnel that ran beneath Boston Harbor, and I felt I was being pushed face-first into an old sorrow. Being a loyal Catholic was starting to feel to me like being friends with someone who's doing something hurtful and refuses to listen when you try to talk about it. There was a similar stubbornness there, as if, in a world where big things changed at the speed of light, the Church was reluctantly reconsidering a few small rules, going along at the pace of a horse-drawn cart. I knew that a lot of people liked it that way, were proud of it even, felt that the Church's resistance to change was a badge of honor in a scattered, trivial, money-and-sex-mad world. I liked tradition, too, and loved some of the old-fashioned aspects of my Church, but the stubbornness and the damage it caused were tearing me in half.

After a while it began to seem to me that my *mission,* if I could dare to use that word, my *protest,* my *quest* had everything to do with the sadness I felt at what had happened to people like Father Welch in the iron cage of rules that was our Church. For me, that Church, St. Anthony's especially, had always been a refuge from the everyday world, a place—so rare in this society— to go and be quiet, a building that encouraged thoughts that went beyond the ordinary concerns of daily life, beyond money and status and looks and growing old, a building that had been raised at great expense to stand as a reminder that there was another dimension of life, other things to be thinking about. I remembered that every time my grandmother passed the church on foot, in a bus, or in a car, she would etch a tiny cross onto her forehead with her right thumbnail. That habit had come to seem foolish to me as I grew older, pure superstition. But now I understood what Nana had been doing: reminding herself that there were considerations that went beyond the errands, hopes, and worries that always swelled up to seem so important, reminding herself that, as my father had recently discovered, one day we all disappear. That was the whole point of having a church, of weekly services, sacraments, prayer. It wasn't supposed to be about keeping the rules and being rewarded with an eternity of bliss, as if you were a student trying to please a strict teacher; it was designed to redirect our attention away from the clamoring fears and hopes that could drown out all thought of anything larger.

And now look what was happening. Only a few years earlier the archdiocesan headquarters, where I was headed that day, had occupied a Tudor mansion close to downtown Boston. But the sex abuse scandal had hit the city in a particularly strong way—the lives of hundreds of people, mostly men, had been destroyed by twisted priests, and that destruction had ultimately hit the Church in its pocketbook. The residence of the archbishop of Boston had to be sold to raise the millions of dollars needed for legal fees and penalties. In order to find priests to say Mass at the churches that remained open, the archdiocese had to go trolling for them in Africa or South America. There was nothing wrong with those priests, I knew, even in spite of my lukewarm feelings about Father Gerencia. Some of them were wonderful men from a strong spiritual tradition. But it seemed clear to me that things would have been so much better if priests whose job it was to keep reminding us, to keep putting the world into perspective, if those priests themselves had grown up in the neighborhood where they preached and if they had one foot firmly in the everyday world, had been able to marry, for instance, or kiss a woman on a park bench without a giant fuss being made. Or, even more, if they could be women who knew the particular concerns of women in the modern world—bearing and raising children, balancing that with a career, understanding their husbands, caring for their parents. It seemed so abundantly obvious that the Church I loved and cherished was shrinking down to a place where it would no longer have the power to remind people of that other dimension, and it seemed clear that so much of that shrinkage had to do with the fact that my Church, in clinging to the old ways, had fallen so far behind modern life that for many people—most of my once-Catholic friends—it wasn't even relevant any longer. They went back to St. Anthony's for the baptism of their child (a formal prelude to the big party), and on Christmas Eve or Easter Sunday, or for a funeral—but it had no hold on their insides.

Thinking that way on the long subway ride was like a splint on my broken courage. It was beginning to seem at least possible that God might be sending the visions not as a way to test my paltry individual faith, not to see if I'd go insane under the assault, not to torment or confuse me, but in order to allow me to make some useful contribution to my Church, helping, alongside people like Father Alberto and Father Welch, to drag it back into relevance. It seemed to me as I got off at the smoky, littered station with its racket of squealing wheels and clanging overhead wires, that despite the barrage of doubts I lived with, it might be a perfectly worthwhile use of my time to act as one small voice calling for that kind of change. I hoped and prayed that Archbishop Menendez would see things that way. That he would listen, at least. That I wouldn't be chased away from the front door.

With the bus ride from the MBTA station, the trip was even longer than I'd expected. The Pastoral Center of the Archdiocese of Boston was housed in a modern, four-story, redbrick-and-glass building set in an industrial park. Except for the statue of Mary near the entrance, it resembled nothing so much as a corporate headquarters.

I entered from what seemed the back of the building, at ground level, near an enormous parking lot. I checked in at a circular desk backed by panels of light wood with a hand-disinfectant dispenser and a framed photo of the pope nearby. After waiting only a minute, I was greeted by a large woman, hair in neat cornrows, whose name

I didn't catch and who said she was Archbishop Menendez's chief of staff. The woman was a bit kinder than the receptionist at St. Ann's but unsmiling and formal, not a person to make small talk with. So I held my nervousness inside and followed her up a set of stairs to a small waiting area. I took a seat there, opened a magazine— *Catholic Living*—and immediately closed it. Said a prayer for Father Welch. For Father Alberto. For my father and my mother and Aunt Chiara and my grandmother, and myself. I needed to use the bathroom but decided to wait.

Soon Archbishop Menendez himself, dressed in plain black pants and a plain black shirt with a small square of white collar showing in front, opened the door to an office and motioned me in. He shook my hand—I was embarrassed at my sweaty palm—nodded as I introduced myself, made good eye contact, and smelled of Ivory soap. The office was bright with sunlight. There were plants on the window sills, a framed, signed photograph of the pope on one wall, a crucifix, an overloaded desk, and a set of bookshelves with titles I glanced at but couldn't quite read. It had a very different feeling, I noticed right away, from Monsignor Ferraponte's office, and Archbishop Menendez had a very different way about him. It gave me a burst of courage.

The archbishop led me to a leather sofa that looked new and sat opposite me in a matching leather armchair on the other side of a glass-topped coffee table. Everything except his desk was perfectly clean and orderly. There was a pitcher of ice water on a tray in front of him and two glasses. He filled them both, handed mine across, then sat back and studied me. I studied him in return and decided that, even in the black uniform, he looked more like a judge or professor than a man of the cloth. Or perhaps a surgeon, nearly old enough to retire. He had that same kind of confidence and brainy energy I'd seen in the OR, as if the winds of doubt never blew across his warm valley, as if nothing on this earth could possibly frighten or upset him.

"It's a good grace to meet you finally," he said after he'd inspected me and had a sip from his glass. "I've heard so much about you."

"How?" I asked. I'd put on my best blue dress, and I smoothed it over the tops of my legs and saw that my hands were shaking.

The archbishop laughed but didn't answer. He set his glass down on a coaster, sat back again, and interlaced his long fingers. I couldn't help but compare him with my father. He was the most clean-shaven man I'd ever seen, his cheeks shining in the window sunlight and his shock of salt-and-pepper hair combed straight back from his forehead in smooth strands. But the difference between them was more than texture of skin or hair color. My father was a man of the body; he

111

loved to work with his hands, his presence in the house felt like that of a block of stone or wood that moved, slowly, solidly, from kitchen table to living room chair, from front seat of the car to the front steps or the garden. The archbishop seemed light, almost translucent, as if he might float away if a window was opened.

"Diocesan gossip," he said at last. "The word around here is that you have a rich prayer life."

"Word?" I said. "From who? What word?"

Another polite laugh, a smile with sparkles at its edges. "Sources never to be named. Is it true? About you having a rich prayer life, I mean?"

"I do, yes, I think so, Your Holiness."

"Let us drop the formal titles, shall we, just for this meeting?"

"Yes, sir," I said. I could feel myself blushing. I hadn't blushed since seventh grade, and it made me a little angry at myself. I didn't want to have come all that way for what would surely be my only meeting with an archbishop, and suddenly go little-girl shy. "Yes, I think I do."

"I admire that," he said. "I envy it. One of the aspects of this job I dislike, and there are many aspects to like, is that it leaves so little time for quiet prayer. I often think of Thomas Merton at the Gethsemane monastery, placing a notice on the bulletin board, pleading with his fellow monks not to elect him abbot for just that reason. He put his prayer life first. The right thing to do."

"He's become a hero of mine," I said, and I barely kept myself from telling him it was Father Welch who'd introduced me to Merton. And then I felt, guiltily, that I was turning my back on Father Welch in his moment of trouble, and I was angry at myself again.

"Yes," the archbishop agreed, "Merton was a radical in some ways, wasn't he, perhaps even a troublemaker. But a Catholic monk to the end and a good one, I believe. . . . Well"—he took a breath and kept his eyes fixed on me—"tell me why you've come."

"I think," I said, and then I stopped, completely intimidated. I tried to remind myself of the pledge I'd made, to accept what came, to emulate Christ's courage, Mary's surrender. I could feel Father Alberto pushing me. I clasped my hands together and said, "For a long time, my whole life, really, I've been having, I don't know what to call them . . . spells, visions, moments, sometimes hours when I'm *taken,* I guess that's the way to say it, taken in prayer. It's been happening since I was a small girl. I had a grandmother who was very devout and I was very close to her, and then later there was a priest at St. Anthony's; he died not so long ago, Father Alberto Ghirardelli. I'd confess to him every Saturday, and then after a while, as I grew older, the confessions turned into long conversations about these spells and other things. I was a little worried that maybe there was something wrong with me. I had friends. I had a fairly normal life, except that my mother died when I was very young, but then there was this other part of me where I'd just go *off*. It worried my father. He took me to see doctors when I was in the second and third grades. I even had some tests done at Mass General, which is where I hope to work one day. I'm a nurse, training to be a nurse, I just finished—"

The archbishop shifted impatiently, the tiniest of movements.

"I'm sorry. I'm rambling."

"It's fine," he said. "You're nervous, it's fine. But tell me exactly why you wanted to meet with me. Because of these moments in prayer?"

"No, no, Archbishop. If it was just that, I never would have come here and bothered you. In fact, it wasn't my idea to come here at all."

"It was Andy Welch's idea."

"Yes, it was . . . and I read about him today in the paper. Just now. On the train." I waited for the archbishop to say something then, but he only shifted his eyes out the window—sadly or angrily, I couldn't be sure—then looked back at me. "I feel like the last year especially, I feel like God has been giving me a specific message in these times of prayer. Instructions almost. It's very intense. Confusing to me, intense, troubling. But it feels absolutely real and clear, and one of the reasons I spent so much time talking with

Father Welch was because I worried it might be something else."

"What is the message, exactly?"

"I feel," I said, and then I had to push hard against a big wave of fear, a hand cupping itself over my lips. "I feel very strongly that God is asking me to become a priest."

I watched him closely then. He didn't laugh, didn't seem in the slightest bit surprised. I decided he must have been given advance notice by Father Welch or perhaps Monsignor Ferraponte. He watched me carefully, unsurprised, unmoved, and, as Father Welch had warned me, impossible to read.

"How?" he asked.

"Excuse me, Archbishop?"

"How," he repeated, "exactly how are these messages presented to you?"

"Different ways. Sometimes I see myself serving at Mass, raising the chalice, speaking the prayer of communication as the host is blessed. Or I see what seems like a photograph of myself dressed in a priest's robes, standing at the altar or in the room where priests get ready for Mass. Or I just get a message, though most of the time it's a message without words. I imagine it's something like what a person feels when he has a true vocation. I'm sorry. It's a difficult thing to explain."

"If it were an easy thing to explain, I'd be less inclined to believe you."

I had to blink away a small rush of tears and then a wave of embarrassment. I'd half expected him to mock me, give me a lecture on the temptations of the Devil as Monsignor Ferraponte had, even end the meeting as soon as he reasonably could. But now he seemed to be saying he believed me. "I would have come forward earlier," I said, encouraged, "but I'm . . . it's strange, Your Eminence, I've taken care of myself my whole life. I grew up in a fairly rough place."

"Where was that?"

"Revere. I learned to take care of myself. I had some fistfights—I even fought a boy once, when he was tormenting a younger cousin. The word in school was not to mess with me. I've calmed down as I've grown older—"

"That's one of the benefits of deep prayer," he said in a joking way. "Not so many fistfights."

I smiled. "Yes. I think so, too. But I'm not, I don't see myself . . . I'm not comfortable making waves."

"I'd be less inclined to believe you if you were."

"And I want to say . . . I think Father Welch is a good man and a good priest. I've been attending Mass at the Paulist Center. I like it there. I'm sorry for what happened, but he's a good man."

"He is a good man," the archbishop said, surprising me again.

"And he never told me about his relationship," I said. "It's not like he put the idea into my head for his own purposes or anything . . . to make it easier for him to be married and stay a priest."

"You don't need to apologize for what's happened," the archbishop said. "For yourself or for Father Welch."

A tear leaked out of the corner of my right eye. The archbishop saw it and looked away. I swatted it with the back of one hand. "You're sure," he asked, and at that moment it seemed like the professionalism holding the features of his face broke apart a bit. He seemed suddenly very human, almost ordinary. "You're sure you might not be getting the details a bit mixed up, that the imagery might not be intended to lead you somewhere else? To a life of a different kind of service in the Church? As a missionary, a nun, a deacon . . . and the robes and altar and so on are just the symbols of that?"

I nodded.

"How, may I ask? How do you know that?"

"It's an interior knowing. I can't say how, but I'm sure of it. I've thought about that, too, I've wondered about it, I even hoped that was what was happening, but it isn't. I can't say anything more except that I feel the presence of God behind it."

"And what is that presence like? How does it manifest itself?"

"A feeling of being surrounded by something that's all-knowing and totally accepting. Totally. The word 'love' can't begin to describe it."

"Does it give you peace, coming here like this?"

"Not particularly, no. The prayer does, not this. But if I didn't try to do this, I think it would be unbearable."

"Have you asked the Holy Spirit for guidance?"

"Many times."

"Have you had other . . . instructions . . . from Our Lord?"

I shook my head.

"Would you be prepared to sacrifice, in the most selfless way, for this outcome?"

"I believe so, Your Eminence. I believe I already have sacrificed certain things."

"You feel God is calling you to be—how should we say it?—the standard-bearer for this new era?"

"I don't have a name for myself," I said, "or for this. I don't even have a name or a face for God anymore. I just know that I'm being asked to do something. I know it like I know that the sun is out today. I'm not an expert on the Church, but even in my lifetime I've seen things change. So I'm wondering, I'm hoping that maybe this might change, too."

The archbishop lightly pinched the tip of his nose once, then a second time, the closest thing I'd seen in him to a nervous tic. He coughed into his hand, took a sip of water. "The changes you're referring to were relatively minor things," he said. "What you're talking about now is major. Almost we could use the word *gigantic*."

118

I watched him lower his eyes to the water glass and work his lips gently back and forth. When he lifted his eyes, they came to rest just to the right of my face. "I'm no expert on the legal system," he said. "But it seems to me that in the law there are certain procedures, certain fixed rules. Of evidence, for example. Of deliberation for the jury. The fact that people stand when the judge enters, that only the lawyers are allowed to present a case, to approach the bar. Correct?"

"Yes, but I'm not—"

He held up his hand again. There was a bit of command in the gesture, the expectation of being obeyed.

"Those laws are not always sensible, but what they do—correct me if you think I'm wrong—is they allow the system—and it's an imperfect system, as we all know—they enable it to function. They steer the procedure away from chaos. They allow things to get done."

"But laws change all the time," I said. "Women can be judges now, for one example. We can sue for equal treatment at work."

"Yes, yes, and rightly so. But even that bit of progress has taken how many years? And in a system that claims, what, two centuries of tradition? Our system, that of the Holy Mother Church, claims a tradition ten times as long. Its rules seem antiquated, even insensible to some, but they exist to allow the functioning of the larger body." The archbishop's voice softened almost imperceptibly. In a less charming man it could have been taken as condescension. "Despite our recent problems, I know Father Welch to be a good man," he said. "He spoke with me about you, as I'm sure you know."

"I didn't know."

"He did. And, at his word, I know you to be a good woman. We have, as I'm sure you can imagine, a number of people every year who come forth claiming to have received instructions from the Lord. It's actually fairly common, and we're trained, all of us who've been spiritual directors, in a kind of vetting process. Ninety-some percent of the time these so-called visions prove to be psychological fixations—caused by mental illness, stress, overwork, a craving for attention, an excess of zeal, experiences that aren't grounded in God at all. The other ten or so percent have legitimate experiences in prayer. I had a conversation with Father Welch about you, it must have been six or eight weeks ago."

"He never mentioned it."

"I asked him not to. We discussed that process in your case. I believe he implemented some of my suggestions for, if you'll forgive me, 'testing' the validity of your experiences. There is little question in my mind—and none in his—as to their validity. As to your interpretation of God's will for you and for the Church, I am less sure, but we could discuss that *ad infinitum* to no avail. To get to the base of my feelings here, I will tell you simply that I took a vow of obedience. I obey the cardinals and the Holy Father. I respect and obey the laws of the Church, even when I question them interiorly. Am I speaking too indirectly?"

"No, Archbishop. But there have always been priests and archbishops and even popes who challenged the prevailing attitudes. Who broke new territory. John XXIII is the best modern example, but there are dozens of others in Church history. Catherine of Siena, Francis of Assisi, Brigid of Ireland—"

The archbishop smiled and turned his glass a quarter turn without lifting it. "Extremely rare examples. And, in the latter case, not even completely reliable."

"I know that, but if I can be blunt, Archbishop, you could risk your standing, your position, and come out publicly in favor of the idea of letting women be ordained. It would be good for the Church, in my opinion. And it would go a long way toward furthering my 'case,' if we can call it that."

"I disagree. It would go a long way toward ruining your case."

"How?" I asked. I sensed the shadow of fear in him then, as though he worried what the more extreme elements of the diocese might do to him if, like Father Alberto, he dared to raise his voice.

"I'd be set upon by the forces of the Church bureaucracy and the American media. You can see the latter at work on today's news. You can see what they're making of the Father Welch situation—a circus. I would become the next story of the month, the next animal act. Just as Father Welch is—and we speak in confidence here, I trust."

"We do. But didn't your office issue the order that he could no longer say Mass?"

"There was, under the circumstances, no option."

"You could have refused to do that or resigned in protest."

"True," he said, and when he paused I sensed his fear again. "In fact, I meditated on that. On my knees, in fact, for the better part of last night. I came to the conclusion that it would accomplish nothing and would erode or end whatever small amount of good I feel I am able to do from this office."

"But isn't that . . . forgive the comparison, but isn't that the way, in history, all kinds of people justified their own behavior to themselves? 'If I speak up, I'll get fired. And it won't do any good in any case.' So the dictator tells them to eliminate or arrest or torture someone, and they do it. Isn't that what Pontius Pilate did?"

"A bit of a strong comparison."

"Yes, of course. Too strong. I don't mean it as an insult. But a kind of violence is being done to the Church, don't you think so?"

"I happen to agree, in a general way, though not exactly with the term 'violence.'"

"But you won't say so publicly."

"Not at this time, no."

The anger—at myself, mainly, my foolish timidity, my tears, but also at his lack of courage—was bubbling up in me, and I could feel that I'd reached the point of saying something else that was too strong. I liked the archbishop and didn't want to alienate him, but a long, rolling wave of frustration had caught up with me. I ducked under it and said, "Tell me what you recommend, Your Eminence."

The archbishop was momentarily lost in thought. He held his chin in one hand. The gesture seemed phony to me, contrived, unoriginal. I turned my eyes away, and they rested on the photo of the pope.

"Again," he said, "I would appreciate very much if we would hold this between the two of us. I'd be happy to give you a piece of advice if my name is kept out of it."

"Of course," I said, but it wasn't what I wanted to say.

"I feel that your only recourse, to return to legal comparisons, is to bring your case before the Supreme Court. In this instance, that would mean Rome. There's an office in Vatican City that handles questions like this. The Congregation for the Doctrine of the Faith. It is that office from which various rulings are issued. For example, several years ago, the decision not to elevate the Virgin Mother to a place of doctrinal equality with her Son—do you remember that?"

"I remember that it made me angry."

"Yes, well, it would have caused hard feelings either way." He sipped from his glass and touched two fingers to his lips. "I think, honestly, that you have little hope. No hope, in fact. But if a matter like this is to be considered at a level where long-standing rules might actually be changed, then it would be considered in that office. These are very conservative people, you understand. The back-bone of the bureaucracy. If the tradition of two thousand years guides me in my thinking, then that tradition *is* the thinking of the bishops and cardinals who advise His Holiness from that office. But you seem determined to see this through, and I feel strangely unwilling to dissuade you." He shifted his eyes away and back. "It's a testament to your presence," he said. "Ten minutes ago I was resolved to offer you a flat, 'No chance,' shake your hand, and say good-bye. But there's something about you that makes me feel such a response would be . . . improper." He looked at the window again and back into my face. "This is the best I can do at the present time. Though—again in deference to you—I would be willing to write a short note to a colleague in Rome, testifying, as it were, that you are indeed a good Catholic and a woman of a particularly rich interior life. My colleague is a cardinal of some influence."

"Could you let me hand carry a copy? I mean, if I go?"

The archbishop could not keep a frown from tugging down the corners of his mouth. I worried for a moment that I'd offended him again, but if I did go to Rome, I didn't want to travel all that way and have nothing in my hand, nothing but the claim of a private conversation. "Agreed," he said. "With the stipulation that you don't publicize it or otherwise spread it around more than is absolutely necessary."

"Yes, of course. It's very good of you to take so much time with me. I'm grateful."

"It's nothing, really." The archbishop pushed his hands down against the arms of his chair, as if signaling that the meeting was coming to a close. But he didn't actually get up. "I made you a suggestion, that's all. Off the record. My way of slipping out of the noose of responsibility. That is what I can offer at this time."

He smiled at me in an indulgent way, pushed down more forcefully against the arms of the chair, and stood, and it was only then that the years really showed in him. Creaky knees. An extra second to get upright. He seemed so much older than Father Welch; I wondered if he'd entered the seminary at a later age, and I wondered what kind of life he might have had before that.

Near the door, he put a gentle hand on my back, for just a second, then took it away. "In this world," he said, "the good people, the people who try to change the stale old patterns—Christ, Martin Luther King, Gandhi—look what happens to them."

"Father Ghirardelli," I said.

"Another on the list."

"It makes some people doubt that there's a God or that He's good."

"Yes," he said, smiling his good-bye and reaching out to shake my hand, "but, for me, quite the opposite. It makes me certain there has to be a better world."

CHAPTER **SEVEN**

After the visit to the archbishop, I prayed and prayed and waited and hoped, but weeks went by without any word from his office and I began to convince myself that I'd fulfilled whatever it was that God had been asking of me. I'd been to see an archbishop, I'd made my case for a more inclusive Church; that's where the story would end. I felt a creeping sense of relief.

I was nearing the end of my schooling, finishing up an obstetrics course—my favorite to that point. Every day I helped women bring new life into the world, I went to church afterward, came home and made dinner for my father, said my prayers, and went to bed. Some nights, by the time I made it back to Tapley Avenue, he'd already cooked a meal for himself and was out with friends—at the dog track, usually, or playing cards at the Revere City Club. The tenderness of our evening at Rossetti's never repeated itself, but there had been, since that night, a noticeable change in the rooms of our house, a softening up of the molds we'd long ago poured ourselves into. He asked me to show him the type of prayer that made me so happy, and I did that, sitting with him in the living room and talking about wordless prayer, about simply letting the mind run and skitter and gently bringing it back with what Father Welch had called "a sacred word." After a week or so my father asked me to show him a second time, and I sat with him again and we talked about it. Since his sister Chiara died, he said, he was having what he called "*un po' di guai*," a little trouble. If he didn't keep himself occupied with a TV show, a card game, the radio, or projects around the yard, his mind would go back, compulsively, to memories of my mother. When he'd been working every day and busy like that, it hadn't been so bad. Now the loss of her tormented him.

"What was she like, Papa?" I took that

opportunity to ask. "You never really told me much."

"*Non volevo parlare di lei*," he said. Of late he'd been avoiding the English language entirely, as though, moving farther into old age, he wanted only to turn his ears back in the direction of Naples and the syllables of his youth. *Non volevo parlare di lei.* "I didn't want to talk of her because I was afraid this would happen. She's with me now all the time, everywhere. I get jealous of other men who wanted to marry her, long ago. I wake up, and I think she's downstairs cooking the eggs. I come out of the City Club, and I think I see her waiting for me in the car. In the middle of sleep I reach over to touch her."

"But what was she like?"

"Like? You've seen the pictures. Beautiful. You look like her."

"I mean, her personality. What was your relationship like?"

"Relationship?" he said, pinching up his face. He understood the word, of course—*rapporto* in Italian—that wasn't the problem. The problem was that the whole idea of a "relationship" with a spouse or lover was a modern notion, and my father was a man buried up to his rib cage in the soil of a very different time. Even if he'd really wanted to walk out of that world, he could never have lifted himself all the way out of the Old World soil. "She was the other part of me," he said after the muscles of his face relaxed, "the other half. You take away that half, and it's like you're walking around everywhere with one arm and one leg."

"But how did she die? How, exactly?"

"How?" he said, "*Il cuore.* The heart." But immediately after saying that he looked away, something utterly atypical of him. He was a person of the most direct eye contact imaginable. Even as a little girl I noticed it and had often been made uneasy by it. Speaking to you at the table or outside in our above-ground pool, he'd fix you with his steady brown eyes and you not only had to look back, you almost couldn't move, couldn't form a sentence for a few seconds. It was as if the force of his whole being was concentrated there in two glistening brown marbles. But then, sitting in our living room, talking about something that had happened twenty years earlier, he flinched. I noticed.

"There's something else," I said.

"Sure," he agreed, but he pronounced the word very quietly, keeping his eyes out the window. "*Certo.*"

"What is it? Tell me."

Slowly, reluctantly, the eyes swung back, and when they rested on me again I knew that I'd just torn the wrapping off some old secret. It was strange, in the one or two seconds before he spoke again, strange to sense the size and weight of it and to feel a new truth uncovered there between us. "*Quando tu sei nata*," he said quietly.

"When I was born? What do you mean, when I was born?" But by then I half knew.

"She died giving birth to you."

"And no one told me?" I said loudly. "All these years?"

"Don't yell."

"Papa! You lied to me about my mother all this time, and you want me to just say, okay, all right, no problem?"

He shrugged, broke eye contact again. "Your grandmother and I and Aunt Chiara, we didn't want you to feel bad about it."

"Why would I feel bad about it?"

"You were big," he said, holding his hands two feet apart. "It was hard for you, coming into this world. Hard for your mother. She broke open. She . . . lost the blood." He waved a hand as if swatting away a wasp from the side of his face.

"But I couldn't help that. It wasn't my fault!"

"Sure, I know," he said. "Everybody knows. But kids, sometimes they think that way. We didn't tell you at first so you wouldn't feel bad. Then, later, we kept not telling you." The eyes wavered and returned and then: "*Mi dispiace.*" I'm sorry.

The apology—another first, a surprise almost as large as our new history—sucked most of the anger out of me. My father seemed suddenly so small there with his square head, rough skin, and bristly hair, the eyes buried in wrinkles as though a child had scratched lines around them for twenty years without mercy. "It's all right," I said. But, strangely, it wasn't. Against every possible current of logic, beyond the anger and surprise, I was feeling what my father and grandmother had worried I would feel—a cold rivulet of guilt. Not that I'd killed my mother; of course I hadn't. But that she'd died bringing me to life. Intensified a hundredfold, it was the type of guilt you feel when someone does you a favor you know you can't possibly repay. Maybe guilt isn't the word for it. *Debt* might be a better word. Something owed, enormous, unrepayable. And made more intense, too, by the hard births I'd seen over the previous weeks, the blood and pain and exhaustion and fierce effort. My mother had gone through that and not just suffered but died in the process.

We sat for a few minutes without speaking, and then I calmed down enough to say, "Father Alberto taught me a different way of praying. Maybe that would be better. For both of us. He said there was an ancient Christian prayer, the Prayer of Giving. You think of somebody—as they're dying, on their birthday, anytime—and when you breathe in, you take every difficulty they have, every sadness, in this world or the next, you take it onto yourself. And when you breathe out, you give them strength, peace, health, joy. He said it doesn't matter if they're alive or dead. Doesn't even matter if they're a friend or an enemy, though it's harder if they're an enemy, naturally. I did it for Aunt Chiara when she was dying. I've been doing it for Mama ever since he taught me. When I go to church, I always start with a few minutes of that prayer. Every time I think of her, I just breathe in and feel like I'm taking every hard thing away from her and onto myself. You'd think it would make your own sadness heavier, but it doesn't, it makes it lighter."

"You see," he said, after a moment, "how strong you are?"

When he said those words—again, it was so unlike him to offer compliments—I remember noticing that the shadows in the room had shifted a certain way and there were ribbons of light on his face from the curtained windows, two of them bending across his bent nose. He held up his hands and made them into fists so that the muscles of his forearms flexed. Forty-nine years of turning wrenches had made his hands and arms huge. "Popeye," his sister had called him. He was a small man, barely literate, but I knew that his physical strength had made him feel like a force in the world. Now he held the arms up in front of himself. "Always I thought strong was this," he said. "Now I see the other kind."

"I don't feel very strong right now."

"Because I told you about your mother," he said.

"It's all right. It will just take a little time. I'm all right."

"It's too late for me now, saying these prayers. I'll never catch up. You can't get strong when you're old."

"Bullshit," I said, surprising myself. I think that, once you start hearing the truth, or at least once you start tearing away the wrapping of old fibs, it leaves you raw, and, for that little bit of time at least, the rawness stripped me of the skin of good-girl politeness I usually lived in with him. Once the word was out—we never cursed in our house—I thought he'd frown and spin into one of his quick fits of fatherly disapproval, the same kind of thing I'd seen when I'd come home late for supper and he'd insist on making me another serving of pasta. But he looked at me again as if seeing a new person there, and he said, *"Va bene. Okay . . . later we'll try,"* and I got up and went to make supper.

THE REVELATION ABOUT how my mother had actually died moved quickly from the realm of surprise into the realm of fact. It made sense of a few small pieces of the past—my grandmother's last words, for one example—but it did nothing to fill the space left by her absence, nothing to change my routine or my prayers, nothing to ease what I'd come to think of as my dilemma. She was, I believed, in another dimension of life, a place that past suffering could not touch. I asked her to send some help, a bit of motherly advice, but I didn't really expect to receive it. My challenges in this life were my own.

Still, I suppose at that point I was looking for a sign, and I think if Father Alberto had been alive, he would have taken me to task for that. I could almost hear his voice: "Cynthia, it's important to be able to say, 'Thy will be done' and 'I accept what you have in mind for me.' But it's just as important to exercise your own free will. Understand? God wants surrender, sure, but surrender doesn't mean you go limp like a tomato plant after a hurricane."

During those days I was half asleep in my passivity—there's no other word for it except maybe *laziness*—waiting for some kind of clear instructions, waiting for God to help me, instead of figuring things out for myself.

At the end of that week, as he'd promised, Archbishop Menendez sent me a copy of the letter he'd written to a Cardinal Rosario in Rome. In it he said he thought there was "a real possibility" that I had a true and unusual communication with God. He said he thought the particular message I was receiving was "some-what suspect," but, at the same time, as he put it, "the power of her presence" was enough that he felt he shouldn't close the door on me completely. After that introduction he went on to suggest, in the mildest terms, that the cardinal might consider meeting with me to discuss my situation—he sent along my name and address—but he emphasized that if I came to Rome, it would be at my own expense, that I was in no way being sponsored by him, the archdiocese, or any particular church. "Your eminence, I leave this matter to your judgment" was the way he closed. "I send this merely to inform you, without recommendation either way."

I read the letter three times, folded it back into the envelope, and set it on the table beside my bed. The tone was so weak and apologetic. On the one hand the archbishop was saying what a good and special person I was, and on the other he was denying any involvement in my "situation," as he called it, and going to some lengths to defend himself against the potential charge that he was in any way sponsoring or supporting a troublemaker.

Reading that letter was especially hard for me because I had no advisers at that point in my life, no one to talk to about my "situation." I never spoke with friends about my prayer life. I hadn't had any contact with Father Welch since the big scandal broke. I'd written him two notes and heard nothing; the Paulist Center wouldn't give out his new phone number; I imagined that he and his girlfriend had moved far away, beyond the reach of the Boston press. But I wondered what he would have said about the archbishop's letter, and I wondered what Father Alberto would have said. I wondered what I was supposed to do then—book a flight to Rome, find Cardinal Rosario, and knock on the door of his office holding the archbishop's letter in one hand and impressing him with my "presence"?

I had an interesting dream that night, one of those dreams that's so vivid you wake up feeling as though you've left your body in another world. In the dream, Father Alberto was standing behind and to the side of me and speaking over my right shoulder. I was overjoyed to feel him there and wanted desperately to speak to him, but all he said was "Be careful walking." Then he said it again in Italian: "*Sta' attenta quando cammini.*" I woke up, and after a minute of readjusting myself to ordinary life, I guessed—incorrectly as it would turn out—that it must simply be a connection I was making to his death.

One week after that dream, I came home and found that my father had set a piece of mail at my place at the table. The envelope was cream-colored, fine paper, and in the upper-left-hand corner were the words *Ufficio del Cardinale Armando Rosario/Vaticano*. Inside, on stationery so thick it almost felt like a piece of cloth, was this short message, in English:

Dear Miss Piantedosi:

Cardinal Rosario will meet with you at 10:30 o'clock on the 8th of September at the address shown above.

Father Clement, Assistant to the Cardinal

I sat holding the sheet of paper in both hands, feeling as though the objects around me—tablecloth, curtains, dials on the stove, the glass jars of vinegar peppers sitting on the counter—were props in a movie set and I'd been jerked out of my real life and thrust into a role. Those ordinary things simply did not fit with the letter in my hand. The Vatican! The Vatican was as familiar to us as the planet Mars, and as distant. It existed, yes, we all knew that, but as part of another world, or at least another dimension of life so far from our own that it might have been a Hollywood creation. I rubbed the stationery between my thumb and second finger, as if testing it for actuality. Without yet believing in the possibility of going, I thought about that date, September 8. Two months after the clinicals finished, five weeks before I took my Boards. It would be possible to leave then, for a short while. But I wondered how much it would cost—plane ticket, hotel, food. I glanced into the living room and saw only my father's legs from the knee down: brown jeans, work boots. He was listening to the news, a report from Afghanistan, another distant planet. I read the note again, folded it back into its envelope, and carried it up to my room.

THAT SAME WEEK, STILL CAUGHT in what felt like a surreal fog, I made a slightly unusual detour on the way home from work. Instead of going to St. Anthony's as I usually would have, I got off the subway—the line runs just inland from the beach—crossed over Revere Beach Boulevard, walked for a little while along the sand, and sat on the seawall, facing east. As is often the case on early-summer nights there, a cool breeze drifted in off the water. I remember that it blew against me in such a way that I had to hold my dress down between my knees. When there's a wind from that direction, jets headed for Logan Airport circle around to the north and then turn and come in to land directly over our long stretch of beach. That night, as I'd enjoyed doing all my life, I watched them make their circular approaches.

I followed one plane as it looped over the Nahant Peninsula and then Lynn Beach and Revere Beach. As it came closer, I saw the green stripe along the fuselage and the lettering. It made me smile because I remembered being at the beach as a very young girl with my grandmother and having her point out a plane that had flown all the way from Italy. It made no sense to me then, that she and the plane had come from the same place far on the other side of the water in which we waded and splashed. My world consisted of two or three square miles; anything beyond that was insubstantial, imaginary, impossible to hold in thought.

I decided, walking home alone from the beach, that it was time to expand my small world, time to have a better understanding of my heritage, time for me to try to do something on my own without the support system of grandparents or parents or friends or teachers or an institution like a college or hospital. It was time, in other words, to cast myself off the comfortable perch on which I'd lived for twenty-two years, make one brave, gracious swan dive, and let God catch me, if He wanted to, before I crashed to earth. I don't know that I took the airplane as any kind of sign. I don't think that was it. I think it was simply the case that some piece of fruit had finally come ripe in me. I'd been thinking about the letter from the Vatican almost without stopping for four days, working it over in my mind, trying to make it real. Maybe seeing the Alitalia jet had been the last stage of that.

When I arrived home, I found that my father had felt like cooking—Italian sausages and peppers—and, as he often did, had left some for me on a covered plate. Before I ate it, though, I went and sat with him for a little while in the living room. He muted the television and looked up. I said, "I'm going to Rome." He nodded, and it was as hard as always to read his thoughts. Was he hurt? Surprised? Relieved? Worried? I couldn't tell. "Will you come with me?"

He shook his head, the *no* not as firm and determined as it had been during our conversation on the beach, but a no all the same.

"Why not? You speak Italian better than I do. We could visit the Vatican, see the sights. You could take me to Naples and show me the place you were born."

Another shake of the head. "My cousin Franco can show you. He lives near Rome now, he can show you."

"Wouldn't you like to see him?"

"Franco?" He shook his head again, as if it were a foolish question or as if there were some old bad blood between them. He held my eyes for another second or two and then turned back to the TV.

More than once since my graduation from high school, my father had made it clear to me that I shouldn't stay at home only for fear of hurting him. "I can take care of myself," he reminded me every few months.

But I saw no need to move out. It wasn't a matter of caring for him, and it wasn't a matter of getting free housing. I suppose it might have been partly a kind of laziness on my part, an inertia that kept me there. I was comfortable with the routine.

140

I liked being close to St. Anthony's and the beach. Lisa had moved away, but I had two friends who still lived in the neighborhood, one married and pregnant, the other with a fiancé, and every couple of weeks we'd get together for a glass of wine or dinner. That, and the occasional night out with nursing school friends was all the excitement I wanted. It wasn't because of any feeling of loneliness that I'd stayed living with my father, and it wasn't about money—I'd been working and saving for as long as I could remember.

I think I felt responsible, in part, for being the only female company in his life. After my mother's death, he hadn't dated anyone and had never voiced so much as a syllable about the idea of remarrying. He'd had a fairly strange relationship with his wonderful mother-in-law. They lived in peace, on the one hand, but on the other they barely said a word to each other through the course of a day. He'd bring in a basket of tomatoes from the garden and place them on the counter near the sink, and the understanding would be that she'd wash them and slice them up into a salad or cook them with onions, garlic, and oil and put them into a canning jar to make gravy in the winter.

I never saw them touch each other, never heard them call each other by name, yet there was a kind of comfort in the way they shared that home after my mother was gone. When my grandmother died, it was as if I took her place. Now my father brought the tomatoes to *me*. We had that same, almost completely wordless relationship, something that would have been awkward with any other person I knew. There was a great comfort in it for me, a sense of home, of my true place.

I went and heated up the food and ate it, cleaned the kitchen as I always did, kissed my father good night before I went up to my room. But I was held in the territory just this side of sleep by a sharp-edged sadness. I wanted to have a richer intimacy with my father, not just a wordless understanding or a moment here and there like the ones we'd recently enjoyed, but an ongoing closeness, the two of us welded together by the shared experience of what it meant to be alive on this earth. Growing up, I'd had no mother, no brothers or sisters, and though I'd always been close to my cousins, aunts, and uncles, I wanted the particular kind of love relationship that goes with daily contact. It wasn't that my father had ever been hurtful to me. He could be kind in his own way, but at my age I wanted more than that. Even though I didn't have a boyfriend or a husband or children or a flashy job or car—the markers for adulthood where we lived—I wanted him to see me in my fullness; that's the only way I can express it. Not just as a grown daughter but as a full human being.

I realized, after his second refusal to consider a

trip to Italy, that I'd never really had that, not completely, not to the extent I wanted. My grandmother had seen me that way. Father Alberto had seen me that way. And I believed with all my heart that God saw me that way. Still, I felt partly cheated. Whenever I bought a cup of coffee in the subway station before getting on the train to come home, I looked at the person in the kiosk. Even if she didn't look back at me, I looked at her, and when I took the cup and thanked her and gave her the money I tried as best I could to make it an exchange between two full souls. That was all I'd ever wanted in my own home. Probably, I thought, I'd never get married, never have the love of a husband or children. That understanding made me sadder than it ever had. My father's small nod, his slight acknowledgement of my kiss, that was all the intimacy I'd ever know.

But I'd made my decision. If I couldn't enjoy the kind of human intimacy I wanted, I'd try to have the deepest possible intimacy with God. And waiting around passively, dreamily, hoping for the courage to act—what kind of partner would that make? What kind of *rapporto* was that?

The next morning when I woke up, ready to make my travel plans, my father wasn't there. On the kitchen table I saw that he'd left a small stack of new bills, all twenties. Eight hundred dollars, a fortune for a man like him. He had set my empty coffee cup on top of the bills and put them in a place where I couldn't help but see them. There was no tender note, no explanation, just a piece of paper with his cousin's name and a telephone number on it; he'd purposely left the house and gone out early, something he didn't usually do, so he wouldn't have to face me. But he'd left all that money, probably taken it from a stash he kept in his bedroom, hidden for some imagined emergency—war, death of a spouse. Sudden departure of the last person left in his life.

BOOK THREE

CHAPTER **EIGHT**

On the afternoon I left for Italy, a perfect September day, I hugged my father good-bye and went out and stood on the sidewalk in the sun. Not only had I never flown on an airplane in my life, I'd never even taken a taxi. It didn't make sense for us. I could walk to church, walk to Broadway to buy what we needed in the stores there. For food shopping I took my father's car. Boston meant a short bus ride to the subway station and then about fifteen minutes on the train into downtown.

But, using part of the money my aunt left me, I'd gone out and purchased a plane ticket and two pieces of luggage—one carry-on, one rolling suitcase—and I felt as though I was starting a new chapter of my life, and so, rather than struggle with the suitcases on the bus and train or accept my father's offer to drive me and make him deal with the airport traffic, I decided to call a cab.

When the taxi pulled up to the curb, I recognized the driver as a girl I'd known in high school. She popped the trunk but stayed behind the wheel. I put my own bags in, and as I slid into the seat and we started away, I turned and looked at the front door and saw my father standing there behind the screen, not waving or smiling, just watching me go. I lifted a hand to him, kissed my fingers, waved. He put both hands up, palms forward, to touch the screen. I had the sense, I don't know why, that I would never see him again.

"Going on vacation?" the driver asked. As soon as I heard her voice, the name came to me: Laura Annina. She'd been one of the cool kids in our class, always flirting with boys instead of paying attention to the teacher, having a couple of minor run-ins with the police at night on Revere Beach. We'd existed in different orbits and never had much to say to each other. I wasn't sure she even remembered me.

But when I told her where I was going, she said, "Well, you were always one of those kids who did things right. And I was always one of those kids who did things wrong. And look at us now. You're going to Italy, and I'm stuck here, still with the same boyfriend. Remember Jinty?"

"Sure," I said. "Handsomest boy in the school."

"Yeah, for what that's worth. I'm living with my aunt, still. Embarrassed to say it, but it's true."

"I live with my father," I said. "There's no disgrace in that."

"Nah," she said, and it was the same *nah* I used to hear at Revere Beach (from a distance of twenty yards or so, cool circle to uncool) when friends asked if she wanted to go clubbing that night or into town or up to Hampton Beach for the weekend. Nah, I can't. Nah, Jinty wouldn't like that much.

"Just, ya know. Things haven't really worked out the way I wanted."

"We're still young."

"Nah, yeah," she said, in a tired voice. "I just never went nowhere, and I'm probably never goin' nowhere. Jinty and I will probably get married someday, if he ever gets around to askin'. And I'll probably drive a cab until we have kids, or maybe my uncle will get me on at City Hall or somethin'. And then you'll see me pushin' a stroller down Broadway and then yellin' for my kids at the football game and then drinkin' beers on the front porch after they leave to get married."

"You could go back to school."

"Yeah, right," she said, and she blasted the horn at a car in front of us and I could tell she didn't want to continue the conversation.

There was something sad in it for me. I knew so many people like Laura, so many friends whose dreams had been stunted while they were still in diapers, who'd put their life in a box and pulled the lid on over themselves, and lay there in the dark believing that was the whole world. Nothing good existed outside that box, or if it did exist, it was part of a system designed for other people, not them. A boyfriend with a car, money for cigarettes—those were the big hopes. There was absolutely nothing wrong with the life Laura lived, except that she seemed so prematurely tired and unhappy living it, as if there were chains on her wrists and ankles that only she could see. I knew her, understood her from the inside. Doing something that made her happier—going back to school, trying to find a job where she could move up the ranks and make more money and have her own apartment, or even telling Jinty straight out she wanted to get married and start a family—those things were as alien to her as becoming a brain surgeon and settling in the suburbs. As alien, I thought, as the idea of going to Rome had been for me a few months ago. There was a comfort in living the way we lived, in seeing people you knew, day after day, year after year, on the streets of the city where you'd been raised. There were fewer surprises in a life like that.

I wasn't so different. At least, not so different in the way I lived on the outside. Inwardly, though, my father was right: there was a streak of bravery in me. Even as a young girl I'd taken the lid off the box of my interior life. I believed there was no limit to what could happen there, and I don't really know where that belief came from. Not from Father Alberto, because I'd felt that way long before my conversations with him began. Not even from my grandmother. Maybe my mother had been a brave woman and had passed it down to me in her genes. Maybe it had something to do with the fact that I was descended from people who'd had the courage to leave the familiarity of their birthplace and sail across the ocean in steerage looking for something better. But Laura was descended from those same people. Her great-grandparents had left the Old Country, too, and traveled to a world where they didn't know anyone besides maybe a cousin or two, where they didn't speak the language, didn't like the food, where they had no place to live, no job, where there was snow and ice instead of olive trees and earthquakes. They'd had the courage to do that, as my own parents had, yet the generations they'd given birth to seemed to put roots down into the soil of eastern Massachusetts and never want to go anywhere else for the rest of their given days.

In my inner life, at least, I'd always been a kind of explorer, unafraid to venture into unmapped lands. So it felt right on that day to finally be matching my interior spirit to visible events. Sitting on the leatherette seat, glancing at the side of Laura's face and sending a silent prayer in her direction that her life, however she lived it, would lead her to a happy place, I felt a perfectly wonderful excitement take hold of me, fingers against my skin. There was a nervousness, yes, but much larger than the nervousness was this thrill at finally breaking out of my comfortable world. Anything could happen to me in Italy, anything good or bad. I'd been standing on the bridge over the Point of Pines tidal inlet all my life, watching the water come in and go out, frozen there, paralyzed by fear but wanting, at the same time, to feel the excitement of being airborne, the stomach-wrenching drop and hard splash. Finally I was making my leap.

At the airport, Laura parked, jumped out of the cab, and set my new bags on the sidewalk in front of the terminal as tenderly as if they were the luggage of a queen. The fare was $19.80, and I gave her a twenty and a ten. She looked up and for a second I thought she'd embrace me. But she only shook my hand in a congratulatory way, said, "You're sweet," and jumped back in her cab to hurry home.

I'd gone past the airport in cars and on the subway thousands of times but never once set foot inside the terminal buildings. When I stepped through the automatic door, holding one bag over my shoulder and rolling the other behind me, the gritty world of Greater Boston shifted, instantly, into a futuristic universe, all glass and metal and echoing announcements. The floor was so well polished you almost could have used it as a mirror. In front of me was a confusion of lines, passengers repacking overstuffed bags, people running, saying their good-byes, standing nervously with tickets clutched in their hands and purses draped over their wrists. For a moment, a small lizard of fear crawled across the back of my neck, and I had an urge to turn around, call Laura to come get me, show up back at the house on Tapley Avenue, and tell my father I just couldn't do it.

But then a woman from one of the airlines came over and asked if she could help, and she guided me into a long line and stayed nearby explaining the whole process. I showed my ticket and driver's license, checked one bag, and then, since I was two hours early, spent a little time in the airport bookstore, where I was surprised to find one of Thomas Merton's lesser-known books, *The Wisdom of the Desert*, something Father Welch had mentioned more than once. I bought it, went to the café area, and had an expensive cup of coffee and a bagel, and sat there reading the marvelous introduction. I still remember this line about the desert monks of the third century: "They sought a God whom they alone could find, not one who was 'given' in a set, stereotyped form by somebody else."

Yes, I thought. That's why I'm doing this.

When the time came, I went through the security line, telling myself I was setting out to find that God, too, and then I was sitting in a black, cushioned chair looking out the window at the Alitalia plane that would carry me across the Atlantic. Half the other waiting travelers were speaking Italian. I observed them carefully, their fine shoes and neatly creased pants, their stylish dresses and jewelry. They were tourists, obviously, having come to Boston on vacation, and that idea seemed amusing and surprising. It had never occurred to me that people in the rest of the world would choose my neighborhood for an exotic trip. Maybe some of them had taken the subway out to Revere or been given a recommendation to eat at Rossetti's. Maybe my father and I had sat near them on our happy night or had seen them walking on the beach. I had an urge to strike up a conversation with a mother and daughter sitting nearby, to ask them a hundred questions about Rome. But, in their expensive clothes and fancy hairstyles, they seemed so much more sophisticated than I felt, and I was afraid of looking stupid. I concentrated instead on listening to the language, realizing that my father's stubborn return to Italian coincided exactly with the first time I'd told him I might go to Rome. Maybe he'd been preparing me, then, all those weeks.

I said a prayer for him. I tried to imagine his life before I came into it: a child in a fascist society with its bluster, violence, and lies. German occupation. American bombs and soldiers. Wreckage everywhere, lines for food, the decision to leave, and then the harrowing boat trip in early adolescence. I knew from stories my uncles told that there had been widespread anti-Italian feeling in 1940s and 1950s Boston. Instead of finishing school, my father had lied about his age and found a job as a laborer on the subway, laying track and stringing wire. An older Italian man had taken him on as an apprentice mechanic, and he'd ended up learning those skills, becoming a master mechanic, and doing that work for almost fifty years.

What I didn't know, what I'd never had the courage to ask, was why he'd waited until age forty-two to marry, then eleven more years to have a child. What had a woman so many years his junior seen in him? "My aunt, she introduced us once at a wedding" was the story. But my mother had been twenty then, a few years younger than I was. My father was thirty-nine. What kind of life made a twenty-year-old, Italian-born beauty fall in love with a man her father's age? And why had I neglected to ask? In the photographs I saw, they were standing close, arms around each other's waists, seemingly in love. But what had the fiber of that love been made of? A common heritage? A lopsided physical attraction? A comfort she took from him, surrounded, as she was, by a hostile, half-alien world? I had wanted to be seen by my father as a full soul. But had I ever really done that for him?

Soon we were being summoned to the gate, showing boarding passes, striding down the long walkway with its bouncy floor. I felt another surge of excitement and then a small jolt of nerves as I actually stepped onto the plane. Again I just did what everyone else did. I found my seat. I saw people stuffing things into the overhead compartment, so I put my bag up there, too, saving out *The Wisdom of the Desert* and a pharmaceuticals textbook. It seemed to take a long time for passengers to settle in, and then the flight attendants gave us a miniclass on what to do if we crashed in water or ran out of oxygen. There was a swelling knot of nerves in my belly as the plane backed out of its parking place and rolled toward the runway. I was holding tight to the arms of the seat.

"First time flying?" the person in the seat beside me asked.

He was a nice-looking man, fifty or sixty years old, dressed in a suit, and he looked as comfortable there as my father did in his chair in front of the television. I told him it was, that I was going on vacation to Rome, and he said, "Rome is simply the greatest city in the world. I've been there dozens of times on business, and my life's dream, when I retire, is for my wife and me to sell our house, and rent an apartment in Trastevere, do you know it?"

"I don't know anyplace there."

"It was the working-class section years ago. Then the movie stars and artists discovered it, and now it's the Italian SoHo."

I nodded and smiled, afraid to reveal how little I knew of the world.

"Rome," he said, as if he was speaking the name

of a lover. "I just want to walk the streets all day for the last ten or twenty years of my life, go into museums, have great meals, stroll in the parks. You're not going to drive, I hope."

I told him I had a distant relative who was going to help me get around. I was hoping he'd meet me at the airport.

"That's wise. The only bad thing about the city, the only bad thing about the country, really, is that the people drive as if they're constantly showing off for one another. It's like a hockey game. Do you know hockey?"

"No."

"In hockey, which is a beautiful sport, the players are constantly trying to show who's tougher. They fight, they whack each other with sticks, they elbow each other in the face. It's exactly the same in Italy with the drivers." But he was smiling as he said all this, making it seem as though Italy, or at least the Italian road, was a kind of comic strip. "You'll have a great time," he said, in an encouraging way. "Which part of the city are you staying in?"

"Near the Vatican. I rented the hotel online. They said it was walking distance."

He assured me it was a good section of the city, not the nicest but safe for a woman traveling alone: "If you keep your wits about you."

It was amazing to me how much speed the plane gathered as we went down the runway, and it was frightening to feel the lift in my belly, the way we bounced from side to side after the wheels left the ground. Once we were airborne, the man took out his computer, but before he began to work on it he said, "A Merton fan, I see."

"Yes. I just bought this one."

He asked if he could look at it and flipped through a few of the pages. "I read him in college," he said, handing the book back to me. "It made so much sense then, the things he was saying."

"And now?"

He shrugged, smiled. "Now real life has taken over."

"What he's talking about seems exactly like real life to me."

"Wait thirty years," he said knowingly, and then he turned to his computer screen and we said nothing after that. Out the window, I caught just a glimpse of the northern end of Revere Beach, and then the coastline of the North Shore, a bright jumble in twilight: I could see water towers, squat gas tanks, gray roofs. A few miniature boats scratching thin white lines on the sea, heading home.

I READ A BIT AND studied the textbook a bit, and then, after the meal, settled in with a blanket. I was thinking, for some reason, of the ways people limit themselves: of the man beside me, of Laura

Annina, of my father not wanting to break his routine and see Italy again. Was it only fear, or were they enviably satisfied with their lives while I was too restless in mine? Maybe, I thought, as I slipped toward sleep, it had something to do with not having a mother. Maybe the spiritual itch started there. Merton, I remembered, had also lost his mother when he was very young. . . .

I was awakened by the attendants serving breakfast. Soon the pilot announced that we could see Italy out the windows on the side of the plane where I was sitting. I looked down and was surprised at how closely it resembled the map. I don't know why I should have been, but somehow I thought the actual land would be messier, the edges blurred.

We landed, and there was a short delay and then the confusion of immigration and customs. A bit like confession, I thought tiredly; that same twinge of concern as you approached it; that same feeling of cleanliness as you walked away. Just beyond the customs zone I saw a man—much too young to be my father's cousin Franco—holding up a sign that said CYNTHIA PIANTEDOSI. Spelled correctly for once. It was a nice way to be greeted. The person holding the sign turned out to be Franco's son, and to my surprise, he also turned out to be a priest. He shook my hand warmly, insisted I call him "Bruno," not "Father Bruno," and also insisted on rolling the larger of my two bags out of the terminal to a small blue van in the parking area. "This belongs to my father," he said in Italian, "but he let me use it today to take you to the hotel. He sends his regards. Tomorrow night we will go to his house for dinner."

"My father told me about you. I had no idea you were a priest."

He smiled proudly, as if having been ordained was the fulfillment of a childhood dream. Beneath the smile, though, lay a shadow of something else—misery, confusion, doubt—that anyone on earth could see. *"Già cinque anni.* Five years already," he said, his Italian so much cleaner than what I was used to hearing at home. "I have a minor position at the Vatican."

In two minutes he had ferried me out of the airport parking lot and into a land of ugliness. I felt a wash of disappointment and then another wash of embarrassment at my own foolishness. For some reason I'd imagined that all of Rome, every bit of it, would be ancient buildings and ruins, and here out the windows what I saw was only modern-day commercial clutter: factories and electric wires, billboards, an acre of old cars crushed and stacked like cardboard boxes, the occasional unattractive apartment building, all gray concrete and flat, featureless planes. And my neighbor on the flight had been absolutely correct: the driving was madness.

Father Bruno seemed perfectly comfortable in

the midst of the madness, though, changing lanes the way some people change radio stations. It was sport to him, hockey on wheels. He raced up to within inches of the bumpers of trucks, then waited for an opening, darted left or right, and went racing along in pursuit of the next bumper. I was curious to learn about the life of a priest in Italy but afraid to distract him, so I kept silent and he kept his eyes on the road and the pretend-happy expression on his face. After half an hour or so he took an exit and curved down from the elevated highway into the city.

"This is more like I imagined Rome to be," I said, wondering what my Italian sounded like to him. A small accent? Noise against his ears?

Another sorrow-lined smile. *"Roma,"* he said. "My home. My father moved here to work at the Vatican when I was very young. He's a lawyer, retired now."

In that part of the city I saw no ruins or elaborate fountains, but there were at least some nice-looking, fairly old, stucco apartment buildings—lemon- and ochre- and apricot-colored, the windows bracketed with brown or green shutters flapping open to either side or closed tight against the morning. We sped past one church. It was squeezed lopsidedly between two younger buildings, as if they were its grandchildren holding it upright: pocked gray stone, worn wooden doors. The sight of it sent a wave of happiness through me. Everything else might be unfamiliar here, but I'd be at home in the churches, I knew that. My prayers would take me beyond superficial differences—language, smells, national habits, down into a quiet unity, a place with no flags or passports or accents.

By the time we'd gone another block we were caught up in a swirling soup of traffic, made worse by cars parked on both sides of the narrow streets, and then we at last broke free and entered a residential district of five-story apartment buildings with graffiti on the ground floors and rust stains by the gutters. There was a sidewalk sale going on, block after block of it. I caught glimpses of women standing beside tables covered with cardboard boxes. Clothes and books, it looked like.

Father Bruno made a left onto a narrower street and double-parked near a sign that read ALBERGO. "This is the place you reserved," he said, with the smallest note of disdain. "Not the best hotel in the city and not the best neighborhood either, but close to the Vatican and you can walk around at night here without worry."

"Thank you so much," I said. "I can carry my own bags in. It's no problem."

"What time tomorrow is your meeting?"

"I'm supposed to be at the Congregation for the Doctrine of the Faith at ten thirty. I'm meeting Cardinal Rosario."

"An important place and an important man," he said, and, when I didn't respond: "I'll come for you at ten."

"That will give us enough time?"

"Oh, yes. It is very close. You can almost walk there. I will be here at ten, don't worry. If you want to see the Vatican now, go to the end of this street and turn left and follow the people."

"Thank you so much again," I said.

"*Niente*," he said. "It's nothing." He nodded and smiled, and when I closed the door he carried his unspoken sorrows away with him into the Italian morning.

I hadn't wanted an expensive hotel and had found this one, Albergo delle Mura, online. The lobby was small but gleaming, all tile and chrome, the people at the desk friendly enough. The room one of them showed me to, up three flights of stairs, was perfectly adequate. I closed the door and sat on the bed, and even though the sink in the bathroom was dripping and the single window looked out on nothing more interesting than the roof of an apartment building across the street, I felt absolutely bathed in happiness. I was in Italy, in Rome! It had thrilled me to hear Italian spoken, to see it on the billboards and signs. The colors and shapes of the cars, the style of the architecture, even the way the people walked seemed fresh and fascinating to me. Tired as I was from the time change and the long flight, I could hardly wait to go out into the city, but I unpacked first, took a shower, changed clothes.

Following Bruno's directions, I walked to the end of the street and turned left. A wall made of thin red bricks, faded and old-looking, slanted up and away from me. As he'd promised, there was what seemed like a river of tourists, so I followed them through the entrance marked CITTÀ DEL VATICANO and into St. Peter's Square: the fountain, the obelisk, the twin rows of stone columns at its circumference, the grand church with the pope's balcony and the famous dome. Seeing it that way, in person, sent another burst of joy through me. After a few minutes in a line that snaked through metal detectors and past two security guards, I stepped through the doors of the church that, in a certain way, stood at the center of my universe. Just inside the front entrance was Michelangelo's *Pietà*. Softly lit, protected by bulletproof glass, it was a treasure sent to us from some finer world. I stood in front of it for a long time. As had been the case with St. Peter's, I'd seen it before, of course, many times, in the book Father Alberto had given me, in photos, in a TV special. But the *Pietà* felt familiar in a way that St. Peter's did not, a way that had nothing to do with books and photos. After a while I understood that for years I'd been seeing it, or some image I associated with it, in my prayers. Something in the folds of white marble whispered to me in a language that was familiar but not quite understandable. I stood there trying to make sense of that, but the connection was vague, a strand of thought linking dream and day. According to the biblical accounts, Mary had been a young girl—fourteen or fifteen, probably—when she'd discovered she was pregnant. Pregnancy without marriage, in her time, meant nothing but disgrace, a future of poverty, misery, and shame. Joseph—many years older and really a mysterious figure—had saved her from that fate. But why had he married her? Pity? Simple charity? Loneliness? An intuition that the child she carried was an exceptional soul? And what had happened to him after Christ's birth? There wasn't a word in the Bible about that. Or about what Mary's life had been like after her husband died.

After a while I left those questions and that magnificent sculpture and wandered around the rest of the enormous church. The nave was crowded with tour groups, nuns, kids, couples with guidebooks. There must have been twenty different languages in the air. I studied everything—the colors and designs of the worn floor tiles, the columns standing there like redwoods, Michelangelo's domed ceiling, the murals and stained glass, the main altar, the side altars, the confessionals, the yellow marble fountains, the resting place of one of my heroes, Pope John XXIII. It was a museum of my faith, and I wandered around examining every surface, every twist of decorative marble along the ceiling, every pew.

After a time I stepped into one of the side chapels, which was mainly empty, and knelt for a few minutes on the hard tile, wishing I could magically summon my grandmother and Father Alberto and set them down beside me there. I wanted to share St. Peter's with them, or, at least, be able to send them a postcard of the *Pietà*. I closed my eyes and pictured Mary's sculpted face. Most likely she'd looked nothing like Michelangelo's marble woman, not so beautiful, not so unlined and unworried. Brown-skinned, not white, occasionally weary or upset. It didn't matter. What mattered to me was that in those perfect features Michelangelo had captured the essence of the human predicament: the sorrows of bodily existence and the confidence of true faith. I told myself that making peace between those two things was the only balance I had to strike. Just that. Be afraid, be nervous, be sad—fine. But lay the blanket of faith over those cold, restless children. Let them rest.

I sat in a pew there for close to an hour, then went and stood in front of the sculpture again, and again it was like listening to music I knew and loved. This is enough, I thought. Even if nothing comes of the meeting with Cardinal Rosario, this is more than enough to justify the expense and the effort of coming here. Just this.

When I left finally, hungry and weary, I sat for a while on the lip of the fountain in the square, looking at Michelangelo's dome and the dark metal doors and the pilgrims filing in and out. I had the thought then—strange for me—that, for the rest of my life I would try to come to Rome on vacations. I'd save up for fifty weeks, then make an annual pilgrimage to this place. The strangeness came from the fast transition—in my mind, at least—from provincial girl to world traveler and from the feeling, so strong, that here, in the heart of the heart of the Church's rules and regulations, those things didn't matter to me at all. What mattered was having a solid building, a temple, that served as an anchor for my inner wanderings. That was what St. Anthony's had always been. Now my world was larger.

I walked out of the square, found a place to have lunch, and surprised myself that I was able, so comfortably, to order pizza and a glass of wine and make small talk with the waiter.

From there I decided, rather than going back to the hotel, to have a second espresso and walk across the Tiber into the heart of Rome. I had brought along a map but had decided, in my typically stubborn fashion, that I'd do without a guidebook. I'd end up where I ended up, see what I was meant to see. And it worked out fine. There were churches, it seemed, on every other block, and, in stark contrast to the United States, all of them were open. The smaller ones stood with so little fanfare in a row of other buildings that I sometimes couldn't tell from the facades that they weren't banks, shops, or residential buildings. I stepped into three of them on that walk, and they were all magnificent—huge oil paintings on the walls, images of saints in golden frames, neat rows of pews, altars made of pink, yellow, brown, or white marble. I said a prayer in each of them and lit candles for my father and mother and grandmother and Father Alberto and Father Welch and Matilda, for the monsignor and the archbishop and for the Church, for anyone who was suffering on this earth. In each place I prayed that something would come of my visit, that I would have the courage to meet with this important man and say what I had to say. And that he would have the courage and good grace to listen.

At last, late in the afternoon, after I'd wandered along a street where it seemed that every third shop was selling ITALIA T-shirts and miniature ceramic Colosseums, I ended up in Campo de' Fiori. It was a few hundred square yards of cobblestone surrounded by somewhat tattered palazzi and narrow buildings and full of fruit vendors and the tables and chairs of outdoor cafés. In the center of the square stood a statue of a hooded figure; for some reason it drew me. A plaque there stated that the figure was Giordano

Bruno. The unfortunate and brave philosopher had been burned at the stake on this spot in 1600 for espousing the heresy that not only did the earth revolve around the sun, but that there might be other suns and other universes in God's kingdom.

Not exactly what I needed to see at that particular moment.

But Campo de' Fiori was a lively place, an even mix, it seemed, of ordinary Italians enjoying coffee at outdoor tables and tourists, wide-eyed like me, wandering the cobblestones with a half-eaten peach or plum in hand and gazing at the scores of architectural details—the cornices and carved eagles, the metal skulls on doorways, the arched windows and stone lions looking down at us from their places beneath flat roofs.

There was a spirit to those buildings that I'd never encountered at home. They spoke of a thousand years of human habitation—everything from the fiery death of Giordano Bruno to the processions of emperors and popes. They'd seen wars, invasions, occupations, bountiful times, and desperate times. Something in their old solidity and the simple beauty of their lines gave me faith that, whatever happened with Cardinal Rosario, whatever happened on this earth, at some point in our eternal travels, everything would be fine. Eventually, eventually, as Julian of Norwich had been quoted as saying in one of the books Father Alberto gave me, "All shall be well and all shall be well, and all manner of thing shall be well."

Julian of Norwich—it seemed strange and wonderful that I should think of her then, because her visions had led her to believe in a compassionate, not a wrathful God, and she'd claimed, openly, that Christ was both father and mother spirit. Life was for learning, she said, not for suffering and penance, and in order to learn we sometimes have to fail and endure. Father Alberto had told me that she'd never been canonized—something he thought was "a monstrous mistake"—but that he prayed to her every day.

Thinking of her, floating around in my small, jet-lagged ecstasy, hungry again and remembering Father Alberto's love of food, I asked a young Italian woman about my own age for a restaurant recommendation. She led me a little way down a crooked lane—*vicolo* is the Italian word: not a street, exactly, and not really an alley—that angled off Campo de' Fiori, and at a bend in the lane she pointed to an awning above a patio that held two or three tables and told me it was a restaurant and the best place to eat in that neighborhood. I went across the patio and through the front door and was greeted by an elderly woman as if I were her long-lost grandchild. There were no menus. I was seated at an uncovered wooden table, and within a minute a waiter started bringing the meal of the day. Mineral water in a bottle and a jug of white wine; an antipasto that included a bowl of cooked lentils, a bowl of fennel, a plate of various salamis, olives, fresh bread; and a bright green olive oil. Then came two different pastas in another large bowl—one very cheesy and the other in a succulent tomato sauce. By then I was more than full, but the waiter hadn't finished. He brought the meat dish—a loin of pork. And then, for dessert, a fruit-and-jelly torte.

I was used to Italian food, of course, but not used to consuming it in such quantity. Still, I've always had the habit of eating a little too much when I'm nervous, and I've always had a bit of trouble with my weight (giving up something for Lent helped; running on the beach in the warm weather helped), and it seemed wrong to refuse any of the dishes the kitchen sent my way. I ate and ate, watching the families around me, listening to the music of the language, letting myself enjoy the way the sounds, tastes, and smells seemed to bring my grandmother back to the table with me. What a mistake it was, I said half aloud to my father, not to have come here with me.

At last, when the steady stream of food seemed to have finally gone quiet, I paid and thanked the waiter and made the long walk back to the hotel with the mad Roman traffic honking and roaring close beside me all the way. I took the stairs up to my room, washed, prayed for only half an hour, then undressed and fell into bed and was enveloped immediately in a wonderful, deep sleep.

I was awakened from that sleep by a persistent knocking. I was so groggy and seemed to have traveled so far from the depths of unconsciousness that I thought, at first, I must have slept all the way through and missed breakfast and it was Father Bruno at the door, telling me we were late for our meeting. But when I looked at the alarm clock beside the bed it read 1:15, and when I peeked outside the windows it was dark. The knocking paused momentarily, then started up again. Hasty taps, persistent, not loud. "*Signorina? Signorina Piantedosi?*" someone was saying on the other side. I wondered if the place was on fire.

I got up and went to the door and called out a question. No words there, just more knocking in a steady rhythm. I hesitated a moment, then unlatched and opened the door. Standing there was a tall man, a stranger, with three or four days' growth of beard and features that seemed somehow un-Italian, one eye blue and one brown. I could see then that he was drunk, and I was starting to slam the door when he said "*Signorina bella*" in heavily accented Italian and reached out and took hold of my shoulders with both hands. From the depths of me I felt my ninth-grade street self rise up, and without thinking about it I kicked him hard, once, in the left knee. He stumbled backward a step, and I managed to get the door closed tight between us and to lock it with shaking hands. I went to the phone, called downstairs, and told the people at the desk what had happened. There were profuse apologies, and the assurance—after a moment—that the tall man had been chased from the hotel and would never return. He'd inquired at the desk earlier, using my name. Was he a friend of mine?

"Absolutely not," I said. "He tried to grab me."

More apologies. "Tomorrow the manager will speak to you and apologize personally," the clerk said.

I went back to bed but couldn't sleep. I thought of the warnings I'd heard in America and realized how foolish I'd been to open the door at that hour. Seduced by the beauty of the city and the kindness of a few people I had met, I'd forgotten the basic rules of safety for a woman traveling alone. Eventually I drifted to sleep and woke up, drifted to sleep and woke up again, and at last, probably at four a.m., fell into a more solid rest and was awakened by the alarm at seven.

After another shower, an hour of prayer, and breakfast—just coffee and pastry—in the downstairs dining room, I went outside and saw Father Bruno waiting there beside his father's blue van. He was wearing an expression that was equal parts anxiety and welcome. The morning was sunny and mild, warmer but less humid than a hot Boston day, and I was surprised to feel a fresh breeze skipping down the street, a wash of wind that didn't smell like big city at all. I hadn't seen any skyscrapers on the drive in or during the previous day's meandering. In places, at moments, Rome felt like a sprawling, ancient village.

"*Mi hai aspettato tanto tempo?*" I asked.

"No, no, no, five minutes, nothing at all. Everything is fine. I came early. I didn't want you to miss your appointment."

I climbed into the front seat, and we cut and swerved out of our graffiti-decorated neighborhood and over to the river, where we made a sharp right turn at a round, fortress-like building.

"Castel Sant'Angelo," Father Bruno said, pointing to it. "There's a secret escape route leading from the Vatican palace to that place. Whenever a pope felt like somebody was going to try to kill him, he hid there."

For a moment it seemed so strange to me, the idea of a pope worried about being killed. There had been no shortage of violence in Revere when I was growing up—fights, assaults, the occasional underworld assassination or gang shooting; I'd done enough reading of history to be familiar with wars and invasions, torture and slavery; I'd seen patients come into the ER with gunshot and stab wounds—so I don't know how I'd managed to preserve my naiveté into my twenties. Maybe *naiveté* wasn't the right word for it. I suppose I simply wanted the world to be populated by compassionate, considerate men and women, so I looked for evidence to support that view and ignored, or half ignored, the darker side. It was part of what had led me to open the door in the middle of the night in a strange city. But I remembered then that Pope John Paul had been shot right in St. Peter's Square. A little more remembering, and I called to mind a conversation with Father Alberto about it, some details: a Turkish man, Agca was his last name; after the first shots, the Vatican security chief and a brave nun had wrestled him to the ground, probably saving the pope's life. "When he recovered," Father Alberto said, "John Paul went to visit Agca in jail to say he forgave him. Who would do something like that?"

Bruno interrupted my musing: "All the important roads into Rome go straight to the end at the churches," he said, trying out his English for the first time. "So the pilgrim, when they coming in Rome, see in front of them first the churches."

I nodded politely to show I understood, but I was having a hard time focusing. I felt a film of sweat on the palms of my hands. Before leaving home, I'd looked up the Congregation for the Doctrine of the Faith on my computer but then decided not to spend more than a few seconds studying the images. I don't know why, exactly.

So I'd go into the meeting with a fresh mind, maybe, not imagining beforehand the place where it would be held or what might be said there. I wanted to keep my thoughts free of all that, to trust that I'd find my way, that the right words would be given to me when I needed them.

"Did you sleep well?" Bruno asked, in Italian again, as if his quick adventure with English had been too terrifying to repeat. "Did you see the Vatican? St. Peter's? Did you find a place to eat? After I drove away I realized I should have recommended someplace. There are too many restaurants here that serve bad food and prey on tourists."

After thinking about it for a few seconds, I decided to tell him what had happened in the night. He was furious. "No more in this hotel, then," he said. "I do not like this neighborhood. It is not safe enough for a person like you. When you're in the meeting now, I will find you another hotel, maybe a little more expensive if that is okay. I will go to this hotel and explain and end your reservation and see if I can get your payment returned to you."

I told him I didn't want him to go to so much trouble, but, in fact, I was happy when he insisted.

"This is the way people do things here," he said with a quick bitterness. "Do they call the police? No. Why? Because then there will be twenty reports to fill out, questions, a black mark against the hotel. They chase the man out and the manager apologizes. Ridiculous! Absurd! What did this man look like?"

I described him as best I could: strange way of speaking, tall and bony, different-colored eyes, and Bruno said immediately, "*Albanese.*" An Albanian.

At breakfast that morning I'd noticed the tendency in Italian newspapers to blame Albanian immigrants for every crime committed in the entire country. I made a small face.

"I'm not prejudiced," he said quickly. "Not at all. We have plenty of our own bad people. But some of the Albanians and North Africans who came here are so desperately poor they'll do anything to earn a few euros. Anything. They'll sell trinkets to tourists on the street. They'll do slave labor all day for next to nothing. If someone sees them drunk and tells them, 'Here's five euros, go up to room 300 and knock on the door and scare the person who answers,' they'll do it. Trust me, I know this. I do volunteer work with these people twice a week; I've heard their stories."

"I believe you," I said, "but what I don't believe is that someone would pay him to target *me*. More likely he just saw me go up to the room and followed me."

"But you said it was one a.m."

"It was."

"And you went back to the hotel at what time?"

"I lost track. Nine, maybe. Nine thirty."

"And he waited three and a half hours before he went up to your room?"

"Then it was just chance."

"But I thought you said he called you by name."

"You're a lawyer's son," I said, trying to make light of it. I wanted to put the night behind me and concentrate on what lay just ahead.

Bruno wouldn't allow it. "It is known that you are here," he said ominously.

"Of course it is. You know it. The people at the hotel know it."

"Cardinal Rosario's office knows it."

"I hope so."

"And other people at the Vatican know it. The Congregation for the Doctrine of the Faith is like your CIA. Anyone who goes there—any foreigner, especially—is seen as a threat to the established order. You frighten them, so they are trying to frighten you in return."

I thought about that for exactly two seconds. "Either you're paranoid," I said, "or I'm naive. The man was a drunk who'd been hanging out in the lobby and heard my name—nothing more than that."

"You should work where I work. You should hear what I hear and what my father heard all those years!"

I thought, for just one moment, about asking if he'd heard of Lamb of God, if that movement within the American Catholic Church was active in Italy, too, but I decided it must be known to the Vatican, and I let the subject drop. As we drove through the streets near the Vatican, Bruno's mad pace was slowed somewhat by the thick flow of cars, trucks, and buzzing motorbikes. I asked him if he'd always wanted to be a priest.

"Oh, yes, always always," he said, "since I was a small boy."

"And are you happy?"

"Oh, very happy," he said. "I have a good job. I have respect. My father is made happy by my ordination."

"You don't wish sometimes that you had a wife and children?"

A twitch of discomfort flicked across his eyes. I was almost sorry I'd asked. "I am still young," he said, as if after ten or so years of the priesthood there would be a chance to reconsider. "Maybe at some point I will miss that kind of life, but for now, I have enough. I have friends, I have work."

"You have God," I suggested, though it was not the type of thing I usually said.

"*Sì, sì,*" he replied, as if having God were a minor consideration.

We went another hundred yards, and he said, "My father is looking forward to meeting you tonight. He was a lawyer for the Vatican at one time, you know."

"I knew he was a lawyer—you and my father

both told me that—but I didn't know he worked at the Vatican. It must have been interesting."

"A universe of dark secrets."

"That's not the way I pictured it. From outside it seems so . . . clean."

Father Bruno made a small laugh. "Where there is great power there are many secrets, and where there are many secrets . . . always trouble. When you speak to a man like Cardinal Rosario, I think, maybe, you should keep that in your mind."

"Thank you," I said, though really I had little idea what he meant.

"For a layperson to meet with him is an honor." He looked across at me so long I almost told him to watch the road. At last he turned his eyes back to the traffic, hit the brakes, swerved, smiled, and added, "An honor and also like . . . a big game of chess or a small war." He went silent a moment, looked over at me again. "He could have been the one who sent that man to your room."

The idea was so preposterous I couldn't think of any response. Bruno glanced over at me once more then whipped us half the way around the left side of St. Peter's Square, just outside the twin rows of columns. He screeched to a stop in front of a partly familiar four-story rectangular block of a building a few hundred yards from the church's entrance. I looked across at him. His face was touched with brushstrokes of what seemed to be awe. It was there, too, in the timid sweep of his arm as he indicated the building. Clearly, in his world this place had some standing, the home of spymasters, saints, and future popes. And, just as clearly, he wasn't intending to accompany me inside and help with the introductions.

"I am going now," he said valiantly, "to find you another hotel and talk to the people at the hotel you are staying in and tell them that what happened is unacceptable, and see if I can get you a refund."

"I appreciate it," I said through my nervousness.

"Will you give me the key? With your permission I can move your bags."

"But they're all unpacked."

"With your permission I will repack them and bring them. Otherwise we will have to travel back there again."

"Fine," I said. I didn't want to focus on the hotel just then. I handed over the room key, tried not to think about Father Bruno packing my underwear into a suitcase. I thanked him, then got out and stood on the sidewalk, ten minutes early. There was no sign on the building, not even a small plaque, and for a moment I thought Bruno had mixed things up. Both sides of the huge wooden front door appeared to be closed tight. The first floor was gray stone, the top three floors the color of an apricot, and the large windows, standing in four neat rows, were tightly shuttered, as if the sun had already swung around and was shining on that side of the building—which wouldn't be the case for several more hours. Father Bruno noticed my confusion. He leaned his body across the passenger seat and waved an arm, pointer finger extended. "There! Over there!" he yelled, jabbing the air. "*Laggiù!*"

I turned. Between where I stood and the double row of concrete pillars stood a gated entrance I hadn't seen. I wondered why Bruno hadn't driven right up to it—for fear that his license plate would be written down in a secret notebook? Until I took a few steps in that direction, it looked to me like a delivery entrance, but when I reached the gates and turned in, I saw two of the famous Swiss guards, unmistakable, almost comical in their red-and-yellow knickers and berets. A street led from the gate into a large paved enclosure. A booth stood on the left-hand side of the street. After a conversation with one of the guards I was allowed to approach the booth. I took the letter from Cardinal Rosario's office out of my purse and produced it for the man sitting there. It turned out to be a kind of magical document: in a moment I was being escorted around the gray corner of the building to the true front door. The Congregation for the Doctrine of the Faith, apparently, kept its back to the street. Another moment and I was led up a wide marble stairway and into a conference room with high-backed oak chairs surrounding a table twenty feet long. Left alone, seated at the table, I felt a familiar stirring in the center of myself, a spark, a shifting. I thought, *not now.* There was, on the wall I faced, a painting that reached almost to the ceiling: St. Jerome the martyr falling to the ground after being struck by a club wielded by one of two brutes with bare chests and bulging muscles. I was staring at it, studying the expression of terror on St. Jerome's face, trying as hard as I could to resist—my palms were leaving wet prints on the exquisitely polished tabletop—when I went spinning away into one of my spells.

There were times, in those strange departures from ordinary five-sense reality, when I'd find myself transported into worlds, or parts of worlds, that were alien to anything I had ever known. I'd never spoken about some of them, not even to Father Alberto, because I was ashamed of hearing the descriptions on my own lips. How could a sane person say the words out loud? Peaceful emerald fields set high above the struggles of earth. Crowded chambers with men and women talking and arguing beneath the faces of Jesus and Mary and various other holy figures. Deep, still, shadowed kingdoms stirred by a colored current or wind—as if I were at the bottom of the ocean. Who in her right mind would admit to those kinds of things after anything other than an LSD trip?

But there were other times when, as if in a recurring dream, I would return to somewhat less exotic "places." There, in the second-floor meeting room of the Congregation for the Doctrine of the Faith, I stepped out into one of those more familiar homes. It was an unpeopled realm, entirely inhuman, painted in pastels, with a steady low humming that seemed to come from movement all around the perimeter. In the center was a kind of sun, or sunlight, that was not too strong to gaze into. It was almost as if I'd somehow made my way down into a blood cell or some subatomic kingdom, where activity and stillness had been joined, all of it purposeful but calm. It was very pleasant to be there, a kind of homecoming. There was no sense of time, only that steady movement and illumination and a feeling of perfect acceptance. It went on and on, and then, at some point, I felt my normal self re-forming around me, withdrawing from that world, lifting up and away from it, without sadness or concern or hurry of any kind. Simply a moving away from that light and that perfect love and coming back to the mottled struggle that is life on earth. It was, I guessed, something close to what being born must feel like.

I opened my eyes. Opposite me at the grand wooden table sat two unfamiliar men, a fairly young priest wearing tortoise-shell glasses and blinking repeatedly, and a much older man in a red robe with gold buttons up the front and gold thread along the seams of his lapels and epaulettes. Cardinal Rosario, most likely in his mid-sixties, had a thin, bony face, but with small sacs of flesh at the jowls and white eyebrows as stiff as the shortest toothbrush bristles. He was watching me with a steely attention. I took a breath and decided, instead of apologizing, to pretend nothing had happened—a trick I'd used dozens of times in school. I asked Mary to give me strength, to put the right words into my mouth, not to let me have come all that way in vain.

"Thank you for agreeing to see me, Your Eminence," I said.

The cardinal nodded, but the nod consisted of a single, quarter-inch movement of his chin. His eyes were like green marbles, unnaturally steady, and I couldn't read anything at all in them. He folded one hand over the other and raised them in front of his mouth, keeping his elbows on the table, and he stayed there like that, barely blinking, his lips hidden from me and his crimson cuffs hanging down from his wrists. "I prefer to speak in English, if you don't mind," I went on. "My Italian is very good. I've spoken it since I was a girl. But what I have to say is so important to me, and I've come so far to say it to you, that I want to speak in the language that is most comfortable to me. Do you mind?"

The priest beside Cardinal Rosario translated, but the cardinal's eyes didn't move from me. I could feel them, like long fingers, pointing, pressing. He made another small nod, and I sensed that the translation hadn't been necessary at all. But when he spoke it was in Italian and in a voice that was quiet and precise, delivered from behind the folded fingers.

"I have been asked to introduce myself," the young priest said, in American English. "I am Father Clement, a.k.a. Francis Giordano, His Eminence's translator and assistant. Niagara Falls, New York, born and bred."

I smiled at him, introduced myself in the same way, and said again how grateful I was that the cardinal had agreed to meet with me. Cardinal Rosario listened to the translation but still didn't move his eyes from my face. I stared back at him, watching for any change of expression. Nothing. "I apologize for that delay. That happens to me sometimes, Your Eminence. It is not something I can control."

Father Clement translated, the cardinal kept looking at me, said nothing, blinked once, waited.

"I'm here," I said, and then I stopped because no words were coming. I could feel my heart thumping in my chest. There was an awkward pause of probably ten seconds, and it seemed to me then that I could sense different aspects of myself—apologetic, brave, frustrated—fighting with one another for the right to speak first. "I'm here because, for the past few years I've been having, in my prayer life . . . I guess I would call them visions." I waited for the translation. "In the visions I feel strongly that God is instructing me to become a parish priest. I'm a lifelong Catholic, from a good Catholic family. I know very well the Church's position on women being ordained. At the same time, after speaking with two good priests at home, I've come to believe that it would be wrong for me to keep ignoring these messages. I've tried to ignore them, please believe me. I have suspected that they might be a trick of the Devil, that they might come from my egotism, even that they might be a sign of mental illness. But after so many conversations with those good priests and after praying about it for a long time, I've come to the conclusion that it's a true message from God and that I have to act on it, whatever the outcome. So I've traveled all this way, alone, at my own expense, in the hope that the Congregation will at least consider a change in this policy."

Before the translation even started I saw a flicker of irritation scamper like a spider across the cardinal's face. As I spoke, he moved his eyes over my forehead, mouth, and neck and then back to my eyes, small, deliberate movements, as if there were a numbered series of dots on my skin and he was following them to draw a picture: one, two, three, four, a demon woman appearing out of the blank page. When Father Clement finished with the Italian version of what

I'd said, we sat, the three of us, in a pocket of silence. A chess game, I thought. A war. And then, in a deliberate, calm way, Cardinal Rosario brought his hands down from his mouth and set them on the table, one on top of the other. The nails were as neatly trimmed and clean as a surgeon's. He spoke a short sentence—"*Non è possibile*"—which I of course understood. But, to be polite, I waited.

"This is not possible," Father Clement said.

The cardinal spoke again, quietly and precisely. On his tongue the Italian language had a gentle, singsong rhythm to it and sounded nothing like the harsh dialect my father and grandmother had been fond of using with each other at home. They were Neapolitans, working people, peasant stock. This man would have had a different kind of upbringing entirely.

"No change can be made," Father Clement said. The cardinal added another few words. "Even," Father Clement translated, "if you were a saint, this could not be done."

"I'm not a saint," I said. "I've never made any claim to be anything but an ordinary woman."

The cardinal's eyes lingered on me. When he spoke again it was in English, the words touched with a small accent but perfectly understandable. "Do you have the children?"

"No, Your Eminence. I'm not married."

"Ah."

"I hope to be someday," I said. "My dream has always been to have a family."

A wisp of amusement went across his eyes, quicker than the light of a fast-passing car on the curtains of a room at night. Cardinal Rosario blinked it away. "You wish to be a wife and mother and also the priest?"

"No," I said. "I don't wish to be a priest. I've never wished to be a priest. In fact, I don't even think I'd be a very good priest. I'm too solitary in certain ways. And probably too selfish. I love my life the way it is, a quiet life. I live with my father. I can walk to our local church, which is a very beautiful church, built by Italian Americans. I like my work—I'm studying to be a nurse. I like helping people who are ill and afraid and in pain. Really the last thing I want is to be a priest."

"Why, then, did you come?"

"May I ask, Your Eminence, if you were having these messages from our Lord, wouldn't you want to act on them?"

"I have never had those messages, daughter."

"But if you did, and if you became convinced that they were genuine, wouldn't it be wrong to fail to act on them?"

Cardinal Rosario pondered the question for a few seconds, his body very still, his eyes resting on me in a way that was cool but not unkind. "Placed against the rules set down by Christ himself," he said, "what are such messages worth?"

"What rules?"

"His own choice of priests."

"But he had no priests then, Your Eminence."

"Of"—the cardinal turned to Father Clement, spoke a few words in Italian, and the priest said, "close associates."

"Mary Magdalene," I said. "Martha. His own mother. Weren't those women precious to him?"

"All the people are precious to him."

"Can't it be said that the cultural standards of his time and those of our time are different in terms of the role of women?"

He shook his head. "The faith," he said, and again he turned to Father Clement for a word and the young priest supplied it. "The faith is timeless."

"Of course, Your Eminence. But over the past twenty centuries the rules of the Church have changed, they've evolved according to custom and the society's evolution."

"*Nelle piccole cose*," the cardinal said. "In small things."

"But there have been many people who effected changes. The story of Saint Clare of Assisi—I was named after her . . . my middle name. Saint Agnes of Rome was an example of going against the mores of the time, a voice for the equality of men and women. Saint Teresa of Ávila was such a powerful figure. Saint Catherine of Siena, who returned the papacy to Rome."

The cardinal was nodding. For the smallest moment I thought I might actually be persuading him with my short list of historical precedents. "Have you ever," he asked in Italian, "performed what could be considered a miracle?"

"Not really," I said. "No, I don't think so."

"You hesitated before answering."

"I . . . I'm in training to be a nurse, as I said. There have been a few times when it seemed as if I could change a patient's condition by touching him or her."

"Bring the patient back to life?"

"I don't think so. I'm not sure. There was one time when that might have happened, but it might have had nothing to do with me."

He nodded, studied me.

"I'm not . . . I haven't come here, Your Eminence, to talk about me."

"You very much care for the Church," he suggested.

"Yes, I do, Your Eminence, very much. And in my part of the world, she is dying."

"Ah," he said, as if my part of the world didn't count for much.

"I am not a radical in any sense of that word. I'm the farthest thing from a troublemaker, you have to believe me."

"And yet at home, I understand," he said, "you have caused there to be some trouble. With your monsignor."

My eyes shifted to Father Clement. It seemed to me that, with the mention of Monsignor Ferraponte, the young priest's neck and face had started trembling; the heavy frames of his eyeglasses were moving in small jumps. I couldn't tell if he was angry, embarrassed, surprised, or frustrated, but he seemed to me to be making an effort to keep the cardinal from seeing his reaction. A chess game, Father Bruno had said, but it was more like poker, and I'd proven to be terrible at poker the two or three times I'd played. In cases where there was even a small bit of deceit or secrecy involved, even for the purposes of a game, I'd always been a miserable failure. I couldn't bluff. I didn't know when other people were bluffing, manipulating, working a strategy.

Once he was mentioned, though, I sat there wondering if it might have been Monsignor Ferraponte who'd actually arranged this meeting or if the monsignor and the archbishop had done it together, for their own mysterious purposes, and I'd wandered into some kind of Lamb of God trap, the consequences of which I could not even begin to imagine.

"If I caused him to be upset," I was able to say out of the depths of my surprise, "it was not from any malice." The cardinal's trimmed eyebrows lifted at the word. Father Clement explained it in two syllables of Italian. "Or any disrespect."

Cardinal Rosario pursed his lips. "Did your spiritual director perform the holy sacrifice in a state of mortal sin?"

"Father Welch?" I asked. "I don't know."

"Ah. But he has left the priesthood, no?"

"I don't know, Your Eminence. I think the archbishop intended that to happen, yes. And I think calling him my spiritual director isn't really accurate. I simply went to Mass at his church and went to him for confession. We had some conversations, we—"

"Perhaps he was using you to justify his own mortal sins."

"I don't know, I don't think so. And I don't know that he committed any sin."

"Ah. And do we judge that to ourselves, what a sin is?"

"I believe the Lord has given us a conscience to decide such things, yes. And I believe Father Welch is a good man."

"Yes, daughter, He has given us a conscience, and He has also given us the rules of the Church in order to guide that conscience, in order to be sure that conscience is not confusing itself."

"With all respect, Your Eminence, I haven't come here to discuss Father Welch. And I haven't come here to get anything for myself. Becoming a priest would give me nothing in the way of material things or a better living situation, and I don't care at all about status. I just feel that my

Church is dying, and I believe that, in the depth of my prayer, Christ is asking me to help keep it alive. We're losing good priests, fine men like Father Welch, and there are thousands and millions of good women who love God as much as you and I do and who are kept from serving their Church in the most essential way, commemorating Christ's last night on Earth. I came here not to hurt anyone, certainly not to offend you. It's a long way for me to come. It would have been so much easier for me to stay home, live my life, pray, go to Mass. I've mentioned a few historical precedents, but I'd ask you now, as a Catholic to another Catholic, one soul to another, I ask you only to consider beginning a process that could change the rules about who can serve as a parish priest and who cannot. Please believe me, Your Eminence, I don't do this for my own ego or even my own wishes."

Cardinal Rosario watched me, unmoved and unmoving. Except for the ticking of a clock on the wall behind me, the room was completely silent. It seemed then, for just a second or two, that he was looking at me as if he were an ordinary man, untitled, unrobed. Some green shoot of possibility seemed to be sprouting on the table between us: speeded-up time-lapse photography of one impossible hope.

But then he said, "Parish priests become the bishop. Bishops become the archbishop. Arch-

194

bishops become the cardinal. The cardinal maybe, one day, becomes the pope."

"I'm not asking for women cardinals, Your Eminence."

"Not now, no."

"I'm asking for the Church to consider a change that would very likely invigorate her around the world."

Cardinal Rosario turned his head halfway in the direction of Father Clement.

"*Invigorire*," I said, before the priest, who seemed momentarily distracted, could translate.

The cardinal nodded as if he'd known the word, but had wanted to be sure. "You breathe in and then out," he said, lifting one hand from the table and swinging it away and then back toward him. "The Church in various places at various times passes through periods of favor and disfavor. History makes those periods. Inside them, our Church," he held his hands apart as if holding a ball, "grows larger and smaller, more popular and less popular. But she doesn't change."

"I ask you," I said, "I plead with you, Your Eminence, only to raise this issue at the next convocation of the cardinals, only to do that."

"No," he said, shaking his head sadly. Then he started to speak in quick, quiet tones to Father Clement, as if the meeting had already ended and I had been dismissed. "Cardinal Rosario," Father Clement said, blinking in his nervous way, "sees in you a good woman. And he respects the recommendation of his friend Archbishop Menendez. Truly respects it. But he says that what you're asking of him is simply not possible, and with respect for you and admiration for your faith, he declines."

"No hope, then?" I said. "Could we meet once more?"

Father Clement translated the question but did not need to translate the answer. The cardinal was moving his head side to side, eyes down, the second finger of his right hand tapping on the top of the left. His eyes came up to me, and he said, "My good daughter, be very careful now here on such a path like this. There are people here who, if they don't see you as I see you, would form the wrong opinion and perhaps wish you harm."

And with that, before I could say anything else, the cardinal blessed me with the sign of the cross and stood and turned away.

I stood also. Father Clement held the door for the cardinal, and as he was doing so, as I was beginning to feel a whole city of hope breaking apart inside me, the bespectacled priest turned almost a hundred eighty degrees and looked at me. Cardinal Rosario was going out the door and couldn't see him. Father Clement had so much pain in his face I thought for a moment that he was going to ask my forgiveness. He seemed desperately to want to say something. I thought I saw him try to speak or smile, but his lips only wobbled and his forehead pinched up like that of a man about to weep. And then he closed the door almost all the way and I listened to their footsteps, out of time with each other, fading in the tile corridor.

I WAS LEFT ALONE IN the conference room. I sat back down and waited there for probably five or six minutes in a kind of daze, expecting someone to come and escort me to the street. The door had been left slightly ajar, and finally I heard sounds in the hallway—voices, passing footsteps—and I made myself stand and go down the stairs and walk out of the building. It seemed strange that they would let me leave unaccompanied, because the whole place—the twelve-foot ceilings, the tile corridor with its dark, heavy-looking doors and huge gold-framed portraits of popes, cardinals, and Church patrons—had a mysterious feeling to it, as if secret work were being done in those closed conference rooms and offices. I retraced my steps along the corridor, down the white marble stairway, past the man at the glassless window with his ledger book sitting open in front of him. He might or might not have acknowledged me; I didn't notice. I was wrapped up tight in a skin of depression, something so rare in my life that for those few minutes I almost felt as though another woman had occupied my body.

I remember stepping out into the air—which seemed suddenly so much warmer than when I'd arrived—and thinking that some message about me must have been sent down to the man in the outdoor booth because he seemed to have been watching for me and he looked at me as if I were an enemy who'd managed to find her way inside the gated compound. She needed to be observed carefully to make sure she left without stealing a gold ornament or spray-painting obscene messages on the wall. Keeping a distance of six or eight feet between our bodies, he escorted me past the Swiss guards and through the huge open gate, then stood there as if to make sure I wouldn't try to rush back in.

I waited on the sidewalk, half hypnotized. Father Bruno hadn't yet come to fetch me, and I realized with a great sweep of sadness that I'd been in the building only about twenty minutes. All that money—my father's and my own—all that effort and trouble: the difficult half hour with Monsignor Ferraponte, the slightly hopeful conversation with Archbishop Menendez, all those talks with Father Alberto and Father Welch, the books I'd read, the hours of prayer in which I'd felt so personally addressed by God, the sting of leaving my father behind—in the span of twenty minutes all of it had been turned to ash.

When Father Bruno drove up, when I climbed into the passenger seat of the van and he started off, I burst into tears and wept the way I hadn't wept for as long as I could remember. My chin was resting on my chest; the tears dripped into the lap of my dress, making spots there the size and color of raisins. I felt like an absolute and perfect fool. Father Bruno reached a hand across and rested it lightly on my back.

We went only a few blocks and then, in the great Italian tradition of food as medicine, he stopped at a small café—more illegal parking—and told me I had to go in with him, stand at the bar, and have an espresso. We did that. No conversation, just the white china cups with a red line around the top, the hot dose of sugary caffeine, the company of a few strangers and a barista named Gino with waxed curls at the tips of his moustache.

Back in the van, Bruno said, "A woman like you going into a building like that. How could you come out happy? Am I wrong?"

"I don't know. Not wrong. No."

He asked me to tell him what the meeting had been about, and I felt then that I had nothing to lose, that there was no hope, no possibility of any good outcome now. I couldn't feel more foolish than I already felt, so I gave him the story, start to finish.

He made no response. It seemed to me that he was pretending to concentrate on the driving, whereas on the two other trips we'd taken, he hadn't given the road more than half his attention.

At last he said, "I have your things in back. I packed up everything and moved you out of the hotel, and they gave me a fifty percent refund. I found you a much nicer place."

"Please keep the money," I said. "For gas. For your time."

"I used it to pay part of the bill at the new hotel."

Without saying anything else, he drove across the river into a pretty, residential section of the city and pulled up at another tall wrought-iron gate in front of what looked to be a small palace. The building was made of white limestone, with at least a dozen windows in the front wall and several balconies where, in a romantic movie, in another era, a young prince and princess might have sat enjoying a carafe of wine on a September afternoon. The grounds were planted with shrubs and small trees, all of them past bloom and waiting, in an orderly silence, for the start of winter. Bruno lifted my bags out of the back of the van, pushed a button that made the gate swing open, and carried them down a gravel driveway, one in each hand. A courtyard huddled there, shaded by trees and a grape arbor. Several rear doors opened onto it. He led me through one of them and, at an interior door, took a key from his pocket.

"I know the woman who owns this hotel. Claudia Maniscalco is her name. It used to be a true palazzo. Her family let it go into disrepair, and she moved back from Milano to oversee the renovations."

He opened the door onto a room that was something out of a futuristic universe. The chairs were curved pieces of thin black metal, cushion-less. The bed was huge and round. On the walls hung framed posters of American movie stars—Humphrey Bogart, Marilyn Monroe, Cary Grant, Jimmy Stewart, Jayne Mansfield.

"Is okay?" he asked, in English.

"Yes, beautiful," I said, though really, it was almost clownish to my eye. Expensive-looking, half absurd. It fit me about as well as a miniskirt or a garish tattoo.

He set my bags to one side of the bed, and then, as if he'd been pondering his response for half an hour, he said, "This is something we talk about often, my friends and I. Not so much about women becoming priests as men priests being able to marry and have a family. And we talk about the fact that even here, even in Italy, people do not take the Church seriously the way they once did. There are some elements within the Church, here and in other places in Europe, that are dangerous now, I think. The people in those groups are like a wounded animal. They can see what is happening. They see that they are no longer taken so seriously, that people are leaving the Church, that the young people are laughing at it. It hurts them, makes them angry, makes them afraid. Normal feelings. But what they do with those feelings is very bad. They begin to see those other people, those who do not go to Mass, those who were baptized and then left the Church, or those within the Church, like you, who are trying to change it, they see them as enemies, as the Devil, or under the influence of the Devil, and once they see a person that way, he ceases to become a full person, and then they can do anything to him, or to her. Anything at all. This is why I worry about you now."

The long oration seemed to have been percolating inside him for years, and was connected, I thought, to the sadness I'd noticed in his face from the first minute. The emotion of it brought his sleepy dark eyes to life, and I saw a resemblance to my father there, just a flash of it.

"We talk about this," he went on, "but we talk about it quietly, in secret, usually with only our closest friends. It is a little bit like living in Communist Russia a generation ago."

"I should just go home now," I said, thinking of facing my father with my head hanging, thinking of the questions he'd ask and the answers I'd have to give. "I should just let things be as they are and live the life I was living."

"You could do that," he said, "yes. But you are in Rome, you are in Italy. You should at least enjoy yourself. Rest now. Tonight I will come take you to dinner at my father's house, but tomorrow there are places you must see. Your Italian is so good, you'll have no trouble. One place you must see is a church, a very special church. It is called Santa Maria in Trastevere. I can make you a small map." He took a pen from his breast pocket and, using a pad of paper that sat next to the telephone on a stylish black bureau, drew me a simple map with the river and main streets and told me I could walk to the church in probably twenty minutes, or he could drive me there now, on his way back to work.

I was suddenly worn out. I thanked him but said I wanted to rest. He wrote his phone number on the bottom of the pad of paper and said that if I needed anything, anything at all, if there was any kind of problem, I should be sure to call him. Then he hugged me against him and left in a way that seemed hurried, as if our quick embrace in a hotel room had made him uncomfortable or as if he didn't fully trust me with what he'd revealed.

I lay down on the circular mattress and stared at the ceiling, which had been painted a dark purple to resemble the night sky. I thought of Laura Annina and I understood her a little better then: if you stayed in your familiar world, if you didn't ask too much from life, if you didn't try to push a boyfriend to marry you or a cardinal to change the rules, you protected yourself from a certain level of pain. There would be unavoidable dis-appointments—arguments, illness—but not very much in the way of failure. You could blame your disappointments on fate or bad luck, the unfairness of class or race or gender; failures, though, would be all your own.

I decided—Father Alberto had recommended this for especially difficult times—to do the Prayer of Giving for myself. I pretended I was outside myself, looking on with the loving eyes of my grandmother, and I breathed in the pain I was feeling and filtered it through that love, and breathed it out again as something else— determination, forgiveness, acceptance. For the first few minutes it seemed a foolish exercise, something forced and false. But I kept at it, as Father had advised me to, and in time, inch by inch, I pulled myself out of the muddy swamp of defeat. Your will, not my will, I said. Your will, not mine. Over and over again until a different kind of hypnosis took hold. Bad, good, neutral— things happened the way they were supposed to happen; it didn't mean I shouldn't have tried. I couldn't know what might come of that trying, what seed of doubt I might have planted in the cardinal's mind, what tiny bit of support Father Bruno and his friends might feel from knowing someone else had made an effort.

I decided, after praying for a long while, prone, on the ridiculous circular bed, that moping around the hotel all afternoon was a bad idea. I would go and see the church Bruno had recommended.

Being in a church always gave me a sense of calm, always seemed to take my life and shift it out from under its cascade of thoughts. So many of those thoughts were useless, or even counterproductive, a waste of energy. Most of them had to do with worrying about things that couldn't be changed, or hoping things would turn out a certain way. I had been able, for one example, to almost completely give up thinking about becoming someone's wife one day. It might happen. Even in the midst of my strenuous attempt to become a priest, I still hoped it would happen. But I didn't worry about it any longer. In that one section of my life, at least, I had turned my hopes over to God. If the right man came along, at the right time, if he asked me to marry him, if I loved him, if I thought we could make a nice family together and live in harmony, that would be exciting and fine. If not, it would be God's will, and I knew I could accept it.

An attitude like that wasn't the same as passivity. It was activity within a bubble of a certain size. If God decided to let that bubble break open and allow me to move out beyond it into the larger sphere of married women and men, that would be wonderful. If not, I had to continue to do everything I could within the confines of my present life. I wanted to feel the same way about pursuing the priesthood. That bubble seemed to have a very thick skin. I felt as though I'd been punching and kicking against it from the inside, trying to break a hole through it, and on that day it had become clear to me that the job would remain unfinished. And yet, despite all my prayers, I wasn't truly at peace with that.

I got up off the round bed and walked out into the courtyard, down the gravel drive, and through the tall front gate, and I felt the residue of the morning's disappointment like a weight on my neck and shoulders. Beginning to shift and rearrange itself beneath that weight, though—and I could feel this, too—was my conviction that the world spun the way its Creator wanted it to spin and that the secret of happiness was to align ourselves with His will. Going to a church always made me remember that. And I was hungry, on top of everything else.

A meal, I thought, a good meal, an hour in a beautiful church, and the weight would begin to seem bearable.

Just outside the gates of what I'd come to think of as the Old Palace Hotel was a very busy four-lane road and, on the other side of it, the Tiber River. In that part of the city the river was sunk thirty or forty feet below the level of the street, with rocky banks and stone walls rising up on either side. As I crossed a marble bridge there—flat, loud with traffic, decorated with carved angels—I noticed a man rowing along in a racing shell like the ones I sometimes saw on the Charles River. He was going fast, facing backward, working very hard, his efforts marked by small circular puddles where the blades of his oars left the water. For a few seconds after each stroke the circular puddles remained visible behind the boat in two neat rows, shrinking. Then, like impossible hopes, like twins with short identical lives, they disappeared.

On the far side of the river I saw a rat squeezing its body down between the bars of a sewer grate.

Glancing from time to time at Father Bruno's simple map, I followed a route that was positively wild with motorbikes, motorcycles, delivery trucks, and speeding cars. There was one brave soul juggling bowling pins at a stoplight—right in the middle of the street. I watched him for a moment—he dropped one pin, laughed at himself, collected donations—and then I went on, eventually turning onto a half-sunken lane and finding myself in a different part of Rome. This neighborhood was loud with traffic noise, too, but there were more pedestrians hurrying along the narrow slanted sidewalks. They carried briefcases or pushed strollers and didn't seem to be tourists. The neighborhood had a feeling of homey oldness; a sign on one worn stone house said *casa di Dante*.

I walked on, passing several small restaurants, until I came to one that seemed right, and I went in and was seated at a table among a crowd of Italians enjoying their midday meal. The waitress greeted me, handed me a menu in hard black covers. Opening it I saw that there were twenty or thirty different kinds of pasta listed under *primi piatti*. When she came again, she brought bottled water, bread, and olive oil in a shallow dish, and I ordered something I'd never eaten before— spaghetti in oxtail gravy. I asked for a glass of wine, too.

The wine was light and delicious, and the tomato gravy had actual pieces of oxtail in it; I was surprised how much taste that little bit of bone and meat added. The bread was slightly salty with a hard crust, the pasta perfectly *al dente*. As I drank and chewed, I looked around the small room at the tables and chairs crowded close together, Italian couples and families at various stages of their meals. Ordinary life, I thought. Decent, ordinary life with its patches of fun and worry. Unlike the one American in their midst, these people weren't trying to change anything, weren't pushing hard against the inside of any bubble, weren't radicals, troublemakers, or fools.

But as I had hoped it would, the meal turned that line of thought in a slightly more positive direction. I thanked the waitress and then, after some wandering around the alleys and narrow streets, cars squeezing past so close I could have readjusted their side mirrors with a swing of my hips, I found the church Father Bruno had marked on his map. Santa Maria in Trastevere, it was called. It was set in an uneven, sloping square with a fountain in the middle. The square was a less trendy version of Campo de' Fiori, and the church was, at least from the outside, much less grand than St. Peter's. Between the plain gray columns out front and the chipped wooden entrance doors, a Gypsy boy, three or four years old, was kicking an empty plastic suntan lotion bottle back and forth as if it were a soccer ball. A woman who appeared to be his mother was half kneeling, half sitting on the pavement, holding an infant against her chest, one cupped hand extended. I put a five-euro coin in her palm, and the woman, so beautiful with her black hair and coppery skin, looked up and smiled. Just before I turned away from her, I saw that the infant wrapped in the folds of her dress was actually a doll.

To either side of the front doors irregular-sized chunks of white marble had been embedded in the concrete walls. There were letters cut into the worn surfaces, Greek or Latin, I guessed, no doubt thousands of years old. Inside, I needed a few seconds to let my eyes adjust. Thick stone columns stood to either side of the nave, though, strangely, they were all slightly different from one another—different types of stone, somewhat different color and shape—as if they'd been salvaged from four or five broken-up churches and combined there to make something new.

There were plain brown pews that looked a thousand years older than the ones in St. Anthony's and orange, pink, brown, and white marble tiles set into the floor—triangles, rectangles, odd chunks arranged in circular patterns. It all seemed so smoky and used, so far from the sparkling neatness and bright lights of St. Anthony's and so far outside the orbit of attention St. Peter's occupied. But when I stepped toward the middle of the nave and looked at the altar, I saw that the shabbiness of the front of the building was just another disguise. Behind the marble altar stood a crescent of a dozen brown wooden chairs like the ones you'd expect to see bishops sitting in at Easter Mass, and above them was a fresco, all arms and faces, the scene interrupted by two windows with winged figures around them. Above that, two-thirds of the way to the ceiling, an incredible mosaic ran all the way to the top of the curved dome.

Midway up was a wide band that had a line of sheep in it, six to each side. Above the band were nine human figures, with Jesus and Mary at the center, both of them seated, bracketed by apostles to either side, all of it against a background of thousands of tiny gold tiles. I had a feeling similar to what I'd felt in front of the *Pietà*: I didn't really need to see the Sistine Chapel, the Colosseum, the Forum. God sparkled in those ancient chips of color and was singing to me through them. That was enough. That might sound like an immature thing to say, an idea born of a few minutes' excitement, but I suddenly had the sense that the real purpose of coming to Rome hadn't been to convince the cardinal or make a pilgrimage to St. Peter's, but to see this church.

I genuflected and walked up the aisle and noticed that, in the part of the mosaic that covered the curved half bowl of the apse, Jesus had his arm around his mother. They were sitting close together, his head a foot or so above hers, their bodies wrapped in robes. You could clearly see his thin fingers resting on her opposite shoulder. That, I thought, that was my Jesus. Not the tortured man hanging from nails on a cross, not the strict young future rabbi turning over tables in the temple, but an ordinary-looking, loving man, the embodiment of God, giving his mother an embrace that seemed to say, there is no distinction here, she and I are made of the same stuff.

On a flat section to the side of that indented, curved ceiling, there was another fresco, this one of Mary lying on a bed with Jesus standing over her. To my surprise I saw that Jesus was holding a baby. After staring at the images for several minutes I thought I understood: Jesus had seen Mary's entire life on Earth from the moment of her birth to the moment of her assumption into Heaven and had been standing close beside her all that time. The baby was himself; Jesus almost seemed to be comforting it against the pain that waited in its future. Caught in a sudden gust of happiness, I sat in one of the hard pews. I could hear the noise of a few tourists who were shuffling around and whispering to one another. I could smell candle smoke. I could sense an older woman farther down the pew running rosary beads through her fingertips the way my grandmother had, as if she were squeezing pits from cherries, one after the next.

Instead of trying to pray, I kept my eyes open and studied the main mosaic in front of me. Jesus and Mary were sitting up straight, but not stiffly straight. They didn't look sad or wounded. They weren't off in some distant realm separated from the sinful world by an uncrossable distance. Something in their posture and faces spoke of a perfect and perfectly compassionate under-standing of the human condition. I sat there for a long time studying them, and it began to seem to me that the disappointment of the day had been reversed. For months I'd been praying and praying for a sign, and in Santa Maria, it seemed, the sign had at last been given. I couldn't have said exactly what I felt I was supposed to do, but something about seeing Jesus with his arm around his mother that way and seeing him standing there holding the baby and looking down at Mary gave me the sure sense that others in the world, including the man who'd designed those mosaics, understood Christianity in a way that had been lost to the Vatican authorities over the past several hundred years.

It was more than simply the role of Mary or the role of women in the Church. It went beyond that. It was an aspect of Jesus himself, the spirit we all revered, some tenderness in him that I'd been imagining since I was a tiny girl, some way of giving his mother her rightful place of importance in the story—that grand, sweeping epic that had stood at the heart of my interior world for as long as I could remember. The hero of that story was more than someone who walked around with a dozen disciples trailing him, doing miracles, yelling at people, eventually allowing himself to be tortured and killed in the fulfillment of a prophecy that had been spoken thousands of years before.

The gesture of him with his arm around his mother rendered him—and her—fully human and real in a way nothing else I'd ever seen or heard had been able to do. It seemed to wash into the gutter all the doubt that had attached itself to me over the past few years. I stayed there a long time, filled up with that new happiness, as if the oxtail gravy at lunch had been spiked with a sweet Roman morphine.

Then I floated back down the side aisle of the church and out through the heavy wooden doors. They squeaked on their hinges as if complaining

"Don't leave, don't leave." I went out past the boy kicking his empty plastic bottle and the woman kneeling there with the black shawl and dress wrapped around her, eyes lowered, hand still outstretched.

I walked into the sunlit square and looked up at the sky, and for a few seconds I felt that my loneliness, the loneliness that had seemed to walk along beside me like an empty shell of a person for twenty-two years, had magically disappeared. Some other spirit was living inside me, a comfort, a twin soul. I felt something that even my deepest prayer had not made me feel: that I was fully, completely, totally lovable, as who I was, a woman walking the surface of the earth. Beyond opening myself to that love, there was nothing I *had* to do, nothing at all.

When I lowered my eyes, the first person they settled on there—another of God's little jokes— behind the large fountain at the center of the square, just his head showing above the stone lip, watching me, was the man who'd come knocking on my hotel door at one in the morning.

As soon as my eyes met his, he turned his back and walked off in the opposite direction. I followed him, I don't know why—instinct, anger, a fierceness fed by my newly discovered lovability, or a desire to find out if Father Bruno was right and someone had sent this person to follow me. He turned onto one of the narrow streets, an alley really, that led off the square, and I kept following him.

I turned into the alley, too, and caught sight of him, maybe a hundred feet ahead, just as he made a sharp left into a much narrower alley. I broke into a run, my shoes clattering on the cobblestones, one or two people in the human river of Romans and tourists glancing at me as I hurried past. When I turned left into the narrower alley, I had to go only about ten steps before I realized it was a dead end. The man who'd been following me must have realized the same thing. Too late. Because there he was, pressing himself into a corner where one of the stone buildings jutted out a few feet from its neighbor. He wasn't very good at hiding. I could see one elbow sticking out. I slowed to a walk and took the phone out of my purse, and as I came to the corner of the building I whirled around and held the phone up at the level of his face. Before he could move, I'd taken two quick pictures.

I could see almost immediately what I hadn't been calm enough to see in that one frightened moment in the doorway of the first hotel room: there was something wrong with the man. Just from looking at his angular features with the splotches of black hair above a high forehead and wide-set, mismatched eyes, I could sense that something wasn't right. It wasn't drunkenness: the expression on his face made him seem like a boy in a man's body. And when I started to shout at him, still holding the phone up, his first instinct was to flinch and cower back into the brick corner almost the way a boy would do if he were being yelled at by his mother.

"*Chiamerò la polizia*! I'm going to call the police!" I said, very loudly. My whole body was shaking. "I have your picture, here, on my phone! And unless you tell me why you're following me, I'm going to call the police and show them this picture."

He made a helpless gesture, half shrug, as if he didn't understand what I was saying, and for a second it seemed he'd try to run off. He made a move to his right, back toward the alley, but I reached out my arm and put a hand against his shoulder and I yelled, "NO! Stop!" and to my surprise he did stop. He stood there, almost a foot taller, a hundred pounds heavier, staring down at me, terrified. "Tell me!" I yelled. "Why? Why are you following me?"

He said something in a thickly accented, trembling voice, three syllables. If it was Italian, it was no kind of Italian I'd ever heard.

I poked my finger into the middle of his chest and held up the phone again. "Tell me," I said, "or I'm going to the police. Is someone paying you to follow me?"

He looked at me without speaking for probably the count of five, said the word again: "*grossetto*," pushed my arm away, and sprinted out of the alley.

I had to stand there for several minutes, taking deep breaths. It was as if the sight of that man's face had awakened some sleeping warrior in me, something that was as far from the Cynthia Piantedosi of my prayer life as I was now from the streets of Revere, Massachusetts. Eventually I calmed down enough to walk back out to the end of the alley and then to the square and then, retracing my steps, back to the hotel.

Several times on that walk I turned and looked behind me to see if I was being followed. Twice I cut down side streets, walked half a block, and then made an about-face and turned back in the opposite direction. But I didn't see the man again, and no one else seemed to be watching me.

AT SEVEN O'CLOCK THAT NIGHT I went out and stood on the sidewalk in front of the gate. After I'd been waiting several minutes, running my eyes over every pedestrian I could see, Father Bruno pulled up in the van and I climbed in. We drove toward the outskirts of the city and then into rolling countryside, green hills and olive groves, vineyards and estate houses perched on small rises. He seemed wrapped in a silent tension. I told him how much I'd liked Santa Maria in Trastevere and thanked him for recommending it.

"A special church" was all he said.

He turned off a two-lane road that ran between

cultivated yards and small houses—a scene that was a more rural version of what I'd grown up with on Tapley Avenue—and onto a paved, unlined street, and then turned again onto a dirt road that curved this way and that, and climbed a gentle hillside.

Father Bruno had seemed upset or angry from the first—I wondered if I had somehow insulted him, if he'd wanted a different response from me in the hotel room—and he seemed to grow more uncomfortable with every mile we traveled. "You have to understand," he said at last, the words practically bursting out of him in rapid-fire Italian, "*devi capire*, my father is a good man, but he has no love for the Church. He believes in God, but he despises the Vatican and everything it stands for. Try not to get him onto that subject, please. And if he gets onto that subject, don't encourage him."

"But I thought he worked there."

"His whole career," Father Bruno said, as if that explained everything.

Another hundred yards, and we turned into the drive of a very nice, modern house, brown stucco walls, red tile roof, large, neat garden with staked tomato plants, a grape arbor, and what looked like cherry and peach trees standing in even rows on the west-facing slope. Beyond them spread a view of the valley and the highway that ran through it. The dry hillsides beyond were spotted with grand estates and vineyards. Father Bruno followed the driveway around to the back of the house and pulled to a stop in a cloud of dust, and waiting there was a man who might have been my father's brother. Same short, stocky body. Same strong arms and neck. The same workman's hands protruding from the cuffs of a white, long-sleeved shirt. Even the same bristly salt-and-pepper hair above a high forehead. Behind him, set in the shade of the grape arbor, was a wooden table with four chairs. I got out, walked over to him, shook his hand, and introduced myself, and he examined my face carefully, almost the way Cardinal Rosario had. "I haven't seen your father since we were schoolboys," he said, "but I see in you his eyes and mouth."

"Did you know my mother?"

"I was in love with your mother. I wanted to marry her. She left before I could ask her, then wrote, a few years later, to say she had married my cousin."

That bit of family history was delivered abruptly and not in a particularly kind way. I had the feeling Franco had been preparing to say it to me from the minute he'd heard I'd be visiting. I was glad when a woman appeared at the back door, younger than Franco by perhaps fifteen years, still quite pretty, with graying brown hair and a somewhat heavy build. She was carrying a platter heaped with cooked greens, and she smiled at me in a welcoming way. She set down the platter in the middle of the table and, turning back toward the house, motioned for me to follow.

Inside, in a kitchen with yellow tile walls and pots simmering on the stove, she told me her name was Lucia, and, without any fuss at all, handed me a tray with four bowls on it, salt and pepper shakers, a bottle of olive oil, and a plate with half a loaf of bread. She picked up another platter that held sliced, juicy-looking tomatoes in olive oil with oregano flakes on them, and before we went out the door she said, in a rougher version of Italian than I'd been hearing that day, "Franco can be a pain in the ass. Don't pay too much attention."

It was all done so simply and straightforwardly, as if we'd been friends forever, or as if we were more than distantly related. I couldn't tell at first if Lucia was Franco's wife, girlfriend, or maid. But when we were out in the yard she said, "Franco, sit," in a certain tone of voice that made me understand they were probably longtime lovers. We started in on the tomatoes, bread, and olive oil and then the greens, and Lucia disappeared into the house and came out again with a huge ceramic bowl of spaghetti. I could smell sage and butter—we were strictly a tomato sauce family at home—as she spooned some onto our plates. Franco poured from a jug of white wine, and for a time his mood softened and the conversation moved fairly easily through questions about my life in America: How was my father's health? How did he occupy his time? What was it like where we lived?

But then, after we'd dispensed with the spaghetti and Lucia had brought out a plate of veal, sausages, and meatballs in a tomato gravy and Franco, I noticed, had drunk three or four glasses of wine, he fixed me with a stern look and said, "You're not a nun, are you?"

"Oh, no. A nurse."

He grunted. "My son," he gestured with his fork in the direction of Bruno, "becomes a priest. Otherwise a good boy."

I couldn't tell if he'd meant it as a joke. There was an awkward pause, matched by a small, awkward smile on Father Bruno's lips.

"Becomes a priest," Franco went on. "Throws in his lot with the crooks and liars. Did you know," he went on without waiting for any response, "that the Vatican secretly owns seventy percent of the commercial real estate in Rome. Seventy percent!" He held his fork up like an exclamation point. "They take in money from churches all over the world, too. Poor people giving a euro, a few pennies. It flows there"—he pointed with his fork down into the valley in what I supposed was the direction of St. Peter's—"and they have their summer palaces, their expensive clothes. Some popes wore shoes from Prada!"

"I didn't know that," I said in as neutral a way as I could manage. What I wanted to say was: You worked for the Vatican all those years. Those pennies and euros went to pay your salary, to buy this land and build this house.

"And you're like him?" Franco asked, gesturing to his son. "Religious?"

"Yes," I said. "I pray a lot. It gives me great comfort. I can go to Mass without thinking about the bad aspects of the Church."

Another grunt.

"In just the same way," I went on, "that I can be an American and proud of my country without feeling connected to the bad things it has done in history. I take a more individual view of those things. There are good people and bad, every-where, in all countries and all organizations. There is good and bad in everyone."

Franco grunted again. He cut off a piece of sausage with his fork, chewed, washed it down with a gulp of wine.

"This is Franco's passion," Lucia said. "His hobby. Some men watch soccer and argue in the bars about the different teams. He reads the newspaper, and anytime he meets a new person, after a while he starts to complain about the popes, the cardinals, and the priests. His son is a good boy, a fine young man, and all his father does is criticize the Church in his presence."

"I said he was a good boy," Franco said, looking

at her. "Would you rather I get upset about soccer?"

There was a rough, teasing tone to their exchange, a kind of intimate banter. It was almost sexual, I thought, and I felt a twinge of envy, a quick, sad thought: I would never have someone to joke with that way.

"You used to work for the Vatican, didn't you?" I couldn't stop myself from asking.

He looked at his son instead of at me, and I wished I'd kept silent. "I did," he admitted. "I was young. I needed a job. Like you and Bruno, I had a great respect for the Church, or for what I thought the Church was."

"And you were disillusioned?"

A bark of harsh laughter escaped him. It reminded me of Monsignor Ferraponte's first response when I'd told him I was being called to the priesthood. "*Disincantato*," he corrected. "Disenchanted. *Sì, disincantato*. Yes, because what I saw there, in the inner circles, had nothing to do with the love of Christ. Nothing."

"Pope John XXIII seemed Christlike to me. Pope John Paul."

He nodded vigorously and said, "*Sì, sì*," before pouring himself more wine. "They were clean men wading across a river of filth."

"That's a little strong, isn't it, Papa?" interjected Bruno.

Franco gave his son a stern look. "If you could see what I saw, you wouldn't say that."

"I see some of it."

"The higher up you go"—Franco swung his wine glass a bit too excitedly, splashing a few drops onto his sleeve—"the worse it is. Even the popes can't do some of the things they want to. It's like"—he turned back to me—"your president. He could be an honest man. I believe he is. But if your Congress is corrupt, if all they think about is power and money, then he will be in handcuffs. Am I right?"

"I don't really follow politics," I said.

"A half answer."

"Franco," Lucia cut in. "Don't let the wine make you mean." She turned to me. "It's because of me, his feelings about the Vatican."

"Sure, because of you," Franco said bitterly. "The Prince of Love, the religion of love, and when they have true love in the world, what happens? They bring out the rule book, like a lead pipe, and hit you over the head with it."

"Now," Father Bruno said to Lucia. "Now, I think, is the time for cake."

She smiled and got up from the table, and when I made a move to follow she flapped a hand at me to stay. The silence that fell over us then was more than awkward; there were dissonant chords sounding in the sweet air, dark secrets and painful memories swooping and darting around the table like swallows at dusk. I wondered if Franco might still be bitter about my mother's leaving, still angry at my father for stealing her away. I wondered if she'd been forced to leave and if she'd seen, in my father, only someone who reminded her of her true love. Franco cradled his glass in both hands, staring at it, and I kept looking at him, wondering how much I could ask. He gave me an almost taunting lift of the eyebrows, as if to say: Go ahead! But for some reason, I don't know exactly why, to change the subject maybe, or to change the tone of the evening, or because I was afraid of what I might learn, I asked, "Does the word '*grossetto*' mean anything to you? Is it an Italian word? Dialect?"

Franco lifted the corners of his lips into a bitter smile. "*Grossetto*," he said, almost laughing. "Sure, it means something to me. It means 'demon.'"

"In dialect?"

Another snort of not very nice laughter.

"He is a cardinal," Father Bruno put in. "Giovanni Grossetto. From Venice. Very conservative."

"Conservative?" his father said, tossing the word the length of the table like a spear. "He's a demon. His people, the Lamb of God people, they're all demons. They want to turn the Church back to the time of the Crusades. Kill the infidels!" he shouted, spilling more wine and glaring at his son. "They'll come for you one day, you'll see. The way Mussolini's *fascisti* came for Moretti. They'll come for you, and then you'll understand that I was right."

"It's not the wartime, Papa. And you were what? Five years old then?"

"Old enough to see and to hear," Franco said, almost shouting now, speaking so loudly I was sure Lucia heard him inside the house. "Three of my cousins died in Africa in the war, for nothing. Two of my uncles were taken away and beaten."

"Not by members of the Church," Father Bruno said.

"No, but the Church stood by. The Church let him do what he did. *Il duce.* They could have stopped him. Lamb of God is a mind-set that grew out of that other mind-set."

"Out of fascism, Papa?"

"Of course out of fascism! The fascist mind-set is not limited to Mussolini, you know, or to Hitler. It's a kind of thinking, a way of looking at humanity. Us and Them. We're right, they're wrong, they're inferior, they're dangerous and poisonous and weak—so we'll eliminate them and then human life will be perfect."

"Most Catholics don't have that mind-set."

"Most Italians weren't fascists, either, Bruno. It doesn't take a majority to change a society, or a faith. Only a small minority that yells, threatens, kills, that is willing to do anything to prove to themselves that they're right."

"Not this again, please," Lucia said as she came out carrying a thin torte with diagonal strips of crust laid neatly over a layer of fruit. She cut slices of it and set them on plates in front of us. "Do we have to have this same argument every time we entertain guests for dinner?"

"It's all right," I said. "It's fine. My father says some of the same things."

"Your father says those same things because his father was taken away and he never saw him again," Franco said. "Did he tell you that?"

"No, never."

"That's why he left Italy. Another uncle took him, and he was smart to leave. Those kinds of things don't happen in America. You don't have a Vatican in America. You don't have this dance between the Church rulers and the people, this Vatican waltz, everything smooth, silky, refined . . . except that one of the partners is holding a knife behind the back of the other. And if the partner tries a new step, something different, creative, beautiful"—he made a thrust with one hand—"in it goes."

"We've had our own troubles," I said. "Different kinds of troubles. We have Lamb of God, too. I was close to a priest, an older man, a friend. He was hit by a car, and there are people who think it wasn't an accident."

"It wasn't," Franco said confidently. "I can tell you from this chair, here, in Italy, ten thousand kilometers away, that it was no accident."

I noticed that when the jug of wine was empty, Lucia carried it into the house but didn't refill it and bring it out again. Instead she reappeared with a pot of coffee, poured four cups, and we drank it with the torte—a succulent *dolce*, all butter and sugar and slices of apricot.

"Are we finished now?" she asked pleasantly, looking at Franco.

"She asked about Grossetto," Franco said.

"Grossetto," Lucia said to me, "Franco is convinced that Grossetto had Pope John Paul I killed."

"Killed?"

"Poisoned. He was about to start an investigation into the Vatican Bank. Grossetto controlled the bank and wanted, himself, to be pope. Many people believe this."

I was speechless for a moment. It was an idea straight out of a script for *The Godfather, Part III*. A fantasy, I'd always thought. A Hollywood convenience. "Is that really possible?"

Franco laughed, bitterly. "I'm sorry," he said. "I'm sorry you came here and had your nice notions broken up into pieces. You have a true relationship with Christ, anyone can see that. Bruno has that. Lucia and I have that, though maybe you're not seeing it tonight in me. The best thing is to hold on to that and forget all the rest of it. Forget the pope. Forget Rosario and Grossetto and all that shit. Religion is like, forgive me, it's like what you do with a loved one in the bedroom. Beautiful but private. You don't invite the other people into that world. You don't need regulations and rules to govern your feelings there."

"Enough," Lucia said. "Look, you're embarrassing her. Enough now." She reached across the corner of the table and put a hand on my arm. "Is there anything you especially want to see in Italy? We can arrange for you to see the Sistine Chapel, privately, if you want to get up early. Franco still has connections there, with the tour guides and so on. Would you like that?"

"Of course, yes," I said. "Bruno recommended I see Santa Maria in Trastevere, and I did, and it was just wonderful. I feel I could go back there a hundred days in a row. I'd be happy to have a job there, mopping the floors. I've never seen a church like that."

"That's what I mean," Franco said. "That's the bedroom. You go into that building and you have intimacy, real intimacy with God. You don't need Mass for that. You don't need the cardinals and the rules."

"But without the Vatican, that place would cease to exist," Bruno said. "You can't just have religious feeling with no structure."

"Stop, please," his father said. "I hear the word 'Vatican,' and my digestion goes bad."

Another painful silence followed. I started to do Father Alberto's Prayer of Giving for the man sitting to my right.

"Do you have a lover?" Lucia asked. "A boyfriend?"

For the smallest moment I had the sense that she might be trying to fix me up with Bruno. I was too embarrassed to look at him, and I think he felt the same way. "I wonder sometimes," I said, "if I push men away. Something about me likes my solitary world so much that when they show an interest in me I step back."

"That will change," she said. "I can see in your face that you will be a wife and mother."

"She predicts the future," Franco said. "And more often than not she's right."

"Maybe it will be an Italian man," Lucia suggested.

I couldn't find any response to that. I was blushing again. I felt painfully young.

For a little while then the conversation faltered. We sipped our coffee and looked around the shadowed yard, and then we took refuge in talk about the weather—drought, humidity, the beauty of a New England snowstorm. It was a way of sewing up the ragged torn cloth of our night together, but I found myself thinking the whole time about marriage and motherhood. Somehow—and this was strange—even with Franco's wine-fueled talk I could sense the bond of love between him and Lucia. He felt perfectly free to spout off in her presence, and she felt perfectly free to reprimand him. And that rough, honest love and her remark about seeing my future—it raised a welt of self-pity in me, a longing, an absence.

At last Lucia stood up, and I helped her carry the dishes into the kitchen, offered to help wash them, complimented her on the meal three times. She apologized for Franco—"His bitterness has strong roots" was the way she put it—hugged and kissed me warmly, said, "I hope we will see you here again."

It was dark outside by then, a few stars sparkling above the valley and a ribbon of headlights and taillights running below us like a red-and-white river.

Franco stood up, somewhat unsteadily, and at the door of the van surprised me by taking both my hands and kissing me first on one cheek, then on the other. "I like you," he said. "Bruno's a religious person. You're a religious person. Maybe I will reconsider one day and start going to Mass again."

"Come and visit my father, he'd enjoy that."

"No, no," Franco said. "He left us. We didn't leave him. He must come back here before he dies."

"I'll try to convince him."

I got into the van, waved another good-bye. Bruno drove us along the driveway, down the dirt road, and as far as the highway before he spoke. "He embarrasses me," he said, "but many of the things he says are correct."

"I can tell he loves you. He reminds me of my father. Gruff, but you can sense the tenderness below."

"Very far below," Bruno said, laughing somewhat sadly.

"That woman isn't your mother."

"No," he said. "My mother left, long ago. Found another man, one who didn't work so many hours. Lucia is my father's girlfriend. She's lived in the house for more than twenty years, since I was a small boy. She's been like a mother to me, a good woman. My father's anger toward the Church comes in part from his love of her, because when my mother left, the Church forbade him from getting married again and so he was caught between obedience to the laws of the Church and obedience to the law of his heart."

"Lots of people are in that situation," I said.

He said, "Yes, I agree," with such sadness that I decided he must have a lover or must have given up someone he loved when he entered the priesthood. But I felt he'd been embarrassed and bruised enough for one night, so I kept quiet and watched the dark hillsides sweep past.

When Bruno dropped me off at the gates to the hotel, I thanked him twice, reached out and took his hand and squeezed it, and climbed out of the van. I noticed that he waited to drive away until I'd gone through the tall gates and as far as the end of the driveway.

· · ·

WITH EVERYTHING THAT HAD HAPPENED during that day, the late-night visit at the hotel, the disappointing conversation with Cardinal Rosario, the wonderful hour in Santa Maria, my half-crazed chasing of the tall man, the strange but enjoyable meal at Franco and Lucia's—it should not have been a good night for prayer. But occasionally the mind exhausts itself, running in circles, chasing happiness, grasping onto this tremor of fear and that splinter of insult, and if you let it, sometimes it will just grow tired of that and be quiet, like a little child who's run around the yard for most of an afternoon, then falls asleep in the flower bed.

I was still on American time and tired, but the child of my mind was still running, so I propped a pillow against the headboard of the circular bed and sat there with my eyes closed and my hands folded, asking for guidance.

As I often did, I prayed for the souls of my mother and grandmother and for Father Alberto, and for the health and well-being of my father. I prayed, too, that night, for Father Bruno, who seemed, like his father, to be caught between his feelings for the Church and his feelings for another human being. I prayed for Cardinal Rosario and the priest in the meeting, for Father Welch, Archbishop Menendez, Monsignor Ferraponte, my Aunt Chiara. In that hour, at least, it wasn't so difficult to accept the idea that God has His plans and ways, that there is an element of surrender involved in the true spiritual path, and that surrendering to God's will often involves pain. I had, I told myself, been practicing that surrender my whole life.

Eventually I sank down, beyond all thinking, beyond what seemed to me a vague vision of my own future troubles, and into a quiet place where I rested for a long time. In that place, my disappointment, worry, and sadness amounted to specks of dust on an impossibly large mosaic. I saw, as if they were set up before my eyes, the billions of lives in that mosaic—long and short, famous and anonymous, satisfied and miserable—there were countless connections among those souls, countless secrets, an abundance of love and trouble. All of it arranged just so in the endless, unfathomable universe. A complexity like that had to have been put into motion by some Grand Designer. To my mind, in that hour of prayer, it seemed clear that our response to that grand design should be a life of obedience, but not the strict, narrow-minded obedience of the Lamb of God people. The obedience I was thinking of was more difficult than that; it was an insistence on compassion and an acceptance of our true calling on this earth, whatever pain that acceptance might hold.

As I came slowly out of the prayer, I said one

Hail Mary, then took off my clothes and lay down to sleep. In the absurd round bed, amid the swirl of a million possibilities, I tried to keep my mind fixed on the image of Jesus' arm around his mother's shoulders. Only that.

CHAPTER NINE

Breakfast was included with the price of a room at the Old Palace Hotel and was served on a second-floor balcony that overlooked the front yard's fruit trees and flowering bushes. Strong coffee with hot milk. A creamy coconut yogurt. Cheese, salami, bread, a pear nectar I liked so much I promised myself I'd find a store at home that stocked it and buy a case. From my seat at a round metal table for two I had a view down over the tops of the lemon and fig trees, across the busy road, across the river, over the roofs of some low buildings, and as far as the dome of St. Peter's. As I ate I found myself listening to a conversation of two couples at one of the other tables. They were talking about taking a trip to Assisi that day, and I had to restrain myself from asking if I could tag along. Two hours each way, I heard one of the men say. But the conversation and the sparkle of excitement I felt about being that close to the birthplace of two of the greatest saints, Francis and Clare, was like a layer of makeup over badly flawed skin. As fascinating as Italy was, the churches, the food, the ruins, and as much as I wanted to see the Colosseum and the Sistine Chapel, I hadn't come to Rome to be a tourist; I'd had a purpose. Foolishly, I'd expected there to be some kind of ongoing conversation with people in the Church hierarchy. A series of meetings, maybe. A movement of sympathetic cardinals and clergy. The movement would come to the attention of the pope. Maybe we'd even have an audience.

It had been a fantasy, of course, I saw that clearly now. Egotistical, too. But I'd been so convinced of the authenticity of the visions, so sure that the messages came directly from God, that it was hard for me to believe I'd gotten one "no" and the case was closed.

I was sitting there with my refilled coffee cup and swirling disappointments when Claudia, the woman in charge of the hotel, stepped out onto the balcony. From the moment Father Bruno had introduced us, she'd been intimidating to me. Tall, trim, elegant, a perfectly proportioned face, black hair held back to show gold earrings studded with what looked like emeralds—deep down, in some hidden compartment of my thoughts, I had to admit that she was the kind of woman I wished, in another life, that I might be. Her English was nearly perfect. There was something regal about her. When I'd spoken to her, checking in, she told me the palazzo had been in her family for five generations.

In her right hand she held a cream-colored envelope. She greeted her guests with a cheery *buongiorno*, then came over to my table and handed me the envelope, keeping two fingers on my shoulder and smiling in a playful way. "Very early this morning a mysterious stranger stopped by and left this for you," she said quietly. She seemed amused, as if enjoying her role as a matchmaker. She gave my shoulder a gentle squeeze and went back inside.

The cream-colored envelope reminded me very much of the letter I'd received from Cardinal Rosario, except that my name, "*Sig. Cinzia Piantedosi*," was printed in pencil in block letters on the front, not typed, and there was no return address. I thought Claudia had been joking about the mysterious stranger and that what I held in my hand was only a gesture she was making to soften the shock of the hotel's high rates. A ticket to a show or a museum. A coupon for a half-price dinner. I thought for some reason that I might be going to hear Andrea Boccelli perform—something Father Bruno had set up as a way of taking the sting out of the previous day's rejection.

I slid the blade of a clean butter knife under the flap. Inside was a single sheet of stationery, folded in thirds. On the top half of the page someone had printed three words in pencil, all the letters lower case:

martino zossimo genova

It made no sense.

I set it on the table and puzzled over the words. Claudia reappeared, pouring coffee, and, after hesitating a moment, I asked her what they meant. She glanced at the sheet of paper for all of two seconds before telling me, "Martino Zossimo. A cardinal in the Church. Famous man."

"And Genova?"

"That is the city. 'Genoa,' you say in English."

"Who brought it, do you know?"

She shrugged, smiled, a socialite used to romantic intrigues. "A young man," she said. "He came very early and sounded the bell."

"Very tall?" I asked.

She shook her head.

"Brown glasses? Heavyset?"

She shook her head a second time, pleasantly, noncommittally. She squeezed my shoulder again, in encouragement it seemed. "Young men can be very attentive here."

When Claudia left me, I took the letter into my hands and pondered it. The writing was irregular and ungrammatical enough to have come from the man who'd been following me—he seemed, somehow, to know my name—but what kind of message was he trying to send? If it was from Father Bruno, he would have written a regular note or spoken to me in person. I thought for some reason of the priest Father Clement, who'd been translating for the cardinal. I knew that he'd wanted to say something there at the end, but how had he found out where I was staying? Why was he writing in code? And the description of the mysterious stranger didn't fit him.

I wondered if it was Father Clement's way of going behind the cardinal's back. Or if it was the cardinal's way of doing what he felt he couldn't do in public. Or if it was some kind of trick.

Martino Zossimo. Genova.

Martino Zossimo. Genova. So strange, that name seemed half familiar, I couldn't say why.

I CALLED BRUNO AND, WITHOUT telling him about the message, asked if I could take him to lunch. I owed him for all his help with the hotel situation, I said, for driving me around the city, for introducing me to his family and treating me to such a fine supper. The least I could do was buy him lunch.

"Of course," he surprised me by saying. "That would be very nice. After last night I thought you'd never want to see me again."

WHEN BRUNO PULLED THE VAN up in front of the gates, I told him I wanted to take him to his favorite restaurant, no matter how expensive it was. "I have plenty of money," I said, "and no one to spend it on but myself."

He paused only a moment before saying, "Vecchia Roma, then. It's in a neighborhood we still call the Jewish Ghetto, though there haven't been a lot of Jews here since the war."

"Did Mussolini send them to the camps the way Hitler did?"

"Not with so much enthusiasm. There was no shortage of bad Italians in those days. Still, Mussolini refused to send them to Germany, and even later, after he was gone, many Jews were saved."

"I was interested in what your father said about the years of fascism. My father never talks about it."

"They were young boys," Father Bruno said. We were stopped at a red light, and two men had rushed out to wash the windshield, sponging and drying it in seconds and accepting a tip with an accented *grazie*. Father Bruno said two words to them in what I assumed was Albanian. As he zigged and zagged in the traffic again, he said, "Young boys, but they saw and heard many things. About Mussolini, the Germans, the war. Mussolini twisted so many minds." He paused, hit the brakes, tapped the horn, went on as if there had been no interruption. "That seems to happen in different places at different times, don't you think so? It's as if an idea infects a population and the infection is spread by some charismatic man with an enormous ego. My father was right: not everyone in the population gets sick, but enough people do to change the direction of a country, and sometimes of the whole world."

He nodded as if agreeing with himself. He reminded me of Franco then—the passion, at least, not the anger. "A country, a family, a Church," he went on. "Sometimes I think about all the thoughts in all the minds of everyone on Earth. It seems to me it's like the air around us. The weather can change from sun to rain, from calm to windy. No one knows why that happens. A bad wind blows through the minds in a country, and everything turns bad. One wonders why God allows it."

He surprised me by pulling the van up to the gate of a construction site and parking on a patch of dirt next to the entrance. There were NO PARKING signs everywhere.

"You won't get a ticket here?"

He smiled, a rare sliver of joy on his square, sad face. "No," he said, "it's the Italian way. We all break the rules. But we break them only to a certain extent. Look, see? If people really need to get through this gate, they can. They'll only have to drive slowly for a few seconds, and that's not too painful even for Italians. They'll squeeze between the side of the van and the far gatepost. Even a truck could go in or out. Right now everyone is eating lunch anyway, even the police are eating lunch. But this is the way we are."

"I noticed it in the way people drive," I said. "Crazy, breaking every rule, ignoring lane markers and speed limits."

"Yes," he said, and there was another spark of joy. "But I think we are very good drivers, very courteous in some eccentric way. We are not a people who follow the rules, or maybe it is better to say that we are creative with the rules."

"Even the rules of the Church?" I asked as we got out of the van and walked shoulder to shoulder along a torn-up, dusty sidewalk. I felt something different with him then. The visit to his family, awkward as it had been, seemed to have pushed us into a new kind of friendship. He was a notch more relaxed, less formal; I want to say *younger*.

"Yes," he said, "even the rules of the Church. Maybe especially the rules of the Church. If you go to Mass here on Sunday, in almost any church you will see a group of men standing at the back, talking to each other. They carry on a conversation that lasts from the beginning of the service to the '*Andate in pace*,' though sometimes they'll fall silent just as the host is being raised."

"That must make it hard for the priest."

"It does, it does." He laughed a short, quiet laugh. "But that is our way. Sometimes if you go into a restaurant, the people will overcharge you. Other times they'll pretend to forget you had three glasses of wine instead of two and they won't add that onto the check. Everything here is done that way. We have a happy chaos. We're not like the Germans and the Austrians. Everything there works perfectly, but there is not so much fun, not so much joy in being alive."

"Maybe," I said, as we walked into a restaurant that had a dozen or so outdoor tables elegantly set with white tablecloths under a pale white canvas tent, "maybe that's why the Lamb of God people came to be . . . in reaction to that happy chaos."

"Yes, maybe," he said, "but there's something about those people that most Italians instinctively dislike. We give respect to the pope and the Vatican, yes, naturally, but then we will go home and do what we please. Look, we have the lowest or second lowest birth rate in all of Europe. Do you really think all those married couples are using the rhythm method? Or abstaining?"

At that point the conversation was interrupted by a waiter, who seated us at one of the outdoor tables. For a moment Bruno—who was wearing, as he had every time I'd seen him, his black pants and short-sleeved black shirt, open at the collar— for a moment, in spite of the clothing, he seemed to me not so much like a priest but like an ordinary young Italian man sitting down to lunch with a friend. In the way he opened the menu, in the way he ordered for both of us, pasta and wine and then a meat dish for what Italians call *il secondo piatto*, the second plate, the weight of sadness and formality seemed to lift away from him. I felt much closer to him because of it.

When we'd sipped our wine and taken the first bites of a delicious and perfectly cooked spaghetti with tiny yellow clams and baby octopus mixed into it, I said, "I received a very strange letter this morning at the hotel." I could see that the news had his full attention.

"Claudia brought it to me at breakfast." I took the envelope out of my purse and handed it across the table, and he set down his fork, unfolded the letter and read it, then handed it back to me.

"Eat, please," I said. "This food is too good to be allowed to grow cold. Do you have any idea what it means?"

He swallowed before answering, sipped his wine, picked at one of the miniature octopuses with the tines of his fork, and then raised his eyes. "Do you remember a few years ago, when there were the G8 meetings in Genoa? Do you remember that the young people rioted?"

"Not really," I said. "I don't pay much attention to the news."

"Well, they rioted in the streets because they felt that the powerful people who run the world were making these giant economic arrangements with each other, trade deals and so on, that benefited them, that increased their wealth, but at the expense of the working people. Because of their greed, they were driving the world economy into

244

the mud. The young people lit cars on fire, broke windows. There was wildness in the streets. They fought with the police and many people were hurt, and some, a few, were killed. Well, this man"—he pointed toward the letter—"Cardinal Zossimo, went out into the streets and spoke to them. Not as a representative of the powerful but as a human being. He spoke to them about violence and how rarely it succeeds in bringing any good change to the world. He said he agreed with them in principle, but at the same time he spoke as a member of the Church hierarchy, the elite, the powerful, asking them to be calm. Some people hated him for that, called him a hypocrite. But many many people, myself included, have a great admiration for him. Think of it, a cardinal going out into the wild streets like that, unprotected, to speak to the youth. Who else has done that in history? Can you think of anyone?"

"There was an archbishop in Central America," I said. "I don't know which country. Nicaragua, maybe. Or El Salvador. I remember he was assassinated saying Mass."

"Yes," he said. "Archbishop Romero. A few brave men and a few brave women do things like that. Cardinal Zossimo, they say, walks through the worst neighborhoods of Genoa at night, speaking to the prostitutes and drug addicts and the boys in gangs. Not trying to convince them to go to church or change their lives, just speaking to them, *seeing* them, which is what the rest of the society refuses to do. He would make a wonderful pope, that man, though the chances of him ever being elected are nonexistent. More likely, I think, he'll someday be killed."

Bruno snorted bitterly and pushed his empty dish a few inches to the side. The waiter came and removed it and took my dish away, too, and asked if we wanted more wine. We did. After he was gone, Bruno said, "You heard my father last night, didn't you? They killed John Paul I. Poison, probably. But of course there was never an autopsy or any investigation. Think of it. Corruption reaches that high up into the Church. It is that difficult and that dangerous to try to change things. Small changes, yes, of course. Mass on Saturday night in addition to Sunday. Confession face-to-face. And so on. Even those things met with resistance, and it was only the charisma of John XXIII that enabled such changes to be made, and now they are slowly being reversed. But the big things? Those things threaten the powers that be. And when people have power and money, within the Church, within the State, they'll do almost anything to hold on to it."

"Including murdering a pope?"

"Yes, of course," he said. "Murder is as human as going to the toilet. Why shouldn't it exist within the Church?"

The waiter brought the meat dishes, sausage and

veal. I touched my finger to the envelope. "What does this mean, then?"

Bruno shrugged. "I am not sure. It could be a trick to get you to go there. Perhaps they want to hurt you, and want you to be away from Rome when that happens, so it attracts less attention. Perhaps they want to do some damage to Cardinal Zossimo's reputation by having him meet with an American radical."

"I'm hardly a radical," I said. "And no one knows me here."

"Not yet, no. But Lamb of God has a huge influence on certain newspaper writers. It would be a simple matter to place a few articles there, saying you are an American, a foreigner, who has come here to destroy the Church."

I watched him cut and chew a piece of meat. I'd always had a not-very-respectful feeling about conspiracy theorists. I could feel that disrespect rising up between us, and I tried to push it back down.

"It could also be," Bruno went on, "that Cardinal Rosario—he's not Grossetto, after all; he has no link to Lamb of God, none that we know of anyway—it could be that he actually wanted to say something different to you than he said but that he couldn't be seen to do that in front of anyone else. He couldn't risk your going and announcing, in public, 'Rosario thinks women should be ordained.'"

"Or it could be Father Clement."

"Yes, perhaps that is the most likely. I know him a bit. We worked together out of the same office for a few months when I was first ordained. A good man."

"He seemed upset in the meeting. I had the feeling he wanted to say something to me but couldn't."

"Yes, well, then probably he brought that note to the hotel or arranged for someone else to bring it. Either he had a sense you should make your case to Zossimo or he reports to Zossimo in secret—or both."

"But how would he know where I was staying?"

"Not difficult. First, in Italy, you must always register your name with a passport when you check in, yes? Second, someone could have followed us there when I took you. Not difficult."

"All this intrigue over a person as small as me," I said. "I can't believe that."

"Small in some ways, yes," Bruno agreed. "In other ways, not so small. I have been thinking about this, Cynthia. Do you really believe the archbishop of Boston would have written a letter recommending you to a cardinal in Rome if he thought you were just an ordinary parishioner, a young woman, a nurse, who happened to be upset about one of the rules of the Church and came to him claiming to have been given messages from

God? Are you that naive? Or are you just being disingenuous?"

"I don't know," I said. "Sometimes I feel I live in my own little shell, set apart from the real world of men and women. I've felt that way ever since I was a girl. My friends would be talking about boys, and then later about careers and marriage and money, and it seemed to me that that shell separated me from them. I felt bad about it, plenty of times. Lonely. Isolated. Wondering if I wanted to feel superior to them as a kind of defense, and not join in with them and have an ordinary life."

Bruno nodded as if he understood, and told me to eat and drink.

"I was followed when I went to Santa Maria," I said. "I didn't want to upset you. It was the same man who came to the hotel."

"Wonderful! How well you've been greeted here in our country!"

I showed him the picture on my phone and he looked at it a long time, then shrugged and said, "*Albanese*," as if he'd known as much all along.

"I confronted him. I asked him why he was doing it, who was sending him. He was the one who said, '*Grossetto*.'"

"Wonderful, perfect," Father Bruno said, with a biting sarcasm that surprised me. "And you confronted him. Excellent!"

"Yes. Men, I've found, don't like to be yelled at in public."

He threw back his head and laughed, and for just a moment I could see the happy, handsome boy he'd been long ago, before his mother ran off and his father turned bitter and he made certain decisions about his life. "You," he said, "are either crazy or touched by God or both."

"Crazy, probably."

"If He needed somebody to change His church, He would choose a person like you. Brave. Stubborn. A bit of a *pazza*. Am I correct?"

"About the stubborn part, yes."

After we'd eaten another bite or two, he asked, "What will you do?"

"I don't know. I don't want to have come all this way, had one meeting, heard one refusal, and then go home. I'm not made like that. I don't like to quit things once I start them."

"A good trait."

"I've been thinking I should go to Genoa and try to see this Cardinal Zossimo."

"How?" he asked. "You will have no letter of introduction this time, no archbishop who knows him personally and recommends you. The cardinals"—he floated one hand up into the sky—"they live above us, unapproachable, protected by layers and layers of bureaucracy."

"But you said this cardinal was different. He came out into the streets. You said Father Clement might be—"

"Yes, sure, he came out into the streets when

thousands of people were burning cars and breaking windows. But it is not as though you will see him walking along the main boulevard there and tap him on the shoulder and ask him to allow women to become priests, and he will say, 'Sure, yes, let's sit down and discuss this.' "

"I think I'll try anyway," I said, put off a bit by the note of condescension. "I have eight more days here before I have to fly home. What am I going to do? Spend that time seeing the sights?"

Father Bruno was shaking his head. "I cannot go with you," he said, as if I were asking him to. Which, in a way, I think I was. "To Genoa. I can't get away."

"I wouldn't ask that."

"But I will drive you to the train station, and if I see this tall *Albanese* with the two different eyes, I will strangle him with my own hands and go to Hell for it. And I will make a reservation for you at a nice hotel so you are not in a dangerous part of the city—there are some bad places—*posti brutti*—in Genoa. I will try, through friends here, to get a message to someone in the cardinal's office telling him you're not as crazy as you seem to be. That is the best I can do. I think it will not be enough. And I think, possibly, it is even dangerous for you to go there. I would ask you not to, but I sense that it would do no good. Am I right?"

"Absolutely."

He nodded and thought for a moment, and then I saw a small ironic smile touch the corners of his lips. He sighed in a satisfied way, as if the meal had met his expectations, thanked me for it, then said, "It has been a strange thing, meeting you, Cynthia Piantedosi. Lucia called me last night and said something about you. She said, 'That woman has a shine around her, some kind of aura. She seems to me to be living behind a disguise.' I told her I thought she was right, I just did not know what was there beneath the disguise. Who are you? A saint? A spy? A radical?"

"The most ordinary girl in the world," I said, and he made an expression I'd seen many times before, something that reminded me instantly of my father. He lifted his eyebrows while closing his eyes and turning down the corners of his lips. It was a facial *maybe,* a gesture of half belief: skepticism and affection blended in a way that seemed perfectly Italian to me.

CHAPTER TEN

The train to Genoa left Rome's Termini Station at a few minutes past ten the next morning. We barely made it. Father Bruno was atypically late. As I waited in a light rain out in front of the Old Palace Hotel, I wondered if he might be trying to keep me from traveling to Genoa by making me miss the express train. But he pulled up in Franco's van, fifteen minutes late and overflowing with apologies. Once the apologies were finished, he focused on getting us through the mad Roman traffic and said almost nothing.

Eleven minutes before the train was supposed to depart, he turned into the station lot, parked the van in a clearly marked bus stop, two wheels up on the sidewalk, helped me carry my luggage into the station, showed me where to buy a ticket and how to validate it in the yellow metal box near the track. As I waited there, he rushed over to buy me an umbrella and then to a little shop to buy a bagful of various kinds of pastries and panini I could take along on the trip. "It's a sin to be hungry," he said, but behind his smile I could see a shadow of worry.

Just before I boarded the train he said, "I have two different friends who are trying to get a message to Zossimo's office. And I've booked you in a very nice hotel that's walking distance to the Curia. Here"—he handed me a manila envelope—"everything you need. A map. The hotel reservation. Good luck, my friend. Please be careful. Call me and tell me what happens."

I gave him a warm embrace, held him tight against me for a few seconds. I turned and climbed the steps of the train, found my seat, first class, in a glass-walled coupé. I was facing three middle-aged Italian women, beautifully dressed and obviously friends. As the train pulled out of the station, I saw that Father Bruno was walking along the platform beside the window, waving to get my attention. He was mouthing something in Italian, rather urgently it seemed to me, then he took his phone out of his pocket and pointed at it and raised it high above his head. I couldn't be sure, but it seemed he might be telling me to call him when I arrived.

"A lover?" one of the women said to me.

"No, a friend, a priest."

She raised her carefully plucked eyebrows. "A priest lover," she said, grinning. "The most appreciative."

NOT LONG AFTER WE PULLED out of the enclosed station and left the center of the city behind, we passed through a stretch of ugliness. The high concrete walls at the sides of the tracks were covered in graffiti. The apartment buildings beyond them showed broken windows, laundry hanging over the sills, clusters of rusting antennas standing crookedly on the roofs. Through the speckling of raindrops on the train window the neighborhood didn't seem quite as desperately poor as some parts of Boston I'd seen, but it had the same feeling to it: no beauty, no luxury, no softness, none of the orderliness you saw even in slightly better off places. I thought how hard it must be to cultivate a spiritual life if you were constantly worried about money and physical safety, and I thought that when I went home, when this whole episode was over, when I'd exhausted every option for acting on the messages I was getting from God, I was going to volunteer in a neighborhood like that and try to get the Church to work harder to change the lives of those people.

I remember thinking about the immigrants Father Bruno said he worked with, Albanians who'd left dire poverty and oppression and come to a place like this. I tried to put myself into the mind of the man who'd been following me. I offered up a prayer for him.

And then we were in the countryside, and I was looking out at herds of sheep in green fields and hillsides with neat rows of olive trees crossing them. I loved that landscape. Like the buildings in Campo de' Fiori, these fields and hills had seen, from the Etruscans to Berlusconi, every kind of human behavior. Thousands of years from now, when we'd lived through another series of foolishness, violence, and hope, it would still be here, offering itself to us. All we had to do was grow our food in soil like this, harvest more food from the sea, build shelter, bear and raise children, pray to our Creator. So much was given to us without our having done anything in particular to deserve it, yet we complicated those gifts in so many different ways. We cheated, envied, stole from one another, divided ourselves into opposing groups. We took more than we needed, ravaged the earth. We found reasons to hate and kill, torment and torture. But somehow—even in that whirling ball of bad energy—love, tenderness, and compassion survived like flowers on a battlefield. I had a moment then, thinking that way, really the first moment in my life, when I seriously considered leaving the Catholic Church. I don't know why I felt it just then, but the feeling was as undeniable as it was surprising. Not a temptation of the Devil, as I once would have assumed, but a kind of breaking down of the walls of the person I believed myself to be. Why, I thought, why be Catholic or Protestant or Jew or anything else with a label and rules? Why not, as Bruno's father argued, just lead a simple life of prayer and work, try to love, try to give, and not do anything at all that separated me from other people?

In a moment the thought had passed, but it left a residue, a thin, silvery trail like the ones left by the snails that crawled out of my father's garden and across our brick walk. Why call myself anything but Cynthia the human being?

The countryside just north of Rome's suburbs had been softly rolling hills, a landscape of fruit trees and fields, stone walls and narrow roads along which trucks and cars scooted like colorful toys. But as the train moved farther from the city, the topography changed again, the hills grew steeper, and there were long, slanting fields planted in what appeared to be some kind of grain, about to be harvested. The rain had stopped by then. On the foggy eastern horizon I began to be able to make out blue mountain ranges rising one behind the next like a series of revelations.

The express train made its only stop at a city that began and ended with *O,* and as we were pulling out of the station there, I looked up and saw that it was an ancient hill town, set on a top-hat-shaped piece of land. As protection, no doubt, against invaders. A few hundred buildings rested on that slanted plateau above sandy cliffs. I saw one enormous church there, towering over everything, and I thought about the people who must have designed and built it, hundreds of years ago. What they wanted was to raise a structure in tribute to the mystery that had given them life—such a simple and straightforward project. Once the building was in place, though, ideas and rules attached themselves to it like insects clinging onto something sweet, eating away at it, using it to fatten themselves and spread disease. We started to move again, and soon the hilltop city passed from view behind us, but I sat there with the three Italian women still facing me in the quiet, glassed-in coupé, and I kept thinking about the church builders. I wondered if all of them—masons, sculptors, painters, architects—had enjoyed a deep prayer life. I wondered if that was the source of their artistic inspiration: a longing to describe what they'd experienced, to use their skill to give physical shape to the fragments of the Kingdom of Heaven they saw in their meditations. And I wondered if it was that link to the mysterious dimension of life, not so much the food or the art, that drew millions of people to Italy year after year from all over the world.

I sat back and closed my eyes, and I thought: Martino Zossimo Genova. Three words on a sheet of stationery, and here I was, going hundreds of miles out of my way, to a city I'd never seen, not having any idea what I would find there. Surely I was a foolish person.

CHAPTER **ELEVEN**

The hotel in Genoa would turn out to be shouting distance from the train station, an easy walk for me, even with the umbrella and two bags. For a few seconds, as I asked directions from a station worker, I had the eerie sense—a slight shadowy weight against my back—that someone was following me. I didn't turn around to look until I'd left the station and headed out into what had become a sunny day. No one.

I cut across a small park with a few red-faced, raggedly dressed men and one woman lying in it, bottles of wine half hidden against their hips. The hotel, one block beyond the park, was called the Savoia, and it had a modest presence on the street, just a four-story brick face with a set of steps and a doorway bracketed by two windows. Inside it was so spectacular I began to worry immediately about the cost.

"Your account has been taken care of," the clerk at the desk informed me when I asked what the rate would be.

"By who?"

The clerk was a young man but dressed in a suit and tie that made him seem like a middle-aged accountant who'd been too long on the job. He checked his records. "Someone who wished not to be named," he said primly.

A cold draft of paranoia touched me then. For a moment, before I remembered that Father Bruno had chosen the hotel, I wondered if this was another part of some elaborate trap.

"A person? An institution?"

"I'm not allowed to say. The manager comes in again tomorrow morning. You may speak with him then if you'd like."

I was chaperoned through the tiled lobby—it was surrounded by reading rooms with leather-covered tables, leather armchairs, dark bookshelves, gilded mirrors, and small stone sculptures behind glass—and into the elevator by a man who introduced himself as Mabu, who said he was originally from Morocco and who must have been six and a half feet tall.

"Could you check with me first," I asked him, "before you send outside phone calls or anyone up to the room?"

"*Certo*," he said solemnly, the word emerging from behind his large jaw as if it had been spoken in a barrel. Of course.

The fourth-floor room he showed me to was an embarrassment of riches, three or four times as large as my room at home. It had enough floor space for an aerobics workout, an enormous bed—not round, thank you—a writing table, a coffee bar, a beautifully tiled bath, and two tall windows looking out over rooftops to the port. I decided Father Bruno must have been so embarrassed by the incident at the first hotel that he wanted to make sure nothing close to that would happen again, but even so I couldn't imagine him paying for this out of his own pocket. Mabu set down my bags as if they were as light as boxes of Kleenex. There were, he informed me, Jacuzzis on the top-floor veranda, and a breakfast buffet would be served each day in the dining room on that same floor, starting at seven a.m. "How long will you be with us, *Signorina*?"

"I don't know. One or two nights at least, maybe longer."

"Very good," he said, and when I tipped him he made a dignified half bow in my direction, closed the door quietly behind him, and left me there feeling like I'd accidentally been given a room reserved for visiting royalty.

I spent a little while standing at the windows, looking out at the port from which Christopher Columbus was supposed to have sailed. It wasn't the prettiest of views, but it was new to me, another door opening onto another piece of life, and after all those years of not traveling very far, every view from every new angle—through train and hotel windows, from the street—held a dancing thrill inside it. To the right the buildings of the city stood along a curve of seashore, pinched between a range of dry hills and the water. A traffic-choked elevated highway came sweeping in from the direction I was looking. West, maybe, though geography had never been my strong suit. West or northwest. Toward France. On the far side of the highway I could see two huge white cruise ships at anchor and then, farther left, an intricate jumble of old rooftops and pastel apartment buildings. The yellowish afternoon light on the hills and housefronts—it was almost golden—and the blues, purples, and grays that daubed the undersides of a parade of puffy clouds reminded me exactly of the colors in the coffee-table book Father Alberto had given me for Christmas so many years before. "I know you'll go there one day," he'd said, and of course I hadn't believed him.

I had thought that they were made-up colors, meant to suggest Heaven, but I saw now that they were real, specific to Italy, maybe, or to moments when you had a particularly strong yearning for the presence of God. As sometimes happened, as I ran my eyes over the view, it began to seem that I was linked to everything I saw. All of it—cars on the roadway, plants in the rooftop gardens, clouds, sea, harbor cranes—shared something with the innermost part of me. I don't know exactly what to call it, an *isness*, maybe, an atomic essence, divine breath. The drunks in the park and the brioches under glass in the train station, the leather handles of the suitcase and the young man at the reception desk, we were all part and parcel of the fabric of existence, God's tapestry. How could anyone who felt that ever hurt another soul?

After a time I sat in one of the upholstered chairs, the blue arms embroidered with lines of gold thread, and I closed my eyes and prayed for the soul of my friend Alberto Ghirardelli. It seemed undeniable to me that such a spirit— particles that had taken the shape of someone so generous, funny, and *alive*—had to continue to exist in some other dimension after it left the body. What form it took there I couldn't possibly imagine—not as a middle-aged man, I knew that; the idea of a static Heaven had never made much sense to me—but I had a strong feeling of his presence then, so strong it almost felt like he was actually in the room. It seemed natural to speak to him as I had once spoken to him in the confessional, so I did that. "It was you who started me on this journey, so if things go bad, Father, you're catching the blame. If you're in a place where you can hear me and help me, please don't let me make a fool of myself by coming here, by failing miserably, by being conceited enough to think I could change something so much bigger than me. Please let me have understood correctly the message in my prayers and not have mixed it up out of stupidity or egotism. I love you. I hope you're at peace."

He didn't answer, of course. And yet simply remembering our conversations helped. I sank down into a quiet space, and in that space all doubt evaporated. It slowly came to seem obvious to me that I was doing what I should be doing. There were no visions, just a quiet room that seemed painted in the same blues and purples I'd seen through the window. I rested there for a long time, simply feeling the fact of my own aliveness and the energy of life around me. It would be too easy to describe that energy as the presence of God. I believe that's what it was, but those words somehow can't match the perfection and mystery any more than the actuality and mystery of time can be captured by numbers on a clock face.

Slowly, in a way that felt absolutely unhurried, I found myself returning to awareness of the hotel room. I moved my eyes over the window trim—the corner seam where two pieces of wood met, a tiny chip in the beige paint there—and then slowly the world of nameable, separate shapes reasserted itself. I said a prayer for my father and mother and grandmother, as I always did, and realized I was hungry. Either something about being in Italy made me want to eat all the time or I was having a late-in-life growth spurt.

I showered and changed clothes and, after a short conversation with Mabu—who held the door open for me—went out in search of a place to have dinner. It took all of a block to realize that Genoa didn't feel anything like Rome. There were fewer of the loud motorbikes, no legions of tourists, no one juggling in traffic, no river running through neighborhoods that still carried the architectural marks of the time of Christ. I soon realized, also, that it was too early to eat dinner. Restaurants in Italy don't open for the evening meal until seven or seven thirty at the earliest, so I stopped into the first church I passed, an old gray hulk of a building, set on a busy corner, that leaned toward the street as if it might fall on its face at any moment. It wasn't my favorite place, large and bland, gray stone inside and out, dim light, a sense not of hope but of past suffering and pessimism. I didn't stay long.

The city itself had a pleasant, understated personality, as if it were suffused with the knowledge that it had been an important metropolis centuries before, in its adolescence, and had grown tired of all that fuss and bother and was content now to be just an ordinary adult. Its squat *palazzi* were half hidden behind clacking trolleys and sidewalk cafés. One grand, tarnished building, dirty with roadway soot, sucked students in and spewed them out again as if it were a huge set of lungs and the young men and women were particles of oxygen.

I wandered and wandered, soaking in the newness, still washed clean, inside and out, by the memory of my long quiet prayer. In that state of mind it was all but impossible to worry or be afraid, ridiculous to look behind me to see who might be following. Franco's tales of Vatican intrigue felt as though they belonged to a different orbit in the spin and whirl of atoms. Nothing could hurt me.

I had Father Bruno's map, with the cardinal's office—the Curia, it was called—clearly marked, but I decided to savor the feeling of being a carefree tourist for a little while and save my business for the next morning. On a bending lane a twenty-minute walk from the Savoia, I found a restaurant to my liking. It was just opening its doors: ten tables, a hundred bottles of wine in shelves against the walls, and a waitress so calm and attentive she seemed to have been set down there from another happy dimension of the universe. Another fine meal, more nervous over-eating, a few minutes of prayer for my father.

Afterward, in the first darkness, I walked back along Via Arsenale, the busy street that led to the hotel. It was a narrow-sidewalked thoroughfare enlivened, even at that hour, by a carnival of cars, buses, motorcycles, students, and two-chair tables in front of crammed cafés. Via Arsenale wasn't the straightest route back. I had to climb a steep hill and make a left turn rather than cutting the corner and going more directly, but Mabu had told me in the hotel lobby that Via Prè, running parallel and closer to the water, was a place to avoid. At night absolutely, he said, but even during the day.

When I returned to the hotel, full-bellied and tired from the long afternoon, Mabu was there to greet me. He said someone had come inquiring, asking when I'd gone out, where I might be found. I thought it might be one of the friends of the friends of Father Bruno, with advice about how best to make an appointment to see the cardinal. "A short man," Mabu said, "with a tattoo here." He pointed to the side of his neck.

"Italian?"

"Yes."

"Did he leave a message?"

"Check at the desk."

There were no messages at the desk and nothing on my phone when I went upstairs. I lay down in the luxurious bed and within two minutes was buried in sleep. I had a dream then, just a piece of a vision of a dream, that seemed to have my mother in it. I'd seen pictures of her, of course. And in my mind's eye, thousands of times, I'd imagined her. But the sense of her in that dream carried no visual image. She was there, for a moment, an instant, one beam of selfless love, and then she was being torn away from me.

THE NEXT MORNING, AFTER BREAKFAST on the top-floor patio and a quick peek at the Jacuzzis, I went out into the city again and soon found the Curia—a slim, three-story gray domino of a building standing between a travel agency and a bank. If it hadn't been for the cardinal's seal high up on the facade and the *X* Mabu had made on Father Bruno's map, I might have walked right past it. I stepped in through a small wooden door cut into a larger door and realized that, like so many other buildings I'd seen in Italy, the street view was only a tiny piece of the picture, an illusion, a disguise. It made me think of the way the human condition pretended to be one thing but was actually something else. Like Santa Maria in Trastevere—worn, almost shabby on the out-side but spectacular within—and like the city of Rome itself, an ancient architectural miracle surrounded by a thick ring of modern mess, it seemed obvious to me at that moment that the life we lived was a kind of stage play. We walked around in costume, a flimsy disguise of titles, status, possessions, personality, and looks that masked an enormous interior universe. On the surface my grandmother had been an old woman with aching hands and teardrop-shaped glasses; an inch beneath that she'd been a giant of a soul, a furnace of love, constantly giving off heat. Father Alberto had been a priest, but beyond that title and those vows and the plain black shirt and pants, his true self shone like a gem in gauze. If you thought about it carefully, you understood that everything they *were,* everything about them I missed, really had nothing to do with their titles or looks or even their habits and quirks. What they said and did was all a kind of code, the surface expression of a deeper Self, radio signals sent out through a static of appearances. In my own case, it wasn't so much that I felt trapped or false in my role as nurse and unmarried daughter. I was more comfortable with myself than I'd ever been. But almost always it felt as though another self deep inside me had not yet found its truest means of expression, the correct code through which to communicate clearly and effectively with the outside world. It seemed—*seemed*—that God was telling me the proper manifestation of that true inner self was the priesthood. But what if, as Archbishop Menendez had suggested, I was getting the message slightly wrong? What if there was some other purpose to my little life?

At that point, though, wrong as I might turn out to be, there was no choice but to go forward, to try as energetically and as honestly as I could to do what I believed God was asking of me. If it turned out that I'd misread the code, I'd be forgiven, I was sure.

BEYOND THE FACE THE CURIA showed the world lay a skylight-topped courtyard, invisible from the street. I could see it as I stepped through the door. Just before reaching it, I came upon a small office on my right-hand side, probably ten feet by ten, an open door, photos of the pope and cardinal on the wall, a religious calendar, a painting of Mary drawn on a wooden slab, and, sitting there like bored security guards, two men. One was a gray-headed layman stationed behind a metal desk. The other was a priest with a Buddha belly, a cascade of chins, and small, chubby hands folded peacefully in his lap. I'd brought with me the letter from Archbishop Menendez, hoping it might at least show me to be something other than a mentally unstable foreigner who'd wandered in off the street. But somehow I wasn't surprised when I handed it to the man behind the desk and it had absolutely no effect. I made a polite, succinct argument as to why I should be allowed to have an appointment with the cardinal of Genoa, but he only squinted at me as if I were a nuisance, an interruption to his busy day, a deceitful beggar with a doll against her breast. Even when I took the liberty of mentioning the meeting with Cardinal Rosario, twice, there was no movement.

All during this one-sided conversation I could feel the old priest watching me. Sitting there a few feet to my left, he studied me at first, really studied me. I could sense it out of the side of my vision, and when I turned to meet his eyes he smiled and looked away. Just at the point where I was giving up on trying to communicate with the man behind the desk, the old priest broke his silence.

"*Il cardinale sta a Roma,*" he said. "The cardinal is now in Rome." He lifted one hand lazily and let it fall. The gesture indicated the complete impossibility of doing anything to rectify the situation. Hopelessly great distance. The iron whims of fate.

"But I was just in Rome," I said. "I came here thinking I might have the opportunity for a brief meeting."

The priest let his eyelids close and lifted his shoulders an inch. In another moment, it seemed, I would be told to leave.

"Would it be possible," I asked him, "to see the cardinal's office, perhaps leave him a note?"

The priest studied me for another few seconds, then smiled, showing a row of false teeth. There was a peculiar stillness about him, as if he hadn't moved from the chair in months or as if he'd come there to that tiny office expecting a visit from his heavenly mother and was willing to wait years for her arrival. He spoke a few words to the gray-headed man in a tone of gentle authority, and the man, reluctantly it seemed, led me out of the office, into the courtyard, then across to a doorway at the base of a set of marble stairs. Instead of accompanying me, he pointed up the stairs, mumbled something that sounded like "*Secondo piano*," "Second floor," and left me there. It was a strange way of doing business.

I climbed a flight—white marble everywhere—then another (as I'd discovered in the Albergo delle Mura, in Italy the first floor isn't counted), and then I saw, cut into a narrow wall, a door upholstered in crimson cloth. I don't know why, since I'd been told the cardinal wasn't there, but I felt one bump of excitement in my chest, a thump of hope, perhaps, or a dim recognition that belonged to another world. I approached the doorway and had almost reached it when another gray-haired man sitting at another desk stood up and stopped me. Before I could say a word he greeted me in English, as if my American passport were open on my chest. He nodded as I spoke, showing that he understood perfectly. I was a Catholic, come all the way from America. I'd had a meeting with Cardinal Rosario in Rome and had come to Genoa to speak with Cardinal

Zossimo or at least see the office where he worked and leave him a note.

"Not possible," the man said, when I was finished. He was bald, bespectacled, pushing seventy, and, even with the padding of a tailored suit, rail thin.

"I'd just like to have a peek at his office," I said, though at the time I had no idea why that meant so much to me.

The man shook his head. "The cardinal is now in Turkey."

"Not Rome?"

He shook his head again. "I cannot let into the office anyone."

"May I leave a note?" I asked.

"Yes," the man said, but with about as much enthusiasm as if I'd asked to borrow plane fare back to America. "Yes. *Sì*. Okay."

He handed me a pad of paper and a pencil, and I wrote a short note. My name, my room number at the hotel, the fact that I'd met with Archbishop Menendez of Boston and Cardinal Rosario at the Vatican and had come to Genoa to have a conversation with His Eminence about an important matter. I folded the note in half and handed it over. The man said he'd be sure to pass it on.

And that was as close as I believed I'd ever get to Martino Zossimo, Cardinal of Genoa. There was nothing to do but leave, carrying my disappointment back down the marble steps, past the small office—the heavyset priest lifted his hand in farewell—and out into the city.

For a while I walked the streets under another cloud of pessimism, a mood very similar to, if not as intense as, the one that had taken hold of me as I left the Congregation for the Doctrine of the Faith. I saw a fountain that I'd been told at the hotel marked the center of downtown, the place where the huge demonstrations had been held. I tried to imagine the cardinal walking out into the melee to speak to the young people there. A few blocks farther along, I came to the stone ruins of what was said to have been Christopher Columbus's house. I stopped for a cappuccino on one of the wide, slanting avenues that was lined with water-stained pastel *palazzi*, row upon row of elegant facades, impenetrable, stoic, perfectly regular. I thought of heading down to see the port—my new friend Mabu had recommended it—but the disappointment lay like a sack of stones across my shoulders, so I headed back in the general direction of the hotel, looking for a place to pray.

After wandering the streets of the old city center—a labyrinth of shuttered windows and closed doors—I came upon a church in the middle of a square where vendors stood in booths selling herbs, honey, and oil. The square felt like a secret place, shadowed and quiet, insulated from the city noise. Strangely enough, the church sat up on a kind of platform, twenty or thirty feet above the pavement at the east end of the piazza, as if it had been propped up there as a protection against the next great flood. On its columned porch hung a plaque saying it was the Church of San Pietro, built in the sixteenth century. Inside, it was all stone and smokiness, with an altar carved from brown-and-white marble and, on the right-hand wall, a painting that depicted the head of St. John the Baptist being carried to Herod's daughter on a plate. I knelt in one of the pews and had a long, quiet prayer, and when that was finished I sat there admiring the marble edging at the tops of the walls and the way the light caught swirls of paint on the canvas. I wondered why it was, in Christian history at least, that the good people, the best people, were the ones who seemed to suffer most. Why was it set up that way? Why couldn't it be that goodness in this life had a reward, not later but now? Why couldn't it even be neutral? Why did Father Alberto have to be struck by a car, John the Baptist beheaded, Jesus and later Peter crucified, St. Sebastian shot with a hundred arrows, and Mary forced to watch the execution of her only child? What kind of coded message was that? Surely evil people suffered, too. But why didn't goodness offer any protection? Was God trying to blow up our neat castle of logic? Was He always doing what He did to Job, forcing us far,

far out of anything that resembled a comfort zone, pushing us into a corner where all we had left was a blind faith in Him, utter, naked acceptance of a path we couldn't see?

Those questions had been part of Father Alberto's favorite theme in the pulpit. "Life always brings us to the idea of humility," he said. "Don't you think so? We have these remarkable brains—capable of curing illness, making space-ships that fly to the moon, building roads across the face of the planet. All good things. But at the same time there is a way in which being able to manipulate and control our surroundings so much better than the animals can, there is a way in which that puffs us up with conceit. We begin to feel we have the right to control *everything*. That everything should be explainable according to our human logic. Well, fine, but maybe there's another logic. God's logic. And maybe the only way we begin to come close to understanding it is to let go of our insistence that things should make sense *to us*. What do you think?" he'd ask his silent, obedient congregation. "Give this some thought, and get back to me."

I smiled, thinking of him. But at that moment, sitting alone in the Church of San Pietro, I missed him terribly.

Afterward, I took a seat at an outdoor restaurant in the square—only a Caprese salad this time— then walked back to the hotel. I'd been there just a short while when I heard a knock on the hall door. I opened it and saw Mabu holding a sheet of paper in his hand. "This person, he call for you," Mabu said, "but we don't know, should we pass the phone to you or wait?"

For one or two heartbeats I thought it might be the eccentric cardinal inviting me for a meeting. But I looked at the note and saw the name there: Father Bruno Piantedosi. I thanked Mabu. He gave a short bow and left me alone.

I called Bruno right away, apologizing for not having let him know earlier that I'd arrived safely and telling him that the hotel was absolutely wonderful.

"*Troppo caro*?" he asked. Too expensive? And I understood from the question that, as I'd suspected, he had not been the one who'd paid.

"Fine," I said. "Just right."

"Have you been able to speak with the cardinal?"

"I've been trying. You're right, it's like trying to speak to a man on a mountaintop."

"How long will you be staying?"

The question touched a sore spot in me. A little bruise. Part of me felt so at home in Genoa, and in Italy, that I wanted to stay and stay, to keep trying for a meeting with Cardinal Zossimo or someone else with the power to bring about change. But another part, a saner part, knew clearly what was going on: I was indulging a fantasy I should have abandoned the minute I left the Congregation for the Doctrine of the Faith, if not back home in Boston. I was a tourist now, nothing more. I was spending money that could have been better spent elsewhere and using up time that should have been used studying for my nursing Boards. I could excuse that for another few days, I supposed. I could go on riding a roller coaster of hope and despair, acceptance and bitterness, telling myself the note at the Old Palace Hotel had been a sign from God, that the Savoia bill had been taken care of by some progressive benefactor, a Church insider who knew what I was up to and completely supported it. Soon, though, it would be time to face facts.

I told Bruno I wasn't sure but that I'd let him know, and I thanked him again for all his help.

"That was a nice lunch," he said in a tone that had so much loneliness in it I promised him we'd do it again in Rome, probably within a day or two.

"Except I pay this time," he said, and I told him I'd look forward to that, said good-bye, and hung up feeling almost as if I'd agreed to go out on a date.

I DECIDED THEN TO CALL my father. I'd been thinking of him and praying for him every hour since I'd arrived in Italy. Twenty-two years old and I'd seen him every day of my life, so it felt strange to be away from him even for that small amount of time. I knew he was perfectly capable of taking care of himself. He was strong, tough, in good health. He knew how to cook and shop. He'd spend his days playing cards or walking to Rigione's Market for coffee, doing small repairs to the car or lawn mower engines, watching television. I missed him, and I suspected he missed me, too, so I placed a long-distance call through the hotel operator and was glad when, on the fourth ring, my father picked up.

I asked him how he was. Everything fine. And then, to fill the empty air, I told him about Rome and the things I'd seen there, the ruins, the river, the beautiful churches. "I went once when I was a boy," he said. "My uncle had a little money, and he took Franco and me there on the train. The buildings were bombed out and burnt, the people were standing in line for bread, and all over the place we saw the American soldiers with their rifles and dirty helmets and chocolate. Some of them spoke Italian. It's hard for me to think that people go there now for vacation."

I launched into a small fantasy then, telling him about some future day when I would force him to come back to Italy with me. I wanted to go to Naples and see the village where he'd grown up. I wanted him to see Rome again—no soldiers now, no burning buildings—and maybe Venice. I told him I was in Genoa and how much I liked the city and that I wanted him to see this place, too.

When I was finished with this improbable plan, there was another awkward silence and I was about to say my good-byes and hang up when my father said, "My friend Bobby, he said something the other day. He said he heard something."

"What, Pa?"

I heard him grunt, and I imagined him pressing his lips together and nodding the way he did. Something in the sound prepared me for what was coming.

"He says he heard you went to the Vatican to try to make women be priests. He made it sound like you're making trouble there, with the Church. My other friends were asking me was it true."

Even through the long-distance line, it wasn't hard to hear the tremble of shame in his voice. The world he lived in was not so different from the tiny Neapolitan village he'd left. What mattered was what people thought of you, what they said about your family. The most important thing was never to bring any kind of disgrace upon the Piantedosi name. Bobby Verano, I knew, was an electrician friend, nominally Catholic, who liked his gossip and his wine and to make himself the center of every gathering. He was just the kind of man whose opinion would scratch against my father's skin.

When my father finished, the only thing I could think to say was "I'm sorry, Papa. It's not true. I'm not trying to make trouble."

"But it's true you went there to make the women be priests?"

"That part's true, Pa, yes."

"Why?"

"I feel God is asking me to do that."

"And you couldn't tell me?"

"I didn't think you'd understand. I'm sorry."

There was only silence on the line.

"I'm sorry," I said again. "The last thing I wanted was to embarrass you."

"All right," he said, but I knew it wasn't all right. He'd be sitting in the grandstand at the dog track or holding a hand of cards at the City Club, and he'd be imagining what Bobby and his other friends thought of him, the widower mechanic with the crazy daughter who never had a boyfriend. A troublemaker, a feminist, a radical girl who couldn't tell him what she was really doing over there in the Old Country.

After we said our good-byes I put the phone back on its cradle and sat in the chair with its gold-threaded upholstery and I had a half hour of feeling sorry for myself. I started out thinking about Bobby Merano and some of the other small-minded people we knew, and I went from there to wondering if Monsignor Ferraponte had been right after all and the whole trip was nothing more than a monument to my huge ego. I remembered something Cardinal Rosario had said: he'd somehow known about my conversation with the monsignor. I remembered the tone of the announcement of Father Alberto's death, the monsignor's small, forced expression of sadness. I remembered things Franco and Father Bruno had said about the Church's dark underbelly—the secrets, the fear, the lines that could be crossed once you decided somebody was controlled by the Devil. I thought of the righteous fury on the faces of the Lamb of God protestors when they were shown on TV.

I almost never felt physically afraid, I don't know why. And even after considering all those things, seeing what the possible connections might be, and realizing, at last, what certain types of people must really think of me, even then it wasn't fear I felt but something else. Sadness, maybe. Weariness. Disappointment. As if the last spots on a lens—my hopeful naiveté—had finally been stripped away and now I would have to face the world—and my Church—as it truly was.

CHAPTER TWELVE

For some reason it was hours and hours before I could get to sleep on that night. Sleep had always been such a dependable refuge for me. I always fell asleep almost immediately, slept deeply, rarely had a bad dream, usually woke up refreshed. But that night was different. I rolled this way and that in the oversized bed. I read some of *Wisdom of the Desert* and came upon this entry:

> Abbot Pastor said: Any trial whatever that comes to you can be conquered by silence.

I tried my silent prayer. I tried to understand what God was telling me through this series of failures. I saw that in the words of another famous Catholic writer I loved, Father Thomas Keating, my "program for happiness" was being stifled. We all have our programs, Keating said, our ideas about what shape we want our lives to take. God has to break those programs apart in order to let us see our real purpose.

Like everything else Keating wrote, that theory made sense to me, but the breaking apart was never an enjoyable process, rarely something we could accept without struggle. Lying there, trying to let the worries go and sleep take their place, I wondered if I'd made a wrong turn at some point and, trying too hard to hold on to my program for happiness, my life as I imagined it, I'd wandered into a spiritual dead end.

I had finally fallen asleep in that mood, discouragement teetering on the edge of despair, when the hotel phone made its odd, tinny sound in the darkness. The clock read 2:13. I sat up, wondering if it could be my father calling at what would be 8:13 p.m. Revere time. But the voice on the end of the line belonged to a stranger.

"Signora Piantedosi?" the man began in quiet, careful English.

"Yes."

"You today came at the Curia, yes?"

"I did."

"I was there. The priest. In the office. The old fat priest. Father Bartolomeo, they call me. You wanted to have the visit with *Cardinale* Zossimo."

"I did, yes," I said, suddenly wide awake. "When I went upstairs, I was told he was away, that I couldn't see him."

The old priest coughed. "Now he is here. Genova. He reads your note. Now he wants to have with you the visit. He is sorry so late."

I pressed the phone hard against my ear. "I can come tomorrow at whatever time. I—"

"No, now. This hour," the caller said. "He wants that you should come to the Church of San Luca. Do you know her?"

"No, I know San Pietro. I know the Duomo."

"No, no, San Luca. You can come walking for fifteen minutes to it from your hotel. He will meet you there."

"I don't know where it is."

"Okay. I will help you. Go across the street from your hotel, straight. An alley there. A *vicolo*. I meet you in the *vicolo* and take you to San Luca."

"Now?"

"Now is the only time for him."

"How do I know this is you? I mean, that it isn't a trick?"

There was a pause, then "You, when you went upstairs today, the man there he says the *cardinale* is at Turkey."

"You were that man?"

"No, I am the old priest, in the office. Now is the time for you to come to the *vicolo*. I am not now there, but in a little minutes I am. You must come alone, please, without telling the people. You come across from the hotel into the *vicolo*. Just go and go. Pay attention to nothing there. I think no one will bother you. You are understanding me?"

"Yes, I am."

"Good-bye, then. *Ci vediamo.*"

I SET THE PHONE BACK in its cradle and sat on the edge of the bed. In the darkness I seemed to be surrounded by a vapor of doubt that was broken only by the occasional muted sound from the street. A car passing. A motorbike engine sputtering like machine-gun shots. An ambulance klaxon, its looping siren so different from the ones I was used to at home. I closed my eyes and asked for guidance. Either it was some kind of trick being played by the people who supposedly found me threatening or it was the eccentric cardinal doing something he felt he couldn't do in public. I said a short prayer, asking that I not be ruled by fear on the one hand or egotism and naiveté on the other. I prayed to be shown some kind of sign. But there was no sign, and somehow I knew, even as I prayed, that there wouldn't be. There were the street sounds, the *plink* of the hotel elevator and the padding of soft footsteps on the corridor carpet. I had, for one moment, an image of the Blessed Virgin, just a white flash of her, and then only quiet. I remembered the way I'd been as a girl, seventh grade, ninth grade, twelfth grade—feisty, fearless, unafraid of confrontation, trusting in my fate, knowing that whatever happened to me in school or on the streets, I could always go home to the warmth of my grandmother, the solid presence of my father, the peace of St. Anthony's nave.

Still I hesitated. A minute. Two minutes. Strands of sleepiness dragged at my temples, but the phrase that kept going through my mind was *"all this way."* As in "You've come all this way, and what will you have to show for it?"

I stood up and got dressed, pulled over my head and shoulders the light cashmere sweater my aunt Chiara had given me the Christmas before she died, decided to leave a note on my desk saying I was going to meet Cardinal Zossimo at the Church of San Luca. And then I went quietly out the door.

Downstairs, there was an unfamiliar clerk at the front desk, snoozing, his head on his hands.

Apparently he hadn't been told about phone messages. Mabu was sleeping there, too, filling one of the big leather chairs to overflowing. The sound of the elevator doors had made him open his eyes. He lifted his huge head off the cushion and looked at me tiredly.

"*Signorina*," he said in his accented Italian. "*Dove va?*"

"I have to go to San Luca. I have to meet someone."

I saw his eyes shift to the clock behind the sleeping clerk. "But *Signorina*," he said, "now is not a good time to walk in the city. There are people now who would hurt you, who would steal from you."

"I have to," I said.

As I went across the tile toward the front door, he sat up and moved to the edge of the chair. "*Signorina*, please."

I thought of telling him that in America hotel guests could come and go as they pleased at any time of day or night. But he was so genuinely concerned, and I was carrying, as if in the fibers of the soft sweater, so many threads of uncertainty, that what I said was "Come with me. Just across the street. I'm meeting someone there in the *vicolo*."

"The *vicolo*? That is a very bad place. And you're going from there to San Luca? *A quest'ora*? At this hour? In all the city of Genoa, this is the worst street a woman like you should walk on at night. *I* am even afraid to walk there at night, and look at me. I am afraid of almost nothing."

"I'm afraid of almost nothing, also," I said. When I kept moving toward the entrance, Mabu sighed and stood up, shook the sleep off himself like a bear shaking off water after a river crossing, tucked in his shirt, and pronounced the famous Italian word "*Allora.*" It means something like "All right, then." But he said it, as Italians often do, with a hopeless resignation, as if he were a soldier agreeing to one last assignment, sure to be fatal. "*Allora,*" he said, "*Vado con lei.* I am going with you."

The front door was locked from the inside. Mabu turned the lever and opened it, and we went out. The air was beautifully cool, touched with salt in a way that reminded me of Revere on certain nights. A young couple, two figures cut from charcoal, strolled arm in arm along the far sidewalk. A few of the stores had kept on an interior light, and there were streetlights and the lights from one passing delivery truck, but for the most part the city was dark and asleep. I said one Hail Mary, took a breath, and with Mabu at my side crossed the street toward the alley. There was no one waiting for us. The alley—its shadowed mouth bordered to the left by an eight-foot-tall wooden construction fence—led steeply downhill toward the water. I hesitated a moment and stepped into it.

"*Signorina*," Mabu said, "please. There is another way to go to the Church of San Luca. A few minutes longer, but much safer. Please."

"I can't," I said. "*Non posso.*"

Our footsteps echoed in the *vicolo*. I saw a church to my right, closed up tight and completely dark, bottles, broken glass, and cigarette packages on the pavement in front of it. One yellowish streetlamp a bit farther on. In its frail light I noticed a rat scurrying down the gutter, a syringe there, sparkling. It was only when we were almost to the end of the alley that I saw a figure lurking in the darkness close against the construction fence.

"*Attenti*," Mabu said. He moved a half step in front of me, and I realized that his huge hands had been made into fists. But as we drew closer I had the sure sense that the figure in the shadows was anything but threatening. It was a man dressed in black, I saw, and then I recognized him. The heavyset priest held out a hand and said, "Father Bartolomeo." His face, as he shook hands with Mabu and me, was a trembling mask of flesh— age and tiredness, not fear. In fact, he seemed, as he had at the Curia office, unnaturally calm.

"Thank you for coming," he said to me. "Now let us to walk."

"I didn't want to come alone."

"*Va bene.* That's fine."

Everything about him spoke of a lack of hurry or the inability to move quickly or both. I could sense that Mabu was confused. When Father Bartolomeo, who'd met us at the T where the *vicolo* intersected a very narrow street, gestured that we would be taking a left and traveling along that street, Mabu mumbled, "This is not a good place."

The priest smiled and nodded as pleasantly as if we were three coworkers out for a noontime stroll in one of the city's parks.

But as soon as we turned off the *vicolo*, I was confronted with a scene that might have been a Renaissance painter's vision of Hell. The street itself, little more than a cobblestone lane, was not navigable by cars. The narrow buildings pressed close against each other side to side, and you could have tossed a clothespin across above our heads from one window to the next. Even at that hour, there were clusters of men here and there, sitting on the stoops or standing against the buildings. I thought of Father Bruno, because some of them looked African or North African or perhaps Albanian, some Italian. Two of them were drunk and arguing in hoarse voices. I heard a man screaming angrily in one of the rooms above. Two women in tiny skirts stood at the corner of a side alley, three-quarters hidden in shadow. Strangely, as our odd trio passed, one of them turned and bowed with such reverence I wondered if she'd recognized the priest and was mocking us. "She's bowing to *you*," Father Bartolomeo said in his untroubled voice. His voice, the woman's bow, the sense of the three of us being linked on this strange errand, *a quest'ora*—there was an odd, otherworldly feel to all of it, and thoughts spun around my ears in quick wisps of puzzlement.

Via Prè was not quite as dark as the *vicolo* had been. The pavement was illuminated by widely spaced lamps and one or two lighted windows on the upper floors. A man hissed at us, then burped loudly and laughed in a way that made the skin of my arms prickle. A mongrel slinked past close against the wall. A little farther along I was shocked to see three small children sleeping on a stoop, bathed in the light of a basement window. They were dirty-faced, poorly clothed, clutching each other as if they were cold. On impulse, I took off my sweater and walked over to them, draped it across them as best I could, and we went on. No one spoke. After we'd been walking on Via Prè for ten minutes, our footsteps tapping out an odd, eerie beat, the alley opened a few yards to either side, forming a small piazza. There on our left stood a yellow-walled church with a narrow street running next to it. The priest led us to the door, but before he opened it I turned to Mabu and thanked him. "Go back now and sleep," I said. "I'll be fine."

He looked down at me from his great height.

"I'll be fine," I repeated. "I'm meeting a good man. The Cardinal of Genoa."

There was a splash of surprise on his broad features. He looked at the priest, and when Father Bartolomeo nodded, Mabu looked back at me and pointed farther down in the direction we'd been walking. "*Va giù*," he said. "Go down there. When you return to the hotel, go in that direction. Then left on Corso Emmanuele, then up the hill, left again on Via Arsenale. That way it will be safe."

I thanked him again and saw that he was going that way himself so as not to have to return along Via Prè.

The priest pulled open the right half of the wood-panel door and we went quietly into a nave that was lit only by votive candles and two small lamps.

I waited for my eyes to adjust, then went and knelt at the altar rail. Outside and in, the church had a shabby, unkempt feel to it, but there in front of me stood a spectacular sculpture of Mary, all in white marble. She had one hand over her heart, her marble clothes were rippling as if in a breeze, and at her feet floated a tumbling mass of young children and one slightly older girl, all of them in various postures of confusion or adoration. Strangely, perhaps, the sculpture made me think of my mother giving her life for me, and I was suddenly afraid. It wasn't a physical fear but something deeper, the fear of not being worthy, of having used badly the life that had been passed on to me at such cost, of having run away from something I should long ago have faced. Perhaps, without meaning to, I had made some enormous mistake, and in the face of Mary's marble perfection that possibility seemed to point toward a great, looming regret. Above her, a magnificent, multilayered mural climbed the walls of the apse and filled the curved ceiling below the dome. It was a kind of medieval Via Prè: there were crowds of bodies, some of them drooping over the edge of the ceiling as if they would fall onto the back of the altar. Above them, in the shadows, I could make out more bodies, thin scraps of cloud, out-stretched hands, angels swirling around the center of the cupola. I knelt there in my small vapor of doubt and worry, waiting, breathing.

After a moment, Father Bartolomeo touched me on the shoulder and led me toward a door at the side of the altar. I followed him into a small room. Inside stood a desk and two hard chairs, a bench; a few priests' robes hung in a half-open closet. It seemed to me a place from a remembered dream, a room I'd been to many times before. The priest turned to me. On his face he wore the same calm expression I'd seen in the office at the Curia. His body moved in the same languid way. He lifted his head as if his eyelids were so heavy he had to put his nose up in the air in order to see under them, and he smiled kindly, showing the poorly made teeth. "Please to sit," he said to me. "Please to wait." Then he made a small bow and left, not quite closing the door.

I tried to breathe calmly, telling myself—and mostly believing it—that nothing bad could possibly happen to me there. I ran my eyes over the room—all dark wood, elaborately carved. There were no pictures on the walls, no religious figures painted there, only the plain wooden desk that looked like it weighed a thousand pounds, a plain wooden cross, the hard-backed chairs, the bench, and one pair of polished black shoes beneath it.

It was several minutes before the door opened again. The man who entered was dressed like a beggar or street person in shabby, stained brown pants, running shoes, and a tan sweatshirt that looked twenty years old. He held out a hand and said, "Martino Zossimo," and I stood and bowed my head to him. He was older than I'd expected, his face round and deeply lined but handsome, the hair thick and gray, the eyes steady, the nose sharp and bent to one side as if it had been broken years before, the ears protruding a bit. It was the face, I thought, of a person at peace. He gestured for me to sit and then sat opposite me.

"I am sorry for all the drama," he said, and, unlike Father Bartolomeo's, his English carried only the smallest trace of an accent. "And especially for the late hour. The situation now, here, is difficult for me."

Though I had no idea in what way it might be difficult for him, I said I understood. I thanked him for meeting with me.

"I have been expecting you for a long time," he said.

"I came as quickly as I could, Your Eminence."

"I don't mean tonight. I have been expecting to meet you for a long time. I have seen you in my prayers. In dreams. I have seen you exactly as you look now."

When he said those words, it was as if a long, sharp sword pierced up through the middle of me, stirring something there, as if the point of it had touched the bottom edge of my heart. I suddenly remembered Father Alberto telling me, more than once, not to be falsely modest. I'd had no idea what he meant. Whatever modesty I possessed seemed to me absolutely grounded in reality, not false at all.

But somehow, and it was very strange, when I felt that piercing it was as if an eggshell, made of thin metal, cracked, broke apart, and fell into pieces at my feet. I had turned my eyes away, but when I looked back at the cardinal, I felt—so surprising—that we were in some way equals. Still, his equal or not, I felt raw and skinless there in the small room.

"You were not afraid to come here on Via Prè?" the cardinal asked.

"A bit."

He smiled in a way that seemed sad to me. "It can be not so safe there in the night, though mostly the people would not want to hurt you but only to steal from you, to get money for drugs or to drink."

"We have those places also," I said.

"I knew that you would not be harmed there. I wanted a blessing for that street," he said. "I walk there often, sometimes three or four nights a week. Often at this hour. Sometimes with Father Bartolomeo and sometimes alone. I wanted you to pass along that street because I knew it would be a blessing for those souls."

For once I had no urge to question or dispute him. I was wonderfully at ease.

"You are here in some danger," he said calmly, "but not from the people like those on Via Prè. Within the Church you have made powerful enemies."

"People have been saying that to me almost from the moment I left the airport," I said. "It's a hard thing to believe."

"You are not afraid about that?"

"Not for myself, no."

"You are sure?"

"Yes."

"It would always be this way, I think," he said.

"People who are like you will always make certain others uneasy. If in this life you are warm, you are kind, your heart is open to the full love of Christ without reservation, then you must always invite hatred. I think sometimes of the mob calling for Barabbas to be let to go free and Christ to be crucified. There is always such a crowd. Always."

He turned his eyes away for a moment, as if experiencing a familiar pain in his body. Then he said, "You have come to tell me something."

"Yes, Your Eminence." In as concise a manner as I could, I told him the whole story as it is set down here—the visions, the certainty I had that God was calling me to the priesthood, and that the Church, the American Church at least, was dying. I told him briefly about my meetings in Revere and Boston, the trip to Rome, the cryptic message that had been delivered to me at the Old Palace Hotel. He listened without surprise and with great care, like a good priest in the confessional, with his eyes to the side and down, but not missing a word or anything behind the words. When I finished, he looked at me directly. "I have people in the Vatican who are my friends," he said, so quietly it seemed he worried there were spies outside the door, listening. "From one of those friends, I knew you had come. I knew about the meeting with Rosario. He is a sincere man, perhaps, but of the old ways. When Christ came to Earth, the old ways, which had been set in place to help and guide people, those ways had become tired and rigid and no longer so helpful. I do not mean the true, ancient spirit of Judaism. I mean the rules, the structures of power, the way the spirit of Abraham and Moses had become corrupted. Christ came exactly to break those things apart and show us again the true path. Now, I believe, now in our Church we have a time like that also."

"It's frustrating, Your Eminence. I've felt caught at moments between the possibility that I'm committing a great sin and the other possibility —that the Church is wrong."

"You could not make a sin of any kind," he said. He looked at me a long time, and it seemed to me that in his silent gaze and in that strange remark he was telling me I should know something that he knew. He said, "I receive messages also, in prayer. If I had the authority to change the Church, I would help you in this, yes, of course. But I cannot." He held out his arms and crossed his wrists in front of him. "I am tied like this," he said, "even in this high office."

"What then, Your Eminence?"

"I am being asked, I believe, to help you in a different way."

"What way?"

He held his eyes on me, and I had the sense that there was something he wanted to say. He broke eye contact, started to speak, hesitated, then said, "We must wait a little more time," he said at last. "We must trust in God."

"I do," I said, perhaps too loudly. By then I was leaning a few inches toward him in the small room. "But God is pushing me to do this, I feel it. I believe that with all my heart. Pushing me always to do this thing, and nothing comes of it for me but more and more disappointment."

He watched me. He tucked his hands into the tight sleeves of his threadbare sweater. It was a gesture only a priest would make. "I am the cardinal," he said, a strange waver of pain in his voice. "But I see in you what I would want to see in me."

I told him, and it was true, that the life I was living was such a quiet life, of benefit to so few people, that at times it made me ashamed. It wasn't that I wanted to do great things and be known for them. It was more a feeling I had that some mysterious ability was going to waste, a spiritual ability, and I hadn't the slightest idea how to change that.

He surprised me by saying "Many women now feel as you do. And some men also. But I think, it will sound to you perhaps typical to say this, I think that there has been lost in this time the understanding of what is not seen."

"You mean the traditional things: women having children? Loving their husbands? Keeping their homes?"

He was shaking his head in disagreement. "For women and for men," he said. "The discussion now, in the Church and outside, has become—" He turned his eyes sideways for a moment, searching for the right word, it seemed, and then said, "has been made too solid . . . too concerned with exterior things. The value of the interior world has been lost now in society, even in most parts of the Church. It is seen as a waste, not productive. But think of what did Christ do. Not so much. Not so very much in the exterior world. A small number of miracles in all his years on Earth. A small number of months of talking here and there. A short life, and look. His message was a very large message, but mostly an interior one, I think."

"But he was Christ. He changed the world so much."

"Of course, yes. But there were the good people before him, and the bad also. And after him good and bad, the same."

"You seem to be saying I should let this go, then, the idea of the priesthood."

"I think," he said, again, with what seemed to me that same subtle reluctance, "I think God is asking of you something else . . . something larger."

"What then? Asking what? Forgive me, Your Eminence, I'm confused."

"You encounter, constantly, every day, many

people. Walking now on Via Prè, you touched the people there."

"I gave one sweater to cold children, that's all."

He was shaking his head. "Because of what is inside yourself," he said slowly, "you change the life of every person who sees you."

I was tired then, confused, worn out. Thinking of how I might have changed the lives of the prostitutes on the corner, I very nearly laughed.

"When the priest says Mass," the cardinal went on, "everything inside of him says this Mass. To the extent that he is good, the goodness is passed across to others not only in his words but in the motions of his body, the tone of his voice, the light in his eyes. When a husband and wife make the love, everything that is inside them makes the love. Their history. Their thoughts and the record of their thoughts. Everything they have ever been is joined, and if their lovemaking produces a child, all of that is passed along to that child. When a mother touches her son, everything of her as a person lies inside that touch. Because of it the atoms change in the son."

"But the external world matters, doesn't it?" I said. "If a woman can't be a priest, if a priest who wants to can't marry, the atoms change in them, too. What they do from then on, the effect they have on people, is changed."

"Exactly," he said, as if we'd been agreeing all along.

"What are you saying I should do, then? Tell me."

Instead of answering, he said, "I watched my sister die. From the cancer. A holy woman. We were very close always. She had a great patience. She prayed, she suffered. She felt despair. I think we see those same things in Christ's life and in the life of his mother and of others close to him. We have Christ's own words, 'My Lord, my Lord, why have you forsaken me?' and we have him then rising in the glory. At the very last, after a great torment, my sister left this world in peace."

"I'm sorry for her suffering," I said. And then, when he just kept looking at me: "So I should wait?"

He nodded, as if I'd finally understood what he'd been trying to convey. "I believe we must both of us wait . . . but not so long now."

"I feel like I've done all the work I can do in terms of what God is asking of me."

"I feel that also, in one way, yes," he said. "But I think that now God will send you a new task." He looked away and back, and for the third time I had the feeling there was something he was keeping himself from saying. "And to me a new task, also." He sighed, as if the vision of the difficulty of these coming tasks was already burdening him. He said, "You have seen this beautiful church?" And it was clear that he didn't want to say any more.

"Only for just a few moments, when I came in."

"Then let us go and pray together before the Holy Mother. That is what we can do now. If you would."

We went back out into the smell of candle smoke and old stone. I started to kneel at the altar rail, but the cardinal took hold of my elbow, opened the silver-leaf gates, and led me through them to the place where the priests stood when they were saying Mass. It was as if, for those moments, in that one place, he was fulfilling the visions I'd been having for so long, allowing a woman into the inner sanctum of the faith, as an equal. If he foresaw some other destiny for me, then at least my visions had been correct to this one extent: I was on the altar, praying. "Here," he said, and we knelt side by side on the cool tile, beneath the swirling marble Mary. "Just a few minutes here we will pray," he said quietly.

And we did that. I bowed my head. After a time I could feel an actual, literal weight slipping off my bones, as if the question I'd been struggling with all those years had at last been answered. In place of that worry and struggle, something much larger than myself and my catalogue of wants seemed to take hold of my mind and carry me up and up. Such a sense of fullness came over me then, a joy much stronger than the joys I'd felt before in prayer. In my arms and legs and hands it was as if I could feel the individual cells singing in celebration, and I understood it to mean that I was in a holy place, in the presence of a truly holy man, and that he had passed on to me some great, mysterious gift. I raised my head and opened my eyes and looked above me at the mural. In the center of the cupola—something I could not have seen from any farther out in the church—was a globe of golden light, a golden quietness amid the swirl of bodies. I felt as though I were being absorbed into it.

When, much later, the light released me and I came slowly out of what I can only call the ecstasy of that prayer, my eyes were closed, my head bowed, and the cardinal was no longer beside me.

I looked left and right, then turned and saw him sitting in the front pew. Walking through the silver gates and down the three marble steps, I felt a twinge of embarrassment: I had no idea how long I'd kept him waiting. He stood, looking, it seemed to me, like a carpenter or stonemason who'd wandered into the church after leaving his labors and now was about to fall asleep. He did the strangest thing then: he took my right hand, leaned over, and kissed it, almost as a lover would. I resisted the urge to pull away. "Give to me," he said, as if asking for my hand in marriage, "your blessing."

"I have no blessing to give, Your Eminence. That's not right. It should work the other way."

"Give to me your blessing," he repeated, very calmly, as if I hadn't objected at all.

"I am not worthy to give anyone any kind of blessing."

"Give to me your blessing," he said a third time.

And then it was as if there were a completely different Cynthia Clare Piantedosi standing there. That name no longer fit; my actual past seemed no longer to drag behind me like a tattered sack of memories. I took hold of his hand in both my hands and I said, "Whatever good I have in me I give to you. May God bless you."

"And you," he said. "And protect you now, and give us both courage."

Then he was leading me to the door. We stepped outside, where it was cool but no longer night-time. The old priest was standing there, waiting as patiently as if it were midday and he were expecting a friend for lunch. I would calculate, later, that he'd been there almost two hours. He smiled at me tiredly. The cardinal said just what Mabu had said: "You should go back by the way of Via Arsenale. Father Bartolomeo will walk with you as far as that street, then it will be safe."

I thanked him. He touched me on the shoulder with the fingertips of his right hand, held them there for a long moment, held his eyes on mine, then turned and went back into the church. I had an urge to follow him and ask if we could see each other again, but for some reason I did not do that.

CHAPTER **THIRTEEN**

As Father Bartolomeo and I stepped away from San Luca and out into the small piazza at the end of Via Prè, I was surprised to see that the sun had already risen, there, behind us, behind the range of hills. I was surprised, too, that, as we turned left and began the short climb toward Via Arsenale, Father Bartolomeo walked behind, not next to me. At first, I'm ashamed to admit, I was barely even aware of him. Still caught up in the magic of my meeting with Cardinal Zossimo, walking along in a spell of self-involvement, I realized only after we'd gone a block and a half that Father Bartolomeo had fallen behind and was laboring for breath. The trip along Via Prè had been slightly downhill, but now we were moving in a different direction, away from the water, climbing a steep rise, and he was struggling.

I stopped and waited for him. Strangely, he stopped, too—in order to catch his breath, I thought at first. But then I understood that, like a bodyguard or acolyte, he was purposely keeping a distance. I motioned him up; he smiled and shook his head. It was a peculiar dance, but I was suffused then with such a profound peace that almost nothing else mattered to me. I turned and went along happily in the morning light, uphill another two blocks until we crested the rise. At that point I looked back at the old priest and I said, "Please walk with me. I'm not in a hurry." Still breathing hard, Father Bartolomeo moved up even with me, and together we turned left onto Via Arsenale. I asked him then if he or the cardinal had been the one who'd paid the hotel bill, and he only lifted and lowered his shoulders, once, chest heaving, face calm.

The air smelled of bus exhaust and baking bread. It must have been only five or five thirty in the morning, but already there were a few cars and motorcycles on the street, the sound of their engines echoing against the buildings' stone faces. We had to wait a moment in order to cross. When we were on the other side, Father Bartolomeo caught his breath and said, "I think it is safe now, from here," and reached out to shake my hand good-bye.

I thanked him for waiting all that time, and he said, "My life is waiting," in a laconic manner that was touched with the gentlest humor. His face was a collection of pouches with two sleepy blue eyes set among them. "The *cardinale*," he added, "a special man, yes?"

"I felt that."

"Maybe someday he will be the pope."

I was surprised, for some reason, to hear the thought put into words. I felt again that strange happiness slice up through the middle of me, a blade of hope, a wound with no pain in it. "Everything would change then," I said.

In response, he made the classic Italian expression I'd seen on Father Bruno's face during our meal at the Vecchia Roma: raised eyebrows, slowly closed eyes, turned-down corners of the lips. The famous Italian *forse*. Maybe. Possibly. We hope so, but probably not. At that moment the gesture seemed to me to encompass the whole of the tradition I'd been suckled on, the idea that life was always as disappointing as it was amusing, that one shouldn't place too much hope in its perfectibility, that the strong river of human fate and behavior might swell and shrink, twist this way and that, turn better or worse in various places in various eras, but it would never really cut an absolutely sinless route through the soil of earthly time.

Father Bartolomeo opened his eyes and smiled a cat's smile, as gentle and kind as an embrace. We said good-bye again. I turned and headed toward the hotel.

From there to the Savoia it was a straight line, less than half a mile. I went past the large gray church I didn't much care for, past the entrance to one of the university departments, then past a string of small shops. Café owners were setting out chairs and tables on the sidewalk, and there were sandwich boards there, too, chalked with advertisements for sales or daily specials.

As I walked, I thought about the odd way the meeting had been arranged—the hour, the location, the fact that I'd been directed through what must have been one of the poorest, roughest sections of the city. At first I suspected it was meant to be some kind of test of my courage or sincerity. But then I decided there must have been another reason: Cardinal Zossimo had wanted me to see or experience something there, the abject poverty, the fear, violence, and want those people lived with, the way they were locked outside the warm enclosure of respectable society—no room for them at the inn. For a cardinal, certainly, pampered and fussed over, and for a middle-class American woman who had plenty to eat, a house, and every material possession she wanted, it would be easy to pretend those lives didn't really matter or that they weren't full, important lives in the eyes of God. The cardinal must have hoped I'd understand that, not just in my mind but viscerally.

Not far from the hotel I looked up from my contented musing and saw that the street and sidewalk had become busier. One of the big orange city buses swept past from behind me, making the transition from invisible to apparent and raising a small hurricane of exhaust and noise a few feet to my left. I saw Mabu on the sidewalk two hundred yards from me, his huge head swinging this way and that as if he were watching for someone. He turned his eyes left and saw me. I raised a hand in greeting and was surprised when he started in my direction. He went slowly at first and then more quickly, and then, for no apparent reason, he broke into a trot. He was shouting something and pointing, but I couldn't make out the words because, behind the dying noise of the bus I heard the whine of a motorbike. It was faint at first—concentrating on Mabu's strange behavior, I was barely conscious of it—and then it grew louder and seemed so close that, without turning to see, I angled my steps away from the edge of the sidewalk. Mabu, trotting like a bull in a field, was pointing and yelling, more urgently now. I had started to turn my head and look over my shoulder—the motorbike was very loud by then—when I felt a rush of air and noise beside me and then a tremendous flash of pain behind my left ear.

And then nothing.

CHAPTER FOURTEEN

When people are brought to a hospital in an unconscious state—as was the case with me that morning in Genoa—they are routinely catheterized for the testing of their urine. "It's how we keep the medical students out of our way," one veteran nurse had told us in our clinical rounds of the ER, but I knew it was more than that. Urine is something we all want to get rid of, naturally, flushing it away as soon as it's produced—as if, like past sins, we want to move it as far from us as quickly as possible. But our sins say a lot about us, and, for doctors and nurses, urine is a rich source of information, too. The liver takes toxins from the blood and sends them to the kidneys for filtering, and anything that's harmful or useless to the body will end up in our urine (though alcohol is metabolized so fast it doesn't show up there). It's particularly helpful in the case of female patients, because it lets the doctors know whether or not they can safely perform certain kinds of radiological exams.

Unconscious, my brain swelling and threatening to bleed, I was taken by ambulance, ironically enough, to the Ospedale San Martino in the center of Genoa. There the doctors did what they always do for a patient who comes through the doors with head trauma—an IV line was started, CT scans were taken, a brain surgeon was called in to review the films and be ready in case emergency surgery proved necessary. I wasn't awake for any of this, of course. I remember nothing of those hours—no visions or dreams, no sense of time or my own existence. Brain trauma produces a state very much like that of anesthesia, though in the case of trauma there's a much greater potential for death, paralysis, or other permanent injury.

The main risk is that bleeding and swelling of the brain will damage the sensitive tissue there—similar to what happens in cerebral hemorrhage or stroke—and then whatever function is controlled by that part of the brain will be lost or impaired.

What happened, in my case, was that two things—my own instinct and Mabu's yelling and pointing—very likely saved me from being killed or paralyzed. He saw what I couldn't see—a man on a motorbike speeding up Via Arsenale, driving with one hand. In his other hand the man had a short length of pipe. Even if his target—the back of my head—had been perfectly stationary, it would have been difficult enough for him to hit it square on, going at that speed. But, hearing the sound of the motorbike, I'd instinctively moved a couple of feet farther away from the street, which had forced him to adjust his course and ride closer to the curb. The pavement was sloped a bit there to allow rainwater to flow into the gutter, and—he was steering with one hand, his eyes were on me—the change of angle made him momentarily lose control of the motorbike. That small wobble and the fact that, just as he swung, I had wondered what Mabu was pointing at and had started to turn my head, made it a glancing blow instead of a direct one—enough to knock me flat on the sidewalk, unconscious, but nothing like what it could have been if he'd hit me dead-on.

I went over sideways, crashing and sliding into

the legs of a flimsy metal chair at one of the café tables. The swinging of the club and the impact caused the driver to jerk the handlebars, which caused the front wheel of the motorbike to strike the curb. The driver let go of the pipe and grabbed the handle, but too late. He went over sideways, too, skidding along the sidewalk in front of me like a sack of grain thrown from a moving truck. By the time he'd gotten halfway to his feet, conscious but dazed and scraped up very badly, Mabu had reached him, and the friendly giant—according to the story I was told, at least—swung his right fist with all his weight behind it. The assailant—Armando Malatesta was his name—ended up in a second ambulance, and then in the next room over in the ER (and then, a few hours later, in police custody).

All this is a little bit beside the point, I guess, and all the details were told to me much later. I was taken by ambulance to the emergency room, treated there, and then moved from the ER to the CT scan, from radiology to a bed in Intensive Care. I lay there for the rest of the morning, medicated, monitored in ten different ways, and as unconscious as a block of stone.

When I finally came to the surface again—a slow, painful procession from darkness to light, through all kinds of shadowy realms of confusion and hurt—I became aware of a nurse in a white nun's habit to the left side of the bed and then a man on the other side, seated, holding my right hand in his. Bent nose. Protruding ears. This man, I realized after a few hazy moments, was Martino Zossimo, much more formally attired than the last time I'd seen him. When the nun saw my eyes open, she summoned the doctors. The cardinal squeezed my hand once, then stepped out of the way so I could be checked—lights shined in my eyes, fingers held up for me to count, the IV line adjusted, a short series of simple questions—was I in pain (yes, very much); could I remember my name (yes, but it was difficult to speak); was there anyone I wished them to notify ("Father," I said, but I could not yet retrieve a name, address, or phone number).

I seemed to fall asleep again for a period of time—God knows how long it was—and when I awoke there was less confusion, less pain. I was very thirsty and a little nauseous but happy to see the cardinal's face staring down at me with an expression of such love it seemed to have a physical force to it. If I'd been able to form the words, I might have said that this feeling was precisely the thing I had been missing in my loneliest moments: the sense of being fully *seen*. It was as if he were looking at all the parts of me, good and bad, petty and generous, insecure and confident, ugly and attractive, and saying *yes* to each one of them. Somewhere in one of the books Father Alberto had given me, I'd read that in certain so-called primitive societies the ordinary greeting wasn't "Hello" or "How are you?" or "What are you doing?," it was "I see you."

The cardinal *saw* me. I saw him in return. He helped me sip from a cup of water, then reached out and took hold of my fingers again, but before anything could be said there were more ministrations by the nurses, another visit from a pair of doctors, a bit of business during which the cardinal was asked to leave the room. There was pain—background music, really, unpleasant but not loud, muted by opium derivatives—and very slowly, like birds who'd scattered away from a footstep, my thoughts formed themselves again into a more or less straight line. At that point the cardinal and I were left alone, and it was at that point, too, that he gave me a sketchy account of what had happened. I looked down at my hand, which seemed unnaturally pale against the red cloth of his sleeve.

"Why?" I asked him. "Who?"

He shrugged, told me the man's name, described him—Italian, mid-thirties, tattoo of a dragon on one side of his neck—asked if I'd seen him before. I had not.

All this was done in quiet tones, with spaces between the questions and answers, the information fed to me in drops, carefully, watchfully, the way you feed bread to someone who's thrown up everything she's eaten for the past three days.

By then my thinking mechanism was functioning well enough for me to thank him for taking time out of his schedule to visit me. At those words I noticed a twist of emotion cross his face. "There's something more," I said.

He nodded, pursed his lips, watched me. We had been speaking the whole time in English, but just then, for God knows what reason, he switched to Italian and said, "*Sei incinta.*"

The word comes, perhaps, from *cintura*, which means "belt," and even in my dazed state I understood it immediately.

"You're pregnant," the cardinal had said.

"But that can't be!" I said, so forcefully that I winced against a jolt of pain.

He didn't speak or move his eyes. The weight of love there was trimmed with a filigree of understanding, as if he were a step ahead and waiting for me to catch up.

"That can't be, I've never—" I said, but at that point I remembered the other fact that can be gleaned from a woman's urine, and I closed my mouth and looked away from him. On some unconscious level I could feel that what he'd told me was true, and a shiver of fear went through me, a ripple of the most absolute unworthiness. Then, beneath the pain, beneath the medication that had dulled the pain, and beneath and beyond the surprise came something else: I understood that I would have to let go of the unworthiness at last, that larger forces work through us if we let them, and that going around in a suit of apology was not modesty at all; it was a lie. Father Alberto had tried to tell me that in a dozen different ways. Now, finally, I understood.

I wasn't thinking then of the problems I would face: trying to explain the situation to my father; the struggles of single motherhood; the responsibility of raising this spirit inside me to adulthood and the trials he or she might face then. It seemed to me, all at once, that the spells, my "mission"— even though I'd misunderstood it—and everything else in my past had, in fact, been pointing to this moment, and I was filled with what I can only describe as pure confidence, a "perfection of freedom" to use Thomas Merton's beautiful phrase. I'd often seen, in my Ob-Gyn clinicals, a certain expression on women's faces just after they'd given birth. A release from the pain of labor, yes, of course; but something more than that, too. We are all of us linked to something so much greater than ourselves, and for that little while, at least, those women understood that, in their bodies. At that moment, so did I.

"It is important now," the cardinal was saying, "to leave Genova. You may not be safe here. You should not raise the child here, in any case." There was a slight hesitation, one exhaled breath, almost a sigh, as if he were letting go of his own last and best-loved program for happiness, his good reputation, his dreams of a certain kind of future, something he'd been holding to tightly for all his adult life. "There are people in the countryside," he said, "my friends. They will find a safe place for us. They will help us."

I felt then as I imagine one feels at her first lovemaking and also at the very moment of death: there was, simultaneously, a sense of surprise, a newness, but also a breaking wave of undeniable familiarity, as if, in some mysterious subconscious realm, this great thing had been experienced or known before.

Because in the grammar of the language I had been hearing since my earliest moments on Earth, there was no ambiguity at all. The cardinal had not said "*Ti aiuteranno*, They will help *you*." He'd said "*Ci aiuteranno.*" Which means: "They will help *us*."

ACKNOWLEDGMENTS

First thanks, as always, to Amanda for her unwavering support and warm love. For several reasons, this was a particularly difficult book to write, one that involved a number of major revisions over a period of years. These kinds of demolition and reconstruction projects are not easy on the author and not easy on the author's spouse. Amanda's consistent good humor and optimism buoyed me in those hours, days, and weeks when it seemed I would never be able to tell this story the way I wanted to.

A very special thank-you to Bonnie Smith, Deputy Commissioner, State of Maine, Department of Health and Human Services, for her generous help with information about a nurse's education and work. No one knows that life better than she does, and as a novelist herself, she was aware of the demands of characterization and plot and how the technical information needed to fit with them. She took time out of a busy work and family schedule to help me on a number of occasions. I could not ask for a better friend.

I should add that any and all errors here belong to me, not to her or any of my other friends, readers, and advisers.

A big thank-you, too, to Gino Mazzone, friend

and master tour guide, whose knowledge of Rome and Vatican City exceeds that of any encyclopedia. Gino used a rest day to do what he does when working—show a curious foreigner around his beloved city and impart a small portion of his vast knowledge. To him and his lovely wife, Stacey, my gratitude.

My gratitude also to those Catholic priests who patiently answered my probing questions about Church doctrine but who wished to remain anonymous. They were gracious enough to discuss difficult matters with a persistent, if respectful, stranger, and I salute them for that.

Thanks also to: Marly Rusoff, Michael Radulescu, and Shaye Areheart for their warm support and help, and to Lynn Anderson for her thorough and careful copyediting, and her tolerance for my ungrammatical quirks and preferences; and to my fine editors at Crown: Kate Kennedy and Amanda Patten. Their insight and advice helped me see this story with clearer eyes.

And my gratitude to my Italian teacher, Simone Gugliotta, for her patience and kindness as I wrestle with the language I love.

Last but not least, thank you to my supportive friends Randy and Bonnie DeTrinis, who know the spiritual life so well and who live it so beautifully.